LOTTIE'S LEGACY

A Deena Powers Mystery

Gloria Getman

Lottie's Legacy
Published by Squirrel Creek Books
786 Meadow Ave., Exeter, CA 93221

Printed and bound in the United States of America.
ISBN-13: 978-0-9854747-0-6
ISBN-10: 098547470X

This book is a work of fiction. Names, characters, places and incidents are either the product of the author's imagination or are used fictitiously. Any resemblance to actual events, locales, persons, living or dead, is coincidental. The author will assure no responsibility for errors, inaccuracies, omissions, or any inconsistency herein. Any slights to people, places or organizations are unintentional.

Dedication

To the Visalia-Exeter Writers

Acknowledgments

This book never would have reached completion if it hadn't been for Mary Benton and Sylvia Ross, who prodded me whenever I fell into doldrums. And it never would have gotten started if it weren't for Marilyn Meredith, who patiently encouraged my first unsteady steps while learning the craft. In between were the many people of the Visalia and Exeter Writer's Critique Groups, who have patiently listened and made suggestions during each rewrite, especially Mary Benton whose skill at finding orphaned words is so appreciated.

I want to thank Sylvia Ross for her incredible graphics work as well as her editing and recommendations for the book. I want to thank Win Doyle for taking time to read the book and make useful suggestions, Roger Boling and Harry Perez for their advice on police matters and Teresa Boyce of Bank of the Sierra, who took the time to explain changes in the appearance of US currency.

Prologue

Saturday, January 31, 1998

Harlan Jones crawled out from under his current shelter behind the cement plant, shook his tattered blanket and rolled it tight. He hated January. It was too cold to sleep outside in a crate or cardboard box, and the dampness made his bones ache. He'd have to find a better place to spend his nights, one with a roof in case it rained.

He squinted upward as the sun peeked over the top of the Sierra Nevada range. It meant he'd have to hurry to make the rounds of trash bins before the good people of Four Creeks were up and about. They didn't like to see him searching through their rubbish, and if the police saw him, they were sure to run him off.

Harlan hitched up his pants after relieving himself behind a nearby tree and tied the short piece of clothesline he used to keep them from slipping. Maybe he'd find a better belt one of these days. He'd found a wool jacket in a trash can on Elm Street. True, it did have a lot of moth holes, both elastic cuffs were stretched out and the zipper was broken, but that didn't bother him.

What did bother him was wet feet, and at that moment dampness crept through the sole of his right shoe. He couldn't ignore it. He ripped a piece from the cardboard box he'd slept in and held it between his yellowed teeth as he rubbed his wrinkled hands together to warm them. After tearing off portions of cardboard to form a makeshift insole, he leaned against the tree, pulled off his shoe and tucked it in place. Sliding his foot inside, he wiggled his toes and judged it good. Mentally, he added shoes to the list of items he needed to scrounge.

Harlan shrugged on the worn backpack that held his belongings. It was another item he'd plucked from an unsuspecting citizen's refuse. With his bedroll tied and flung over his shoulder, he hustled down the railroad tracks that cut through town.

The best trash bin for breakfast was behind Avila's Quick Mart. He often found Mojo potatoes there, discarded when the deli case was cleaned out at midnight. He'd have to hurry if he was going to get to Avila's before the kid came to open the store. Avila looked away when he saw Harlan, but not that kid. He yelled and threw stones at him.

'Course the kid didn't really scare him much. He couldn't yell near as loud as Harlan's old man. Now there was a yeller. He didn't just yell, though. He'd beat the crap out of Harlan. Many's the time when he was a boy, his old man'd get drunk, and Harlan would be spitting blood before he was done. Some nights he ran away and hid in a neighbor's barn or empty chicken coop. Didn't matter where, so long as he escaped the old man's fists.

Ah, there it was; the beautiful green bin. He trotted over to it and lifted the cover to survey the pickings. Sure enough, right there on top was a black trash bag. Propping the lid with one hand, he stretched to reach it, but his arms were too short. His old man called him a runt, and maybe he was right about that.

Just then a dingy-blue, Honda Civic skidded into the parking lot. It was the kid with the straight black hair and sallow complexion. He sprang from his car and scooped up a rock.

"Get outta here, you freak." He heaved the stone, hitting Harlan's arm.

Harlan dropped the lid and scooted around the corner out of sight.

"Shithead," he muttered, rubbing his arm.

As soon as the kid was inside the building, Harlan edged back around the corner and lifted the lid again. On tiptoes, he snagged the sack, tore it open and searched the contents. Right on top was a white cardboard tray of cold Mojos. He grabbed a fistful and fled.

The limp potatoes didn't last long in his stomach. By mid-afternoon he was so hungry his belly ached. He gleaned a few oranges from an orchard on the west side of town, but he had to be careful not to eat too many, 'cause they'd give him the runs, and taking care of business could be a serious problem. As he searched the orchard, he noticed a dark cloud-bank creep across the sky and felt a chill breeze. It meant rain and snow in the mountains. It would be the second time this week. He dreaded another night in the wet.

It was near dusk when his thoughts drifted to the empty pigeon pen behind Lottie Weston's house. Though the walls were half screen, and it still smelled of pigeon droppings, the roof didn't leak. 'Course there were mice in it and fleas too, but if he wrapped up in his blanket, it wasn't bad at all. Getting there was the tricky part. He wouldn't risk following the main road. Someone might notice where he was headed. No one bothered him if he kept out of sight.

Cutting across a vacant field and through a plum orchard, he climbed a fence where a horse was pastured. He thought about Lottie along the way. Long years back, he and Lottie had been in the same school. That was before his old man sent him to work for the Barnes ranch up the canyon. Old man Barnes wasn't much better'n his dad, 'cept for regular meals. The Army was the best time. The guys started calling him Jonesy. He didn't mind. He liked that name better anyway.

Jonesy pushed those thoughts aside when he spotted Lottie's house. It sat in the middle of a half-acre lot with two leafless mulberry trees in back. The shaded windows were dark. Looked like Lottie

3

wasn't home. He'd sneak into her pigeon pen. It'd be warmer there.

As he eased open the screen door, the hinges squawked, and he heard mice scurry. Inside, he shucked off his backpack, shook out the bedroll and picked a spot to prop himself. He sat with his back against the wall and tucked the blanket tight around his feet in case a mouse tried to skitter up his pant leg. A draft came in from over his head, and he pulled his black stocking cap down to protect his ears.

Jonesy'd barely settled himself when he heard Lottie's back door slam. Lottie *was* home. He craned his neck to peer through the screen. Though it had started to sprinkle, there was still enough light to see her silhouette. She hunched her shoulders as she headed toward the open shed where she kept firewood covered with gunny sacks. Her steps were plodding and deliberate, like someone unsure of her footing. She was a big woman, lots bigger'n him and heavy too. He'd sure hate to have her mad at him.

A few minutes passed before he saw her come out of the woodshed with an armload of firewood and disappear into the house. He settled back against the wall. It was going to be hard to sleep with an empty stomach.

Seconds later, a shriek came from the house. Jonesy raised himself and stretched his neck. Lottie burst out the back door, the firewood still in her arms. Someone taller than her came from behind and grabbed her hair putting her off balance. She stumbled, dropped her load and fell to her knees.

Jonesy watched, paralyzed with astonishment. In a flash the silhouetted figure bent over and muffled her scream. The attacker's arm rose with a dark object in his hand. A car passed on the road in front of the house, and for a split second light illuminated the assailant's face. Jonesy gasped in recognition.

A dull thud made his stomach quiver. Lottie slumped like a rag doll. Jonesy ducked and closed his eyes tight, his heart hammering in

4

his chest. He pulled the blanket over his head and wished he'd never come to Lottie's house.

Chapter 1

Tuesday, February 3, 1998

The early morning fog was beginning to lighten as I drove my dad's black Explorer into the parking lot of Powers Investigations. I climbed out of the SUV and clutched my jacket to me as I walked toward the door. The Spanish style building sat on a flat spot carved out of a hillside overlooking Ortega Bay, a moderate-sized city in Southern California. A chill ocean breeze carried the muted roar of the distant freeway that travelled along the beach front. Leaves of the eucalyptus trees across the street rustled, and through the mist I could see the roof of the old mission and the tops of palm trees surrounding it.

It had been a little over a month since the death of my father and the first time I'd been to the office since the accident. We were partners in the agency. That is, until my Jeep Cherokee skidded over an embankment on a mountain road and he was killed. I was driving. At least that's what I'd been told. I didn't remember. The concussion I'd received wiped out any memory of the event.

What I had on my mind that morning was to locate the records related to a case he'd been working on at the time of his death. Pausing on the steps, I opened the mailbox and grabbed the mail, then unlocked the door, stepped inside and deactivated the alarm.

In an uncanny way, I half expected to hear Dad's voice call out to me from his office. Instead, slivers of gray light seeped around the curtains that covered the windows of the reception area. I quelled tears as I moved to let in light and open a window to flush out the stale air.

It was time to pull myself together, if not for real, at least I'd pretend.

I glanced at the envelopes in my hand, two get-well cards from friends, and a statement from Harrison Memorial Hospital. I was considering whether or not to open the bill when I heard the crunch of tires on the gravel outside. The door flew open and Judy Amrine stood silhouetted in the doorway with a Starbuck's sack in her hand. The faint scent of coffee drifted my way.

"I figured I'd find you here," she said. "I stopped by your apartment. Deena, it's a little soon to be starting back to work, don't you think? A concussion is nothing to scoff at."

Judy was a spunky gal who'd been widowed, stepped out in the job market for the first time in middle age and was invaluable as our part-time secretary/receptionist and full-time surrogate mother. She was tall, stout and dressed in faded jeans. Emblazoned on the front of the blue sweatshirt she wore was the message, "Grandma Rocks." Her hair, a brassy red with roots faded to gray, ruffled as a breeze swept across the room.

"I had to get out of the apartment. It's too quiet." Quiet wasn't what I really meant. With Dad gone and my two dogs at my friend Francie's ranch, the silence was suffocating. "I thought I'd see about Dad's notes on the warehouse fire he was investigating. If the insurance company doesn't receive a final report soon, we might not get paid, and the hospital would like some money." I held up the envelope with the bill for her to see.

Judy closed the door, walked over to her desk and set the sack down. She opened it and took out two Styrofoam cups. "What about those headaches? They haven't gone away, have they?"

"No." I had to be honest. In the last month I'd spent most mornings with nausea and a headache that hung on like a bad cold. I'd been either medicated or depressed. Or both.

I turned away and gazed through the window at the horizon of the blue-gray ocean. From where the office building sat, the swells and white-caps couldn't be seen, but I knew they were there. The one constant. Nothing else would ever be the same.

Judy's weight registered in the chair behind her desk with a squeaking groan. "You could hire another investigator. You have a good client base in the insurance companies. It wouldn't be the same of course …." Her voice cracked.

I knew she missed Dad almost as much as I did, but right then my own load of grief was all I could carry. I turned around to face her. "It's a possibility."

In truth, I was at loose ends, still untangling the duties of next-of-kin. Dad had made me a full partner when I'd received my license a year earlier. I'd worked under his watchful eye for three years. Unlike most investigators, I had no experience with police work. My knowledge of the law came from the time I'd spent proof reading law books, and later, working in a law office. Now I was on my own.

I walked over to the desk and picked up one of the Styrofoam cups. "After I send the report, I plan to take Dad's ashes to Four Creeks where my grandparents are buried. I'll spend a week with Aunt Madge. We need some time together." I raised the cup in salute. "Thanks," I said and took a sip before heading toward Dad's office. "I'm going to look for that file."

From what Dad initially told me about the case, the insurance company wasn't satisfied with the fire department investigator's report. The cause was deemed electrical, but the report was inconclusive as far as arson was concerned. Tri-Counties Indemnity wanted arson ruled out before they paid the claim. The CEO thought a private investigator would have more time to scrutinize details.

I took a deep breath as I passed through the doorway. The sight of his empty chair gave my heart a twist. He was sixty-four, the age when most people are thinking about retiring. Yet he never mentioned it. The firm had a good reputation because of him, and I wondered if our clients would have the same confidence in me. Most likely, I'd have to earn it.

I went to the desk and fished his keys from the center drawer. All the file cabinets for the agency stood along the wall adjacent to the door. It put them out of sight from anyone who entered the building, but still convenient for the rest of us.

My office was on the other end of the building, and I kept only the files I was currently working on in my desk. I was about to unlock the cabinets when I heard the phone ring in the outer office.

"It's your aunt," Judy called.

Aunt Madge was my dad's only sister, younger by two years. She lived in Four Creeks, some two hundred miles north in the San Joaquin Valley. I reached for the extension, certain she was calling to pin me down about when I would arrive.

"Hi Madge. It'll be just a few more days …"

She interrupted. "Deena. Thank God I found you. When I called your place and there was no answer, I was frantic." Her voice quavered. "I just don't know what to do."

My normally composed aunt didn't sound like herself. "What's the matter?"

"It's simply awful. All those questions. It was so humiliating." Her voice squeaked. "I've been arrested."

"Arrested?! What for?"

"Murder." She broke into sobs.

I switched the receiver to my other ear and hoped I'd misunderstood. "Did you say murder?"

"Yes. And that man tried to confuse me," she whimpered.

"What man? Calm down and tell me what happened."

"The policeman. He was rude." Sniffling came through on the line.

"When? Today?"

"This morning." Sounds of muffled nose blowing followed.

"Madge, what makes the police think you're to blame?"

"I have no idea."

"There has to be a reason. Who was killed?"

A pause and more tissue rustling.

"Madge?"

"Lottie Weston. Her body was found in the canal by her house Sunday morning."

"Refresh my memory. Am I supposed to know her?"

"That concussion must have wiped out more memory than just the accident. Her son, Freddie, was in your graduating class."

After a second it clicked. "Sure, I remember him. His mother was murdered? That's terrible. I think I met her once after a football game at Four Creeks High."

"Deena, what should I do?"

The desperation in her voice was disconcerting. "I'm sure it's some sort of misunderstanding. I'll pack a bag and leave right away. If necessary, we'll talk to an attorney."

I hung up at my end. I didn't believe for one minute my aunt was involved in a murder. You don't get out of bed one morning after living a pristine life for sixty-two years and plot such a thing. This was *my* aunt, the lady with silver hair and a bottomless cookie jar. It made no sense.

Judy stood in the doorway between the two offices, her brown eyes full of concern. No doubt she'd listened in.

"Madge is in some sort of trouble," I said. "I've got to go to Four Creeks sooner than I'd planned." I started toward the door with Judy at my heels, then paused and reached to squeeze her hand. "The report will have to wait. Lock up, will you?"

"Sure, honey."

During the ten minute drive to the apartment Dad and I had shared, my mind raced. As soon as I was inside, I phoned Francie Waite, a friend I'd met through a bicycling club. She lived about twenty miles inland on a small ranch with her husband and two sons. They'd been kind enough to care for my dogs while I recuperated. After the accident I was in no shape to manage them.

When I told her the situation, she pooh-poohed the prospect of my aunt committing *any* sort of crime. "Don't worry about your dogs, Deena. They're getting along fine with everyone here, even the cat. Just look out for Madge."

"I'm anxious for their company. I'll come by to get them as soon as I get Madge's problem straightened out. It shouldn't take more than a few days." I thanked her and we hung up.

I stood in the middle of the bedroom for a minute to organize my thoughts, then snagged my overnight bag from the closet shelf. Opening it on the bed, I tossed in several pieces of clothing and filled my cosmetic case with items from the bathroom. I went to the closet for what I think of as my on-the-job bag. It was soft-sided, well padded and big enough for my camera, binoculars, notebook, laptop, tape recorder, and various other smaller items. Maybe even a snack. All the essentials of a modern-day investigator. I own a Walther PPK that I carried in a shoulder holster, but wore only if I was on surveillance in a questionable neighborhood. I didn't need the weapon or the computer this trip, so I locked them in my closet safe.

Finished packing, I stowed the luggage in the Explorer and returned to the apartment for the box containing Dad's ashes. It was on the mantle awaiting the trip home. I put the needed documents in my purse, tucked the box under my arm and closed the door. Out in the carport, I strapped Dad in the passenger seat as best I could, climbed in and turned the key.

As the SUV climbed the freeway entrance, I wondered if Madge felt the way I did, as if Dad had been plucked off the earth by an alien spacecraft. It was so strange. We were laughing one day and the next, he was gone. I'd come to understand how people felt when someone was lost at sea. Our attorney, the executor of Dad's estate, had taken care of the cremation arrangements while I was still in the hospital.

On the long drive inland my mind wandered, trying to dredge up memories of Freddie's mother, Lottie Weston, from the year when Dad and I moved to the ranch to help my grandparents.

What I remembered about Mrs. Weston wasn't much, only that she was tall, had dark hair, a nice smile, and a scar below one ear. Which ear, I couldn't recall. What could be the connection between Lottie Weston and Aunt Madge that would bring the police to her door? Speculation was fruitless.

A car cut me off and brought my attention back to my driving. I pushed all other thoughts aside and turned on the radio to a station with some upbeat music.

After three hours—record time for me—the Explorer rumbled across the railroad tracks that cut through the town of Four Creeks.

Chapter 2

Four Creeks was nestled against the Sierra foothills. It had doubled in size since I attended high school there. The majority of its businesses lined Main Street: two hardware stores, a branch of Bank of America, a barber shop, saloon, and a real estate office. Tucked in between were several antique dealers, boutiques, and three or four restaurants. The side streets held businesses related to agriculture plus the post office and library. On the west side, a nine-hole golf course was across the street from a shopping center with nationally known stores and fast-food places. The town is still known for the orange groves that surround it in every direction.

I pulled into a parking space in front of Four Creeks Police Station, a squatty brown building on the corner of Main and Plum Street. Two basketball-sized white globes with the word "Police" printed on them stood sentry on either side of the cement walk leading to the door.

I breezed in and through a waiting area to the counter. Behind it at a desk, sat a young woman whose waist-length, black hair shone in the light from a high window. She wore a frown as her fingers sped over a computer keyboard. Her name plate identified her as Elena. I estimated her age at mid-twenties. She flashed me a smile and continued typing as she spoke into the mouthpiece of a headset. After a few seconds, the conversation was over.

"I'm here to see Madge...I mean, Margaret Hatcher," I said as I pulled out a Powers Investigations business card and pushed it across the counter toward her.

Elena rose from her place, and her smile faded as she read my card. She waved me to a line of chairs in the waiting area and wandered off down a hallway. I picked the cleanest-looking chair, sat and glanced around the room. A major-sized cobweb dangled from the corner above the door where I'd entered. Framed certificates and a variety of plaques decorated the opposite wall. Most had something to do with marksmanship. I couldn't read them very well from where I sat, and at the moment, didn't give a damn anyway.

A minute later, Elena returned. "Lieutenant Walker will be with you shortly."

"Is that Buzz Walker?"

"Lieutenant Avis Walker," she corrected and went back to her desk.

Now there was a name that tweaked my memory banks. How long had it been since I'd seen him? A quick calculation made it twenty-two years. My thoughts drifted back to pubescent yearnings and evenings I'd spent with him in his '70 Chevelle. There could only be one Avis Walker. He knew Madge, and that made the charges against her all the more ridiculous. I sat drumming the arms of the chair with my fingernails, and as I did, my temper began to sizzle.

A couple of minutes passed before Elena motioned to the hall. "Third door on the right."

I marched to his door, entered without knocking, and stepped in front of his desk. "I want to see my aunt, right now. How could you possibly arrest that sweet old lady? Why, she was your sixth grade teacher." I drew a deep breath, ready for another salvo.

Buzz Walker rose from the seat behind his desk, hands raised, palms exposed. "Whoa, whoa, whoa. Hey, when I was in her class, I thought she rode to school on a broomstick." He motioned to a green leather office chair. "Sit down, Deena. Cork your steam. It's good to see you. You look great. How long's it been? Twenty years?"

"All of that."

I was about to reiterate my demand when he sat down, leaned back and gazed at me. "You always did have a short fuse," he said. Little lines around his eyes crinkled with a half-smile. "I didn't arrest your aunt. I had her come in to answer a few questions."

I took a seat, perplexed. "Where is she?"

"I imagine she's at home."

Deflated, I stared at him. Flecks of gray had invaded his dark hair. He was still good-looking, still trim, and from his sun-leathered skin, I suspected he still preferred the great outdoors. Probably even wore cowboy boots.

"Madge called me and said she'd been arrested in connection with a murder."

He shook his head. "She misunderstood. She was seen in a heated argument with the victim, Mrs. Weston, the day before her body was found. She had to be considered...well..."

His comment raised my ire. "A suspect? How can you say that? What sort of argument?"

"They were overheard in the library. There were witnesses. Threats were made."

The muscles of my neck tightened. "Threats? What sort of threats? What witnesses?"

He put on his police lieutenant face. "I can't tell you that and you know it."

"There must be other suspects. Have you questioned them? And what makes you so certain it was a homicide? Maybe I should..."

Before I could continue Buzz rose from his chair like a sea monster and stepped around the desk, hands on hips. He was taller than I remembered. His blue eyes narrowed as he loomed over me. "This is a police matter. Stay out of it. It's none of your business."

I stood and drew myself to my full five-foot-four height. Madge *was* my business. I wanted answers, but knew better than to challenge a bull in his own pen. I turned on my heel and left. I'd simply have to find out for myself.

I returned to the SUV. No doubt about it, when Buzz Walker's blue eyes turned green, it was time to get out of the way. No use trying to pump him for more information. That part of his personality hadn't changed.

I wondered if he harbored a grudge. Our high school romance had ended abruptly. I sort of dumped him. No. Actually, I did dump him. He'd started talking about marriage and babies, and I didn't want to spend my life stuck out in the boonies on a ranch like his mother. I took off for college like my tail feathers were on fire and never looked back. Now I'd have to deal with him if I wanted to clear suspicion surrounding Madge.

Relieved Madge wasn't in jail, but no more enlightened, I turned the car in the direction of Indian Hill. As I did so, a cloud of guilt drifted over me. Since college I hadn't spent near enough time with Madge, especially in the last five years since Uncle Henry died. Most years Dad and I visited for a day or two during the holidays, and I'd kept in touch with phone calls. But Madge wasn't a wallflower. She'd developed her own social life as a member of the local garden club, the Women of Colonial Heritage and with a group of fellow retired teachers who enjoyed golf. A retired teacher, she been married to Henry Hatcher, an attorney, older by several years. He built her a comfortable ranch house on the side of Indian Hill, and though childless, they'd lived happily ever after. At least that's the way Madge told it.

Minutes later I pulled into her circular driveway. Branches of the fruitless mulberry trees that stood in her yard were bare, but before the hot summer arrived, when temperatures ranged between ninety and a hundred degrees, their leaves would provide much needed shade.

Her house, with its soft, muted shade of green, had been a second home to me. As a kid I'd spent part of nearly every summer in Four Creeks, splitting the time between Grandpa and Grandma Powers at the ranch and Aunt Madge and Uncle Henry in town. They'd treated me to trips to the nearby national parks, picnics and fishing at the lake, a favorite of Uncle Henry's.

I hauled my luggage out of the Explorer, entered the house, and set my bags near the front door. Madge was in the kitchen. She was wearing her usual well-washed apron over denims and a red knit shirt. It was her favorite color and a shade that complimented her silvery curls. She'd managed to keep a trim figure probably because she continued to do most of her own yard work.

A platter of homemade cookies and another of muffins lined the counter separating the kitchen from the dining room. Baking was Madge's way of handling stress. It didn't matter that no one could eat all the goodies she made, though Uncle Henry certainly tried.

"Hello," I said as I shrugged out of my jacket and laid my purse on the dining room table. Madge rushed to greet me, spatula in hand. She hugged me like I was a prodigal daughter.

"What took you so long to get here?" she asked. Despite her smile, she looked tired and worried.

"I stopped at the police station. I thought I'd find you in jail."

"Oh." Her chin dipped.

"You said you were arrested."

She cocked her head to one side. "I panicked when he looked so stern. It felt like a real arrest. All I could think of was to call you. I resented all those prying questions Avis Walker asked. He used to be such a nice boy."

She reached for the platter of cookies. "I think these are your favorite."

I'm a sucker for chocolate chip cookies, so I chose one and slid onto a stool at the counter. "Madge, we need to talk," I said between bites. "Lieutenant Walker said Mrs. Weston and you had an argument the day before her death. What did you argue about?"

"Don't talk with your mouth full, dear," she said as she returned the platter to its place. "Everyone called her Lottie, but her name was actually Carlotta. You probably didn't know that."

I didn't, but she was stalling.

"The argument."

"Nothing of consequence. And none of that man's business."

Madge went to the stove, lifted the lid on a kettle and stirred the contents with a long-handled ladle. I detected the aroma of her special vegetable soup, another favorite of mine.

"It *is* his business. His job is to investigate her death. He said someone witnessed the dispute and reported it to him."

Madge stiffened. "Oh, questions, questions. I simply can't stand any more questions." She put down the spoon, pulled a tissue from her apron pocket and muffled a sob.

Her distress was upsetting. My aunt was a feisty lady. She'd spent thirty years glaring down rebellious sixth graders. It wasn't her style to dissolve into tears. I rose from my seat, stepped around the partition and put my arms around her. "Okay, Madge. It's been a hard day. We'll talk about it later."

The ring of the wall phone startled both of us. Madge reached for the receiver, listened and handed it to me straight-armed, as though the caller had said a dirty word.

"It's Avis Walker," she said. "I recognize his voice. I don't want to talk to him."

When I took it, she grabbed the muffin tin and stuck it in the sink

18

of soapy water. I hesitated for a second undecided whether my greeting should be cool or conciliatory. Finally, I simply said, "Hello."

"Deena, I wanted to apologize," he said. "I meant to tell you how sorry I am to hear about your father."

"Thank you. I guess Madge told you what happened."

"Yes. I was wondering when the service will be held?"

"We haven't discussed it yet. I'm not sure there's going to be one."

An awkward silence followed.

"I'll give your condolences to my aunt."

"Yes, do that. Thanks." He ended the call.

Not a warm exchange, but no spears and daggers either. I turned to Madge. "He simply wanted to extend his condolences."

"I gathered as much." She rinsed the pan and set it aside.

Buzz Walker had given me the opening I needed to broach a delicate subject. "I think we should lay Dad's ashes to rest in the next day or so."

Madge turned from the sink, wiping her hands on a kitchen towel. "That's too soon. How will his friends know about the service?"

"I wasn't planning on one."

"Why? People will want to pay their respects."

"He's been away from this area so long ...." I couched my words, not wanting to come right out and say I thought all his friends were probably dead. "I doubt there's anyone who'd remember him."

Madge's forehead creased as she folded the towel. "There certainly is. There's...." She leaned back against the sink. Tears welled in her eyes, and I saw her struggle to think of a name.

"It's hard for me to believe we might be the only ones to care," she said, her voice cracking. "We should at least put a notice in the local newspaper."

19

I couldn't deny her wish. "All right, I'll take care of it. I guess I'd better unpack." A lump formed in my throat. Madge was the only family I had left. My mother died when I was seven. My grandparents were long gone. I had no other aunts or uncles. There were probably some second cousins somewhere, but I never knew them. The thought was sobering. I picked up my bags and headed to the guest room.

The room I usually occupied had been redecorated since my last visit. The bedroom walls were pale peach, the carpet a dark green. Fluffy peach and green curtains matched the bedspread. A small desk and lamp stood adjacent to the door. Both were new. When I envisioned the hodge-podge furnishings in my apartment bedroom, the contrast was striking. My battered luggage looked out of place.

After arranging the contents of my cosmetic case in the bathroom, and shoving the bag containing the tools of my trade in the closet, I opened my overnight bag on the bed. I slipped the better garments onto hangers and put the rest in the dresser, then headed back to the kitchen, thinking I'd help prepare lunch.

When I rounded the corner from the hallway to the living room, I overheard Madge talking on the phone. "Frankly, I can't say I'm sorry she's dead. She was a malicious woman and a disgrace to the whole town."

Chapter 3

Madge's comment halted me. I was more than surprised at her words. It wasn't like her to be mean-spirited.

"I know you feel the same way," Madge continued. "But I can't talk now, Irma. Deena's here unpacking her things. Another time, perhaps. Goodbye."

She turned and discovered me standing in the living room facing her. I guess it was obvious by my expression I'd overheard. "Who's Irma?" I asked.

"Oh, she's just a busy-body here in town."

I returned to my seat at the breakfast counter. "Madge, you've *got* to talk to me about this whole situation. It's the only way I can help you. I *have* to know about your relationship with Mrs. Weston, about her and the people she associated with."

I thought Madge was ignoring me when she went to the cupboard and took out two bowls. She filled them with steaming soup and placed them on the counter. "I'm not certain there's much I can tell you."

I doubted her claim. After a lifetime in Four Creeks, she probably knew more about her neighbors than they'd care to believe.

"I know one thing for sure," Madge admitted. "If there'd been any legal way for the city fathers to make Lottie be less conspicuous and get rid of her twelve cats, they would have jumped at it. She was a blot on the landscape, walking around in torn clothes the way she did, as if she didn't have a penny to her name. We all had to look the other way and tolerate her behavior."

I didn't remember seeing anyone like that when I'd visited. Why hadn't I heard about her before? I accepted a spoon Madge offered and dipped into the soup. "Was it so bad someone would kill her?"

"Oh, I doubt that," Madge replied.

"There has to be a motive. Did someone have a deep-seated grudge against her?"

"A grudge? I wouldn't say that exactly. But ill-feelings? Oh, yes. There was plenty of that. Irma . . ." Madge's mouth snapped shut.

"What about Irma?"

"I'm not going to talk about Irma behind her back. You'll have to ask her yourself. Eat your soup." She placed a basket of rolls on the counter.

I bristled at Madge's sixth-grade-teacher command. I wasn't a twelve-year-old, and I wasn't going to let her get away with it. "Not so fast. Tell me her last name and I *will* talk to her."

"Last name's Foster."

I broke open one of the rolls. Irma Foster might not be willing to talk to a stranger with no real authority. But in casual surroundings? "Since Irma doesn't know me, you could invite her to lunch tomorrow and introduce us."

Madge took a seat, picked up her spoon and peered at me over soup-steamed glasses. "You want me to invite her *here*?"

"Sure. You can tell her you want her to meet your niece. It's logical." I bit into the roll.

Madge's shoulders drooped. "Oh, all right, but you're not going to like her. She's a chain-smoker and a bitter woman." Her brow creased as she gave me a sharp look. "I'll call her in the morning."

"How come I've never heard you mention her before? Have you known her very long?"

"Irma and I were in school together."

"That's a long time to be bitter."

"She wasn't always like that." Madge dipped her spoon into the soup and lifted it to her lips.

"What made her change?"

She swallowed and said, "Irma had some tough breaks in life."

"Like what?"

"For one thing, her father was killed in a tractor accident when she was in tenth grade. She had to quit school to go to work. Farmers never thought about life insurance in those days."

"Is she married?"

"Not any longer. Frank Foster died eight years ago."

It seemed improbable that Irma, like Madge, past prime-time, would turn to murder. On the other hand, if she had a score to settle, arrangements could be made. Stranger things have happened. I pondered the possibilities as we ate in silence for several minutes.

"Just for the record, where were you last Saturday night?" I shoveled the last piece of carrot into my mouth.

Madge expelled a sigh. "Well now, Miss Detective, I was right here watching one of those classic movies until bedtime."

I mimicked her tone. "And what was the movie?"

She put her finger to her forehead. "The one with Humphrey Bogart and what's-her-name... Hepburn."

"You mean *African Queen*?"

She wagged her index finger in my direction. "That's the one."

I nodded and wolfed down the last bite of the roll. "Great soup," I said and wiped my lips. I slid off the stool. "I better call Judy to let her know I arrived safe, and then find some place to gas the Explorer." I pluck my purse off the dining room table and headed for the door. "I won't be long."

"Wind's kicking up," she replied. "Better take a jacket."

Out in the Explorer, I dug my cell phone out of my purse and tapped in Judy's number. When she answered, I filled her in on my session with Buzz, and the lack of information I'd been able to wring out of Madge.

"You can't help people who won't help themselves," Judy counseled.

She solved most puzzles with a maxim of some sort.

"Any messages on the machine?"

"No, only a couple of hang-ups."

"I'll keep you posted." I closed the phone.

There were two stop lights in Four Creeks. One of them halted me in front of the high school. It sported a new paint job, a battleship gray with blue trim. It was a mellow tan during my school days. Dad and I moved in with Grandpa and Grandma Powers at the ranch when Grandpa became sick with cancer and needed Dad's help. As a result I spent my senior year of high school at Four Creeks High.

Each time I returned for a visit, I'd see more changes. I'd passed a new housing tract on my way through town. A closed sign hung on the empty building of Tremain's Market, perhaps a victim of the warehouse grocery movement. The mini-mart was still there, but with a new owner.

The sign read Avila's Quick Mart. I pulled in next to a pump, fished my wallet out of my purse and headed for the double doors that greeted me with cigarette ads. Inside, to the left, stood a chest-type freezer filled with a variety of tempting ice cream selections beneath a glass cover. The cash register counter was on the right. Behind it, between the cigarettes and packages of film, was a photo of a fleshy man exhibiting a proud smile and holding a massive white fur ball. The cat had a flat face, tiny eyes and a blue ribbon. The same rotund fellow waddled toward me down the aisle and took his position behind the counter.

I pointed to the white cat. "That's a great picture."

His face lit up with a smile nearly as broad as his girth. "My only claim to fame. Sir Winston. He's Persian. The picture was taken five years ago. I still have him, but he's too old to show. You have a cat?"

I shook my head. "Two dogs." As I sorted through my wallet, looking for a twenty, I noticed the *Delta Sun* in a newspaper rack next to the gumball machine. A report about the Weston murder was on the front page. Pulling out a copy, I laid it on the counter, ready to pay for it and the gasoline.

The big fellow tapped the page. "It's a darn shame about Lottie, isn't it? Makes me mad. The paper don't say it's her, but everyone's talking about it."

My attention sharpened. "Oh, did you know her?"

"Sure, everybody knew Lottie. She was the town oddity. You must be new around here."

I smiled and nodded. "Visiting family."

"Some people thought of her as an eyesore," he continued, "the way she dressed, but I never thought so."

"She was a friend of yours?"

He shrugged. "In a way. She came in every Thursday about noon. Never bought much, only a candy bar and a lottery ticket. But we both loved our cats and swapped tales." His belly jiggled as he chuckled at his own joke.

I gave him an appreciative grin. "Did she show her cats too?"

"Nah, but she kept a bunch, all kinds, mostly she rescued strays. I wonder what's going to happen to them. She asked my advice sometimes, like when one of her kittens got sick. I gave her a sample of medicine I'd used. By the way, I'm Max Avila." He offered his hand across the counter.

"I'm Deena Powers." As I took his hand, a door slammed in the back of the store. I flinched and let go.

Max scowled. "My nephew. That's Eddie's way of clocking out." He shook his head. "Kids. I felt sorry for him 'cause his dad committed suicide. He was a Vietnam vet." He leaned over the counter as if telling me a confidence. "Had those awful flashbacks, you know."

I nodded, thinking not all casualties happened on the battlefield.

As he straightened, he said, "So when Eddie got married and didn't have a job, I hired him." He shrugged. "Now he's got a baby. Hasn't changed him much."

I didn't know how to respond, so I tucked the paper under my arm, matched his shrug and told him the pump number.

When I returned for my change, I'd thought of another question to ask him about Mrs. Weston. But by then, there were three teenage boys in the store. Mr. Avila watched them in an overhead mirror as he handed over my change. Not a good time for questions. I pulled out my business card and slid it across the counter to him. "Maybe we could talk about Mrs. Weston again."

He ignored me.

I pushed through the door and was digging in my bag for my coin purse, when I bumped into a tall balding man in a dark gray business suit. We apologized in unison, and I headed for the car.

"Deena?" he called after me. "Deena Powers?"

I turned back and recognized Russ Treadwell, one of my classmates from Four Creeks High.

"Russ. I'm sorry. I wasn't paying attention as to who I was knocking down." I returned to shake his hand.

Russ had become an attorney like his father before him. He was Madge's attorney, and I hadn't seen him since Uncle Henry's death. His tall lanky frame hadn't changed any and neither had his broad smile.

"Are you visiting or here to stay?" he asked.

"Just visiting." I started to ask about his family.

He interrupted. "Say, I need to talk to you. Are you staying with your aunt?"

I nodded. "Yes."

He reached for the door. "I'll have my secretary call and make an appointment. Got to hurry. Don't want to keep the mayor waiting. Good to see you, Deena." He disappeared inside.

What an odd encounter. He wanted an appointment to talk about family? Or what?

Chapter 4

After settling in the Explorer, I scanned the article about the murder. In a few words, it stated that the body of a woman had been discovered by a jogger at six o'clock Sunday morning. The victim was found floating in an irrigation canal on Orchard Drive. Identification was being withheld pending notification of next of kin. Evidence of trauma led the police to believe it was a homicide. An investigation was in progress.

Disappointing, but all that could be expected after only a couple of days. I folded the paper, laid it aside and started the engine.

My father's ashes were still waiting to be delivered to the mortuary. I pulled out and drove to the north side of town where Van Dyke's Mortuary was located next to Four Creeks Cemetery. When I arrived, I took the box that held Dad's ashes from the seat next to me and went to the door. A sign above a door bell asked me to ring for service. I did, and after several moments a woman in a black business suit answered.

"May I help you?" she asked, eyeing the box under my arm. Her pale complexion made me think she spent too much time indoors.

"I'm Deena Powers and I have the ashes of Wallace Powers. I think you're expecting them."

She stepped back from the door. "Come in."

I entered and handed her the box while I dug an envelope out of my purse. "Here's the appropriate paperwork."

"We're so sorry for your loss," she said with the correct degree of grimness in her expression. She identified herself as Mrs. Van Dyke.

"Have you chosen a date for the service?"

"As soon as the obituary appears in the local newspaper." Although I'd decided to give in to Madge's request, I still doubted anyone would take notice.

"Let's go into the office." She led me through a dim hall to a room furnished in dark mahogany. After I'd settled in a leather chair, she said, "That would be next Monday's edition. We can submit the notice to the paper for you."

Fifteen gut-wrenching minutes later, I was back in the Explorer, having related the highlights of my father's life to a stranger. It's one of those duties a person must endure when a loved one dies. Having left his ashes behind, I felt a new surge of loneliness, as though he'd still been present in the box.

At Mrs. Van Dyke's direction, I stopped at the cemetery to let the manager know the family burial plot would need to be ready the following Tuesday.

With my duty completed, I returned to Madge's house and helped her prepare dinner. She served pan-fried fish, carrots and cauliflower. Madge knows I dislike cauliflower, but every time I visited, it was on my plate at least once. She must have thought I'd change my mind.

During dinner, when I tried to talk about Lottie Weston, Madge changed the subject. She chattered on and on about the garden club and the Women of Colonial Heritage. She'd taken on the role of historian for the Vista de los Rios chapter, and invited me to return for their colonial tea in May. I knew the event would involve a colonial costume, something I'd rather avoid.

At the end of my first day in Four Creeks I didn't know much more than when I arrived. I crawled into bed that night and fell asleep with visions of Lottie floating face down in muddy water.

In the wee hours of the next morning, a nightmare crawled out of my subconscious. I knew it was a dream even as I tried to wrench myself from its grip. In it, I was speeding down a winding mountain road with a blur of pine trees on both sides and snow on the ground. A sense of something ominous made me grip the wheel, muscles taut. A sharp curve appeared ahead. Apprehension escalated—until I jackknifed up in bed, frantic for release from the suffocating panic.

I got out of bed and paced the floor for several minutes. It didn't take a shrink to figure out that the accident and the nightmare was related. But dreams are not reality. That's what I told myself. The sensation of menace could symbolize the loss of my father.

I crawled back under the covers, tossed around a little, dozed off and woke with a headache the size of Chicago. It was still dark outside. Sitting up, I braced my forehead with the heels of my hands and groaned. Relief was ten steps away. Jerking back the covers, my insides quivering, I stumbled to the bathroom. I flipped the light switch and scrunched my eyes against the brightness. The bottle of pain killer Dr. Nichols, my neurologist, had prescribed was in my cosmetic case. I dug it out and fumbled to open it. The safety cap wouldn't budge. As I twisted it in vain, my impatience flashed. I threw the blasted thing in the sink. It ricocheted, hit the mirror, and landed on the floor. A wave of nausea hit me as I watched it roll behind the toilet. I leaned back against the wall, slid to the floor, and pushed up the toilet lid—just in case.

I hate to vomit, have always hated it, especially the residual burning in the back of my nose. In a momentary fit of absurdity, I wondered if tonsils might block that pathway, but there was no use wishing them back. They'd been gone since I was nine.

I sat a few minutes with my eyes closed and struggled to control the nausea. Absently, I ran my fingers through my hair, touching the three-inch scar that was a memento of the accident and wished my memory would heal too.

Groping for the bottle, I clutched it and rose to my feet. With a pinch and a twist, the lid came off, and I rattled out two white tablets.

A minute later, lying on the bed, I stared at the ceiling and waited for the pain to ease. Perhaps the nightmare was my brain trying to restore my memory. I closed my eyes and concentrated. Nothing came. Transient amnesia, Dr. Nichols called it. I might remember someday— or not.

Could I have done something to change events that day? If only I'd talked Dad out of the trip to Dell Fisk's cabin. If only we'd waited a day or two for better weather. If only . . . . It was no use. A person could spend all day in such a futile exercise. I lay quiet for several minutes watching the red numbers on the digital clock change. After a while, the pain eased. I rolled over and drifted to sleep.

When the anemic winter sun filtered through the window and found my face, it woke me. It was past eight o'clock, and I detected the inviting aroma of coffee. After a shower, I dressed and went into the living room to look for the morning paper, eager to see if it contained more information about the Weston murder. I didn't find one.

"Madge, don't you take a newspaper?"

"Only the local," she called from the kitchen. "I gave up on the *Delta Sun*. I don't like their politics. The *Creekside News* came Monday. I've already tossed it. Sorry. What would you like for breakfast?"

My stomach still felt uneasy. "Toast and coffee will be fine, thanks," I said as I took my usual seat.

Madge was dressed in denims and a tan flannel shirt with the long sleeves rolled up. She placed a cup of coffee in front of me and a

31

minute later, a plate of toast and a jar of jam. I couldn't resist a spoonful of her homemade strawberry jam.

"I think I'll go to the library to see if today's newspaper reports anything new about the murder investigation," I said. I had in mind using the big Four Creeks map I remembered hanging on the library wall to locate the scene of the crime. I thought Freddie Weston had lived on the west side of town, but had only a vague notion of the location after so many years. I felt sure the police would be contacting Madge again, and I needed more information before we talked to a lawyer.

Madge raised her eyebrows as though surprised. "All right. I'm going to do some weeding in the backyard, but I'll call Irma first and have lunch ready at noon."

After the last swallow of coffee, I wiped jam off my cheek and put the dishes in the sink. I thanked her, slipped into my jacket and grabbed my purse, ready to leave.

As I reached for the doorknob she said, "Don't be late. I don't want to spend my day listening to Irma complain."

Outside, the sky was overcast and the air was cool and damp. I climbed into the SUV and let the windshield wipers swish away the dew before leaving.

From the stop sign at the bottom of Indian Hill, I made a right-hand turn, and then a left onto Citrus Street, buzzed past the post office and found a parking space in front of the library. The building was a one-story rectangle of gray brick, just as I remembered it from my school days.

I stepped out of the SUV and followed a walkway leading to the double doors. Inside, a large glass display case contained an exhibit of antique china. It was flanked by a colorful bulletin board announcing various community activities, including a promotion for Daffodil Days.

A red-haired woman in a blue turtleneck sweater stood behind a high counter and was engaged in a rapid-fire conversation with a chubby woman opposite her. She was clad in pink stretch-pants, matching sweatshirt, plus pink socks and sneakers. The sight of her brought to mind the Easter Bunny.

"You just never know about people," the librarian said. She shook her head as she chewed a piece of gum. "I was shocked."

In a town as small as Four Creeks, it was easy to guess what they were discussing. I spotted the newspaper rack, ambled over and extracted the *Delta Sun*. I chose a table near the counter. Eavesdropping might harvest better information than the newspaper.

The woman in pink gave her pants a hitch. "Yeah, the whole town is in an uproar, wondering if Madge Hatcher did it. I heard Lottie's head was bloodied."

The librarian flicked a scanning wand across the inside cover of a couple of books, snapped them shut and placed them on a nearby cart. "And to think they argued right here in the library only hours before she was killed. It's hard to believe such things can happen practically under your nose."

"You heard them argue?"

Clearly, Pinkie was eager for more detail and so was I.

"I witnessed the whole thing," the librarian continued. "Lottie shuffled in here wearing that dirty black coat, and parked her folding wire cart right over there by the door where somebody could trip over it. You know, the thing she drags, I mean dragged, around town."

Pinkie giggled. "I guess I shouldn't make fun, but the way she kinda waddled, made me think of a gigantic black duck."

The librarian swiped the bar code on another book and added it to the stack. "Anyway, she went to that round table by the back wall." She pointed her wand in the general direction. "And when she sat

33

down her coat fell open. I could see her belly through a hole in the front of her dress."

Pinkie put her hand over her gaping mouth.

"Pretty soon Madge Hatcher arrived, dressed like she was going to church, wearing a navy blue pantsuit and matching beret. She went over to the table and sat down. It was a heck of a contrast, I'll tell you."

Pinkie wrinkled her nose. "Could you hear what they said?"

"Most of what Lottie said anyway. Mrs. Hatcher had her back to me. I heard Lottie say she'd known Mrs. Hatcher more than fifty years, and she knew what Lottie wanted. I told the police every word."

Pinkie leaned forward. "I heard there was yelling?"

The librarian nodded. "Lottie said she wasn't the only one with secrets. Then Mrs. Hatcher really got mad. She jumped up and almost knocked over the chair."

"What'd she say?"

"Oh, something about she'd fight tigers to protect her family, and she'd get a lawyer. I didn't hear every word, but she sure was upset. She shrieked and told Lottie she'd be sorry. Then Lottie said, 'I'll get what I want. I always have.' Isn't that something?"

"I'll say. Were you the only one who heard them?"

"No. Mr. Richards was over there reading the paper, but he's nearly deaf, you know." She indicated a table where I was sitting.

"He always comes in as soon as I open," she continued. "And Irma was back in the historical section."

"Irma? You mean Irma Foster?"

"Uh huh. She was closer than me. She probably heard it all."

"You think the police questioned her?"

"I suppose so. I told them she was here."

As if the two women realized they might be overheard, they moved to the far end of the counter beyond the computer and lowered their voices. Still, I heard Pinkie ask, "Did Lottie have any family?"

I turned my attention to the article in the *Delta Sun*. It gave few additional details, stating:

> On Sunday morning a body believed to be Carlotta Weston, a native of this area, was discovered in a canal near her home on Orchard Drive. Jogger Will Hastings, who reported the finding to the police, stated, "I jog along here every day and never expected to see something like that." Lieutenant Avis Walker acknowledged evidence of trauma led the police to believe the woman was the victim of a homicide. An investigation is underway. Mrs. Weston lived at 5797 Orchard Drive, Four Creeks.

I made note of the address and glanced around for the map I was expecting to see. It was gone, and in its place was a new section of children's books. I replaced the newspaper and headed for the door, but slowed my pace as I passed the desk. The two women were still buzzing.

"You're kidding," Pinkie said aloud.

"Shhhh. I'm sure Thelma wouldn't say it, if it wasn't so."

Pinkie leaned in. "Then you think it's true that Lottie had twins?" she whispered. "But how could she just give one away? I can't imagine."

I pushed through the swinging doors to the outside. Amazing what you can learn in a library, if you're quiet.

Chapter 5

Everything I'd heard might be gossip, but I couldn't help wondering how Lottie Weston could be a threat to our family. Also intriguing was Lottie's comment that she wasn't the only one with a secret. What sort of secret would Madge have? I couldn't fathom even one.

As I returned to the SUV, my cell phone jingled. It was Madge.

"Irma can't come to lunch today," she said. "She has a hair appointment this afternoon."

Frustrated, I checked my watch again. "It's only eleven. I'll pay her a visit before she gets away. What's her address?"

"Maybe she doesn't want to talk to you. Ever think of that?"

When I didn't comment, Madge expelled a sigh. "She lives north of the Fair Buy Market on East Flores Avenue. Drive north on Benson, and turn right after the railroad tracks. It's a bright yellow house with green trim. I don't understand why she hasn't had it painted since she moved in. It's dreadful."

I knew Madge could criticize Irma's taste in paint for several minutes, and I wanted to be on my way. "Thanks a lot," I said. "I'll see you in a little while."

"Wait," she interrupted. "Do me a favor. Pick up a pint of sour cream at the market on your way here. I'm making beef Stroganoff for dinner."

"Sure thing." I closed the phone.

As I drove along Flores Avenue, a gray cat meandered across the street in front of my car. The houses in the neighborhood had a similar appearance, except for a two-story at the end of a cul-de-sac. Half of them had white columns in front while the others were designed with horizontal ladder railings. All the lawns and shrubs were trimmed, and a few had colorful flower beds. Norway pine seemed to be the favorite landscape tree.

I had no trouble finding Irma Foster's house. It really was a flag-down-a-plane yellow. As I pulled to the curb, I noticed that besides the cat, there were no signs of life on the street. However, there was no shortage of backyard dogs. As soon as I closed the car door several started barking. After a pause to check my purse for a notepad, I approached the house and pressed the doorbell.

A moment later the door edged open, and Irma, nearly six feet tall and over two hundred pounds, glared at me. Her age was likely early sixties. She was wearing blue slacks and a matching long-sleeved sweater. Her unnatural blonde hair was styled in an old-fashioned pageboy. More striking was the gray complexion of a long-time smoker and the scowl on her face.

I countered with an Avon-lady smile and stuck out my hand. "Hello, Mrs. Foster. I'm Deena Powers, Madge Hatcher's niece."

"I guessed who you were." She didn't take my hand, but let the door swing open. No smile. "Your aunt called and said you wanted to talk to me about Lottie Weston. I don't know why. I guess you can come in, but I haven't got much time."

She stepped back and waved me into a dim entry hall leading to her living room. An oak entertainment center dominated the sizable room. A picture window revealed her patio with pots of geraniums and cyclamens in full bloom, undaunted by the cold nights.

She motioned to a plush maroon chair while she took a position on the couch, leaving several feet of space between us, indicating it was not going to be a cozy chitchat.

While she lit a cigarette from a package on the coffee table, I considered whether she was strong enough to wield a blunt implement with lethal intent. Here was a woman with emphysemic lungs, no doubt, and she suddenly decides to commit murder? How likely was that?

I decided on a friendly approach. "I'm glad we have a chance to talk in private."

She took a puff and slowly blew out the smoke. "Get to the point. I have to leave soon."

Clearly, she wasn't buying my technique. "I understand you witnessed the argument between my aunt and Mrs. Weston." I smiled, hoping I'd made the statement sound casual.

Her face blanched. "How'd you know that? The only person I told was Lieutenant Walker."

"I'm sure you're aware my aunt was questioned. I'm looking out for her interests, and it would help if you told me about it."

"Why don't you ask her?"

"I did. What she told me was pretty sketchy. She was awfully upset by the questioning."

"I gave a statement to Lieutenant Walker. I don't like repeating it."

I ignored her intended brush-off. "Did you see Mrs. Weston enter the library?"

"Hah, I saw her, all right. Saw her before she saw me. She came in with that thing on wheels she dragged around town. Parked it beside the IRS publications, waddled over and plopped herself down at a reading table near the wall. I didn't want her to see me, so I ducked behind the last bookshelf."

"Why didn't you want her to see you?"

She took a fierce drag on the cigarette. "Because she'd speak to me, and I'd hate to have anyone think I'd associate with the likes of her. She took a sadistic joy in that sort of thing, making out she was just like everyone else."

"You knew her pretty well?"

She ignored my question. "I peeked between the books and saw she was wearing the same old dirty, black coat she always wore. And those shoes, worn down, looked like she'd walked through a chicken pen." She wrinkled her nose. Another puff.

"Was my aunt there when she came in?"

"No, she came in later. I couldn't believe it when she sat down at the same table."

"What did she say?"

"She said, 'What is it?' No greeting, just 'What is it?' Her face was set grim-like. Then Lottie said, 'Don't want to be seen with me, do you?' or something like that. I would've said hell no. But Madge didn't say anything."

"Then what?"

Irma repositioned herself forward a bit as though warming to the subject. "Madge said, 'I came, didn't I? Tell me what you want.' It wasn't the least bit friendly. And Lottie said, 'Don't get short with me. I've known you more than fifty years. You already know what I want.' She pushed a piece of paper across the table, but Madge ignored it." Irma stabbed out her cigarette in an ashtray on the table beside her.

I leaned forward. I didn't want to miss a single word. "What did she want?"

"Well, I didn't get all of it because my hearing isn't so good, and the librarian started talking to someone at the desk, but I thought I heard the name Deena." Her eyebrows lifted. "I guess that's you."

"My name? They talked about *me*?" I tried to hide my surprise.

"Maybe. Madge had turned in her chair, so I couldn't hear her as well, but I heard Lottie say she had the right."

"The right about what?"

"I don't know, but she said something about a legacy, and Madge laughed out loud and spoke up. She said, 'What kind of legacy would you have to leave? You barely keep body and soul together.' That's what she said." Irma nodded as if confirming the statement and shifted her weight. "Madge got real mad when Lottie said, 'I'm not the only one with secrets. I could tell people about you.' Her face got red. She fairly shouted. Everyone could hear her. She said, 'You think I'm easy, I'm not.' I guess she feels like she still has some influence in town."

"The argument was about money?" It didn't make sense. I leaned back in the chair. "I don't get it."

Irma gave me a sideways glance, and helped herself to another cigarette, but didn't light it. She tapped one end against the package. "That's about it."

"I heard there were threats," I said.

"I guess you could say that. Madge didn't mince words, said something about a lawyer. And Lottie said, 'I'll get what I want. I always have.'" Irma slid the unlit cigarette back in the package. "Hah. Ain't that the truth." She stood and motioned to a wall clock. "I have an appointment."

I had no choice but to leave. I didn't want to alienate her when I had more questions. I'd have to find a way to talk to her again.

It was noon, and the sun had broken through the overcast skies. Back in traffic, I was so busy pondering what I'd heard, I almost drove past Fair Buy Market. At the last second, I made a quick turn into the parking lot.

Without much thought, I picked a spot to park, all the while wondering what Lottie Weston wanted that Madge wouldn't give her, and what connection it had with me. Madge had some explaining to do.

Inside the store, it took me a couple of minutes to locate the dairy section and pick out a container of sour cream. When I approached the checkout, I noticed a young, dark-haired guy standing behind a buxom cashier. She had big brown eyes and frizzed blonde hair. A label on her striped shirt read, Hester. I was thinking about spring and a young man's fancy, when I heard him whisper to her, "I'll be over as soon as Maria and the kid are asleep. I've got something to show you. It won't be long now."

The clerk scowled. "Okay, okay, just get out of here, Eddie. If the manager sees you hanging around, I could lose my job."

He winked, gave her behind a pat and scurried out the door.

She shot me a furtive glance, grabbed my sour cream and scanned it. I paid and left, speculating about whether this fellow was Max Avila's nephew, Eddie.

Out in the parking lot, I saw him climb into a faded blue Civic with a dented back fender. "What a louse," I muttered, feeling sorry for his wife and baby.

I slid into the Explorer and decided to search for the scene of Lottie Weston's murder before returning to Madge's. It was on Orchard Drive, the paper had said.

I turned west out of the parking lot onto Orchard Drive which led from the store to the town of Creekside, a distance of about five miles. As I drove, I realized most of the orchards I remembered were gone, replaced by houses planted in half-acre plots.

The number of houses thinned out, and after about a mile, I spotted a place where a culvert passed beneath the road, and an irrigation canal snaked across open fields in both directions. I pulled off beyond it next to a field where winter rains had yielded a crop of knee high weeds and got out. The area I surveyed was too far out of town for sidewalks.

On the north side of the road, not far from the canal, stood a small California bungalow style house with faded green siding. A brown lawn, dormant for the winter, flanked the uneven sidewalk leading to the front door.

On the other side of the road, seventy to seventy-five yards east, was an even older home with tall leafless trees in the back and a chain-link fence around the front yard.

I walked over to where the culvert opened to the canal. It was about eight feet across with sloping sides to a depth of around five feet. Besides tall, wild grasses and debris, it had a little over a foot of water in the bottom.

I crossed to the other side of the road. There, the canal narrowed and the water was deeper. The grasses on the left bank had been trampled. Native brush and small trees on the opposite bank shaded the slow moving water.

I sat sidesaddle, so to speak, on the concrete barrier between the road and the water below. I thought about Lottie floating there, if indeed it was the location. Had she drowned, or was it a blow to her head that killed her? Maybe she was semi-conscious and unable to help herself. I wondered what her last thoughts might have been.

I thought about Dad and wished I'd been with him when he died, but I was barely conscious myself at the time. He was surrounded by strangers. That's the way it is with traumatic death. At least he wasn't alone like Lottie. No one should die alone. I lingered a bit and stared at the water, then gave myself a mental shake and stood. I had to pull myself out of the gloom and focus on the present. The police would find Lottie's killer. Buzz was right. It was none of my business. Madge couldn't possibly be an actual suspect. I'd take care of Dad's memorial service and get back to my life in Ortega Bay. My life. Who was I kidding? My life had been adrift since the accident.

Behind me, I heard a car slow and turned to see a light blue Civic pull into the driveway of the bungalow. In seconds, the dark-haired guy from the market emerged from the car and disappeared inside.

I climbed back into the Explorer and made an illegal turn around to head back the way I came. As I drove past the older home with the fenced yard, I slowed. The mailbox number was the same as the one in the newspaper. It was easy to see how somebody could get away with murder in such an isolated location. Houses were spread out with stretches of open fields all around.

I pushed on the accelerator an glanced at the grocery bag in the passenger seat. Madge's sour cream would be getting warm from the sun shining through the car window. Time to deliver the goods and ask Madge some questions.

Madge was in the kitchen when I stepped through the front door. I saw her note the time before asking, "Have you had lunch?"

"No. I haven't." The house was filled with a mixture of delicious aromas of cooking beef and spices. I handed her the sour cream, and she handed me a salad with tiny shrimp and sunflower seeds sprinkled on top. A fork, salad dressing, and a package of bread sticks were waiting on the counter. I gave my salad a dollop of dressing, sat and dug in.

"I didn't think Irma would invite you to lunch. She's as tight-fisted as they come. Did you find out what you wanted to know?"

With a forkful of salad poised in front of my mouth, I glanced at her face and caught a glimpse of uneasiness.

"Not as much as I'd hoped. I needed more time, but you're right, she sure didn't think much of Lottie Weston."

I wanted to ask Madge why my name was part of the argument, but hesitated. If she knew Irma overheard their dispute, I might not get

43

any more information out of either of them. On the other hand, how else would I find out?

I paused to open the package of breadsticks. "Irma was in the library the day you and Lottie argued. She overheard some of what was said." I tried to sound casual. "She thought she heard my name mentioned. Why was that?"

Madge was at the stove with her back to me. I watched the familiar little flinch she always exhibited when surprised.

"I don't know why she'd say such a thing," she said over her shoulder. "It's not true at all." She jabbed at the pieces of beef in the frying pan with a slicing knife.

Madge was lying and I knew it. But why? I bit into a breadstick.

As though realizing she was doing something odd, she laid the knife aside and reached into the utensil drawer for a spatula. "Irma is quite hard of hearing, you know."

She turned toward me, her lips pressed together, a scowl on her face. A deep breath. "Oh, I might as well tell you. It can't hurt Mel. He's dead now. Mel was engaged to *Irma* before he married Lottie. It was a dirty trick, what Lottie did, and they weren't teenagers." She held the spatula out like pointing a ruler at a student. "They were grown women."

"Wait a minute. Who's Mel?"

"Melvin Weston. Lottie's husband. I can't say I blame Irma for the way she feels." She turned back to the frying pan and flipped the meat.

I was stunned, not only by Madge's outburst, but by the information. "You mean Lottie lured Mel away from Irma? How did she do it?"

Madge faced me again. She wagged her head from side to side. "Lottie breezed in here from out of town, and within a week she was wearing Mel's engagement ring. I don't know how she did it, but I can

44

imagine. It was a scandal, and Irma never got over it."

"But she married what's-his-name Foster."

"Yes, she did—a year later. In the meantime, everyone was embarrassed for her. In a town this size, it was awful. Frank Foster was no prize. He was a Korean War vet who came home missing a leg. They lived on his parent's ranch, and she had to work like a man. He took to drink, and rumor was he occasionally knocked her around."

"I'm not sure why you've told me all this. You think Irma wanted to kill Lottie after all these years?"

"Fffft, no. But if someone cuffed your ears on a regular basis, you might have lost your hearing too."

She still hadn't answered my first question. I took another bite of salad and was about to restate it when her face brightened. "Oh, you had a call from Dell Fisk. He needs to speak to you. I put the number by the phone." She pointed the spatula toward the wall phone.

"Judy must have given him your number." I finished the salad and put the plate in the sink before grabbing the slip of paper.

I headed for the bedroom and stretched out on the bed with my cell phone.

Dell Fisk was a family friend as well as our attorney. My dad met him while they were in the Army, and they'd been friends ever since. He gave me a job in his office when I needed one and sent his clients to our firm whenever they required our type of service. Sometimes it was related to an errant spouse, and I was the one stuck sitting for hours parked outside some motel waiting for something to happen. Not my favorite way to make a living.

Dell's greeting was warm and husky. He said the weather had turned clear and warmer, and I should return to Ortega Bay to enjoy it. "Also, I have some papers for you to sign."

"Could you mail them to me? I'll be here for a couple weeks."

45

"Sure, but I need to discuss your father's estate with you."

"I'm a bit tied up right now." I explained about Lottie's murder and Madge's predicament.

He exploded with laughter. "That's crazy. What is she—seventy?"

"I agree, it's ridiculous, but there's something strange about this whole thing." I related the incident in the library. "A witness said my name was mentioned."

"Is that so?" His tone changed. He wasn't laughing anymore. "Hmmm." He paused. "Honey, I doubt your aunt is guilty of anything worse than living in a town that thrives on gossip."

"Probably. Still.... Anyway, Dad's service isn't until next week. You know I hadn't planned on one, but Madge insists." I ended the call by assuring Dell I'd see him as soon as I got home.

The phone rang in the kitchen. "It's for you, Deena," Madge called.

I reached for the extension. A woman's voice introduced herself as Carmen Trout, secretary for Treadwell, Barns and Bates, Attorneys at Law.

"Mr. Treadwell asked me to arrange an appointment for you. Would this coming Saturday at one P.M. be convenient?" She was efficient and to the point.

"I think so," I said as I dug for a pencil and paper in the night stand to make a note.

"Good. Then we'll see you at one."

"Wait." She'd hung up. Rats. What did he want to see me about?

Chapter 6

The next morning I was sitting on the bed, wrapped in a towel and clipping my toenails, when my cell phone signaled a call. It was Judy Amrine. She didn't give me a chance to say hello.

"Deena. Someone broke into the office during the night. The door frame is splintered. I found it when I came to check for mail. The police are on their way. What's going on?! We've never had something like *this* happen before."

I groaned. First the accident, then Madge's trouble and now a burglary. What next? "No use speculating," I told her. "I'll be there by noon. I'll call you as soon as I reach the city." As I closed the phone, I felt a rush of adrenaline. Judy was not the excitable type. I dreaded what I'd find.

I grabbed fresh underwear from the drawer, pulled on a pair of jeans and glanced out the window. Wind buffeted the bushes outside, and the sky was slate gray. I slid a sweater over my head, made a quick application of makeup and ran a brush through my hair. After I tossed my medication and toiletries in the overnight bag along with my clothes, I was ready. I grabbed my camera. I'd need photos for an insurance claim.

Since I'd be in Ortega Bay anyway, I figured I might as well see Dell and sign those papers. It was too early for his office to be open, but I called his number and left a message on his machine to let him know. I grabbed my bag and jacket and headed down the hall.

I found Madge in the kitchen dressed in her robe, making coffee. "I heard your phone jingle." She looked at my bag as I put it by the front door and shot me a questioning look. "Going somewhere?"

I slid onto my usual stool and related Judy's phone call.

"Good gracious, Deena. That's what you get for living in a big city." She popped bread into the toaster and poured a cup of coffee for me. "You better have something to eat before you leave."

"I may have to stay overnight." I sipped the hot coffee and formed a mental to-do list. Besides signing those papers for Dell, I'd stop at the apartment and pack more appropriate clothing to wear to Dad's service. And I could pick up my canine friends on my return trip. I'd imposed on Francie's family long enough.

I looked at Madge's carpet. It was the color of pistachio ice cream. Not a good shade for my rambunctious pals who hadn't learned to wipe their paws. Madge's yard wasn't fenced either. However, she had a chain link kennel in the back yard, a leftover from when she and Uncle Henry owned a golden lab named Murphy. The enclosure had been converted to hide the trash can, lawn mower and other garden equipment. Maybe it could be returned to its original use.

"Madge, would it be all right if I brought my dogs with me when I come back?"

She passed me a plate of buttered toast. "I remember you have a longhaired Chihuahua named Mutt. Not a very nice name, if you ask me. You have another dog too?"

"A little over a year ago a friend gave me her black-and-tan Dobe when she had to move back east. His name's Jeff. I thought I told you about him. They've both been at the Waite's ranch since the accident. If I leave them there much longer, the boys won't want to give them back."

Madge's gaze darted toward her living room and her hand went to her throat. "A Doberman? Oh, my."

She probably envisioned the end of her Hummel figurines. After a thoughtful pause, she nodded. "Sure. It'll be okay. We'll manage—

48

somehow."

I wolfed down the toast and gave Madge a hug. "Thanks. You're a dear." I pulled on my jacket, grabbed my bag and headed out to the Explorer.

Madge followed and stood in the doorway, ready to wave goodbye. As I opened the car door, I noticed her uneasy expression. "What's troubling you, Madge?" I asked, ready to reassure her Jeff was a well-behaved dog.

"Why you, of course. Your office burglarized. Why don't you move away from the city? There's too much crime. It's quiet here. Four Creeks is a peaceful town."

I smiled at her, thinking, yeah, except for murder. "I'll be back tomorrow for sure." I slid in and buckled the seat belt.

At the bottom of the hill, I turned left and was headed south when I spotted Buzz Walker coming out of a barber shop on Second Street. I was in a hurry, but the stop would be worth it if I could glean something about the investigation. I pulled to the curb and got out.

The fresh haircut made him look younger. I had to admit he was handsome with his Ray-Bans and navy blue police uniform. As I approached him, I noticed his shoes. Sure enough, cowboy boots. Not exactly regulation. He wasn't aware of me as he opened the door of the police cruiser.

"Hey, Buzz," I called.

He stopped and turned in my direction. "Hi, Deena."

"How do you get away with that?" I asked as I drew near and pointed to his boots. He gave me a deadpan stare. I wasn't going to get a rise out of him, or at least he wasn't going to let on.

He took off his dark glasses and slipped them into his shirt pocket. "What can I do for you?"

"Have you gotten the coroner's report on Mrs. Weston yet?"

He stiffened, his eyes wary.

"Truce, okay?" I stuck out my hand. "I'm worried about my aunt. I don't think she slept well last night." In truth, I had no idea how Madge slept, but engendering a bit of sympathy never hurt when fishing for information.

He relaxed and took my hand. "Okay. Truce. Mrs. Weston suffered blunt force trauma to the right side of her head."

"Is my aunt still a suspect?"

He dropped my hand like a hot brick. "The investigation is ongoing."

He wasn't giving me anything, drat him. "And her funeral?"

"I understand it's Saturday."

I nodded. "I have some urgent business in Ortega Bay, but I'll be back in time to attend. People shouldn't die without someone to mark their passing." I was about to leave when a thought struck me. "By the way, when you talked to Irma Foster, did she say anything about my name being mentioned during the argument in the library?"

"No, she didn't. Why do you ask?"

"Because when I talked to her yesterday, she said she thought she heard my name."

His jaw worked and his face flushed. "What are you doing, sneaking around asking questions? You stay out of this, Deena Powers. You're out of your league!"

"Okay, okay." The truce didn't last long. I back-pedaled in a hurry. "The only reason I was talking to her was because I'd heard she was there, and I wondered why they argued, and when I heard one of them said my name and Madge wouldn't tell me why." I took a breath. "I thought you might know."

He glared. "Keep your nose out of my investigation. You just be a good girl, and go back to the city and hunt down adulterous husbands or something."

Good girl, my rosy red . . . I turned on my heel, stomped toward the Explorer and fumed for the next twenty miles. But later, when my blood pressure settled, I couldn't help but reflect on the familiar warmth of his hand, something I didn't want to acknowledge, but couldn't deny. I banished thoughts about the two of us holding hands in the local movie theater. After all, I had no regrets about leaving Four Creeks back then.

Chapter 7

I stopped along the way for gas and a bag of granola at a place with an easy off-ramp. By the time I merged onto the Coast Highway, the clock on the dash read 12:15. A bank of clouds blotted out the sun and obscured my view of the Pacific. I called Judy and we agreed to meet at the office.

When I pulled into the parking area, I saw her leaning against her car. She had on her usual blue jacket, hat and scarf. I slipped the camera strap over my shoulder and climbed out. As I walked over to her, the wind coming off the ocean made me shiver.

She pushed away from her resting spot and stepped forward. "The door was open when I arrived this morning," she said. "I didn't go in, just called the police."

"What happened to the alarm system we're paying for?"

"The officer said it's antiquated and easy to disable."

When we reached the door of the building, I stopped to examine the splintered frame. "Looks like he kicked it in," I said. A partial shoe print was visible on the door itself.

"Seems like he wasn't concerned about making a lot of noise," Judy said.

She was right. Our building was isolated where it sat on a corner. A new warehouse on the left partially blocked the view of the street in front. On the opposite side, the street led downhill to the main part of town. And across from our parking lot, a sharp incline led to a stand of eucalyptus trees.

"The police looked around inside before they let me go in," Judy continued. "They were here over two hours checking for fingerprints and shooting pictures. Judging from their expressions when they left, they didn't have much to show for their time. One of them left his card." Judy fished a business card out of her coat pocket and handed it to me, then led the way inside.

At first glance it didn't look like much had been disturbed, but when we entered Dad's office my stomach went into a knot. "Oh my God!"

"I haven't moved anything. Thought you should see for yourself."

I almost retched. Our security system was pathetic. File drawers were open and folders scattered across the floor. The contents of Dad's antique oak desk had been dumped out. His cassette recorder lay on the floor, smashed as if someone had stomped on it. And black fingerprint dust covered nearly every flat surface.

Judy looked at my face and at the disorder. "Yeah, that's the way I feel too. But your office isn't as bad, if that's any consolation."

With my heart still pounding, I went to the other side of the building and into my office. She was right. It was obvious my desk drawers had been yanked open and rummaged through. But I never kept anything of value in my desk. I kept anything I was currently working on in my laptop.

As I returned to Dad's office, my anger came to a boil. I was so pissed it was a wonder I didn't have a stroke. I imagined the thief standing at the cabinets pitching the contents in every direction.

I took a deep breath. Steady now, I told myself as I surveyed every aspect of the room. My focus stuck on one empty file drawer. "Where's Dad's camera?"

Judy's attention shifted in the same direction.

I held up an index finger, a signal I was concentrating. Dad's camera bag was similar to mine. The drawer was where he stowed his camera and several different lenses. I mentally walked through our apartment. I didn't remember seeing his bag there which meant it ought to be in the drawer in front of me.

Judy knew it too. "Maybe it was an easy snatch. The computer would have taken more time and trips to a vehicle."

"Perhaps." I pressed my fingers to my temples. If it was the camera he was after, why tear the place apart? No common burglar would rummage through papers to find valuables? There had to be another reason. I put the lid on my emotions and set about snapping pictures from different angles.

Grim-faced, Judy began gathering papers. I pitched in, and soon the floor was clear with everything stacked in piles on Dad's desk.

"It may take a day or so to get the door and alarm system fixed," I said. "I can't leave these files unsecured."

"Your apartment isn't a good place. You won't be home. You can store them in the spare room at my house. The computer too."

"I appreciate that. Thanks. But it would take a truck to move these cabinets. I'll go to Staples and get some cardboard file boxes."

While I unhooked all the computer apparatus, Judy located an empty box in the storage closet and filled it with items from her desk.

It took two of us to carry the heavy computer monitor to her car. "We definitely need an upgrade," I huffed as we strapped it into the back seat of her VW Beetle.

Back in the office, I called the alarm company, then our insurance carrier and left Judy behind while I went after the boxes. On the way, I mulled over what had happened and tried to look at it through an investigator's eyes. Had this person been in the office before as a client? But it didn't make sense that a client would break in. If someone needed a record, he could simply ask for it, or get a subpoena. If it was related to an investigation, which one? Prior to our ill-fated attempt at a weekend getaway, I'd spent several days at the courthouse and the library researching old property records for a mining claim. Dad had been putting in some long hours working for Tri-Counties Indemnity. We planned to have our work completed before leaving.

I parked, hot-footed it into the store, bought a dozen file boxes and was back at the office in fifteen minutes. After we had them assembled and filled, I tugged open the last drawer. It held a couple dozen of Dad's audiotapes, recordings of case interviews. I was sure they'd been in order before the burglary. Now they were scrambled. I'd have to match the dates on the case papers to the ones on the interview tapes before I'd find the one I needed for the final report for Tri-Counties Insurance. I scooped them into a box.

It took a good deal of cramming to get those boxes into the Explorer. When we finished, Judy opened her car door. "I called Mitchell's Doors and Windows. They said they'd send a carpenter to check measurements this afternoon and install the replacement door on Saturday."

"Thanks for taking care of it. I'll meet you at the house."

I watched Judy pull out, climbed into the Explorer and leaned on the steering wheel. A break-in was the last thing I needed when I should have been concentrating on Madge's troubles and Dad's funeral, not some lunatic who had it in for us for some unknown reason. I indulged in a few minutes of self-pity, then reached for a tissue, gritted my teeth and squared my shoulders. "Enough. I hope the dirtball gets what he deserves for all eternity." I turned the key.

By the time I arrived at Judy's, she'd pulled a hand cart out of her garage. It was one she used to haul garden supplies into her back yard. It made the job of unloading much easier than the loading. We stacked the boxes in her spare room along with the computer and afterward settled ourselves at her kitchen table with cold sodas.

Gloria Getman

"Stay here tonight," she said. "I'd feel better knowing you weren't alone in that big apartment."

I glanced at her face and realized the burglary had unsettled her more than first apparent. "Sure. Maybe I'll have time to start sorting the files. Right now I'd better wash up. I have a three o'clock to sign some papers for Dell Fisk."

It took ten minutes to catch a parking place within a block of Dell's office. The building, red brick with a Spanish tile roof, had two towering palm trees plus several poinsettias flanking the entrance.

He greeted me with a bear hug, then held me at arm's length, his blue eyes glistening, and told me how great I looked.

"I miss your dad," he said. "He was a great pal and a pretty good golfer too. I still can't believe what happened." He waxed nostalgic, slipping one arm around my shoulders. "We were in basic training together before we shipped out for Korea, but you already know that. I was the best man at your folks' wedding. All those years.... Why, I remember the day they brought you home." He released me. "Tell me, are you going to be all right?"

I settled into one of his leather client chairs. From old pictures I knew Dell's hair had once been a sandy shade. Now a fine gray fringe ran around the back of his head. He was still handsome in his own way. His wide toothy smile, bronzed head and face were synonymous with the label "Uncle."

"This has been a really bad day," I said. Like the great old friend he was, Dell listened to all my woes.

After I described the break-in, he scowled. "This burglary." He scratched his chin thoughtfully. "I don't like the sound of it. Be careful, honey. Whoever it is may be dangerous."

With reading glasses perched on his nose, he uncovered a file from a stack on his desk and launched into a candid disclosure I never

56

expected.

"I wish I had good news for you, but I'm afraid what I have to tell you is a mixed bag. The probate may take as long as eighteen months, and then the deed to the office building will be yours. There's no mortgage. But other than his G.I. insurance, there's little cash."

I was astounded. "I thought he had a nest egg saved for retirement."

Dell readjusted his weight in the chair and hesitated a few seconds. "You know your father gambled from time to time. While we were in the service he never passed up a poker game, but when he married your mother, and you came along, he quit. After she died, he started in again. Loneliness, I guess."

I knew about all of it. I'd been aware of his late night poker parties and trips to the race track. He never acted like it was a big deal and always returned in high spirits, like he'd won a hat full of money. He gambled away everything he and my mom had saved. When reality hit, he joined Gamblers Anonymous.

"Lately though," Dell continued, "I guess the old devil returned to him. He gave me power of attorney over some of the financial matters to protect the business. The balance in his bank account after the accident was a shock to me, enough to pay his hospital bill, but not much more, and no other savings I could find."

I gulped. "Exactly what is left?"

Dell's eyes glistened. I suppose it wasn't easy to break such bad news to the daughter of an old pal. He took a deep breath and sighed. "The office building, his car and the G.I. insurance, plus there's about fifteen hundred dollars in the bank. You already know what's in the business account."

"Lordy. That's barely enough to pay Judy this month."

"I have the claim form here for his G.I. insurance. You can sign it today and a check will arrive in a few weeks."

I sat in silence for a couple minutes, mentally chewing my nails, trying to soak in the reality. Zombie-like, I signed the legal papers Dell laid on his desk before me.

"When do you figure you'll get back to work again?" he asked as he returned my file to his cabinet. The sound of the drawer closing brought me out of my trance.

"Soon," I said numbly. "I plan to spend at least a week with Aunt Madge after Dad's service. There's a report on a warehouse fire that should bring some money. And I turned in an insurance claim for my wrecked car."

"I could make you a loan."

I mustered a weak smile. I knew he'd say something like that. He was that kind of guy, like a real uncle. He'd handled my divorce— gratis. "I appreciate the offer, but when I get back from Four Creeks I'll contact my usual clients to let them know I'm available. If necessary, I can probably pick up a little per diem with another agency.

He looked at me over his glasses. "Anything else you need?"

"Dad's Explorer. Legal, I mean. I'm driving it now. My Cherokee's in the wrecking yard."

"That's an easy one. All I need is a copy of the pink slip and registration."

We hugged, promised to meet for lunch when I returned, and I thanked him for taking care of financial matters while I was incapacitated. Despite the bad news, I assured myself things could be worse, though I wasn't sure how.

I turned up Bayview Drive toward the big sand-colored apartment building that was home. Like so many buildings in the area, it was perched on the hillside. It had a Mexican tile roof and arched windows.

I liked the ambiance, a place I considered a cool, quiet refuge from the world. But since the accident, it held a sense of vacancy I couldn't define, and misgivings about the single life bubbled to the surface.

I unlocked the door, disabled the security alarm and headed for the bathroom. Lifting those boxes had added a backache to my usual headache. I took the bottle of Advil from the cabinet and gulped the tablets down with water from the sink before turning my attention to the closet.

My intent was to pick something suitable to wear to Dad's service. I didn't own a black dress. My navy-blue business suit would have to do. I opened a suitcase on the bed, filled it with a few warm garments and extra shoes and laid the suit on top.

After closing the lid, I knelt on the closet floor and pulled back the carpet to uncover a small safe I'd had built into the floor. It was big enough to store my laptop, shoulder holster and PPK. After the burglary, the way I was feeling, I put it on. My loose all-weather jacket would cover it nicely.

The pistol had been a gift from Dad for my thirty-ninth birthday the summer before. He'd taken me to a gun shop and told me to pick out what I wanted. It was a rite of passage. Afterward, I'd spent numerous hours at a shooting range getting comfortable with it. However, the idea of ever having to use it to protect myself gave me chills.

As I left the building, I had a creepy feeling between my shoulder blades, like I was being watched. I studied the bushes bordering the complex, and after a few seconds, concluded it was Mrs. Molvitz, a curtain twitcher, who lived in the upstairs apartment. She was the resident busy-body. I was simply feeling edgy.

"I don't know about you, but I'm hungry and tired," Judy said when I stepped in through her back door. "I'll warm some leftovers, and we can relax with a video."

"Sounds good to me, but first I need to use your phone book."

"It's right there in the living room on the table."

I put my suitcase in Judy's spare bedroom, then located the number for Tri-Counties Indemnity and dialed. A woman with a distinctive whiskey voice answered. I asked for Walter Pearson, the CEO who had engaged my father's services. After a moment's wait, a man came on the line.

"Mr. Pearson, this is Deena Powers."

"This is Dennis Colton," he interrupted. "I'm Chief Financial Officer here at Tri-Counties. How can I help you?"

"I'm Wallace Powers' daughter."

"Ah, yes. Sorry to hear about your father's untimely death. Was he insured with us? Is there a problem with the settlement?"

"No, you've got it wrong. My father was investigating a warehouse fire for your firm. I've been going through his files and came across a letter from Mr. Pearson." The fact was I hadn't found any such letter *yet*. "I wanted you to know I intend to complete the case file, and send a final report as soon as possible."

"Miss Powers, you don't need to do that," he said in a crisp tone. "When we heard about what happened to your father, we engaged another firm to complete the investigation. It was concluded in December. It wasn't arson, and we've settled the claim."

"I see. Could I have the name of the firm, so I can officially close the file?"

"That's not necessary, Miss Powers. Good day."

An annoying buzz filled my ear. Drat him! He didn't have to be rude about it. What'd he say about December? I knew for certain Dad was still working on the case then. Was Colton lying or mistaken about the dates? Either way, our firm deserved to be paid for Dad's work. I was sure he was still owed for his expenses. Still fuming, I went into Judy's guest room, shed my jacket, stuffed the pistol under the mattress, and hung the holster on a chair.

I joined Judy in the kitchen, and while she pulled a couple of dishes from the refrigerator and put them in the microwave, I told her what Dennis Colton had said. "Did you transcribe *anything* related to that case for Dad?"

Judy shook her head. "I'm sure I'd remember if I did."

"I don't know what the deal is, but I don't intend to let him swindle our firm. We need every cent of what Dad had coming to him."

The buzzer on the microwave went off.

"What are you going to do?" She put the two plates and silverware on the table.

"I'm going to find his file notes and taped interviews to prove my claim."

As Judy scooped a ladle of chicken casserole onto our plates, she studied my face. "Is there something you're not telling me?"

I heaved a sigh and broke the news about what Dell had revealed. We sat in silence for a few minutes and picked at our food.

"No matter," Judy said. "I'm not going to abandon you. I have savings. I'll survive—at least for a while."

When we finished, she put the dishes in the dishwasher, and we settled ourselves in her living room. She started the movie, but we didn't watch much of it.

"There's something I can't get out of my head," I said.

She muted the TV. "You mean about the burglary?"

I shook my head. "Do you remember Ben Fraser, Dad's partner when he worked for Ortega Bay PD?"

"Sure. Your dad introduced him to me at a benefit the department put on for the city playground."

"The day after I got out of the hospital, I went to the Sherriff's Department to ask for a copy of the accident report. I ran into Ben. He told me that when he heard what happened to us, he rushed to the ER, hoping to see Dad. But it was too late. He talked to the highway patrolman and learned there was a second set of tire tracks at the scene. The officer thought the tracks were made by the person who'd called in the report. I'm not so sure, and I don't think Ben was either. Considering what's just happened, I wonder if someone deliberately caused the accident. It's possible, don't you think?"

Judy's eyes narrowed, but she made no comment. Maybe she thought I was grasping at straws and trying to rid myself of the guilt I felt.

A short time later, I gave up on the movie and went to hook up the computer system in her spare room. I switched it on and sifted through several months of documents on the screen. I found a file dated October 1st of the previous year. It was a letter to Tri-Counties Indemnity, accepting an assignment to investigate and confirming the fee. It meant Dad had been on the case at least eight weeks prior to the accident.

Judy stuck her head around the door frame. "I'm going to bed. I have a book better'n that movie."

"Okay. I think I'll take a stab at organizing some of these files," I said, pointing to the load we'd hauled in earlier.

She disappeared.

I sat cross-legged on the floor and pulled the first box next to me. By midnight I had half the files in order. I stretched and yawned. I'd have to take the remainder with me to work on later at Madge's.

The light was out in Judy's bedroom. I crawled into bed, hoping to sleep, but instead the ugly scenes of the day replayed like an old movie. After an hour, I gave up trying to make sense of it, rolled over and drifted off.

Sometime before dawn I had the same freakish dream. As before, I knew it was a dream, but I couldn't stop it. I woke, drenched in sweat and sucking air like I'd been drowning. The headache that followed was ferocious. I dug in my bag for the Advil bottle and padded to the nearest sink. I gulped down the tablets, and then sat in bed with the covers pulled up to my chin as I tried to banish the heebie-jeebies. The only road I knew like the one in my dream was on the way to Dell's cabin retreat.

Chapter 8

By eight o'clock the next morning, I'd loaded the remainder of the boxes into the SUV, filled the gas tank and was on the road. The sun was shining and from the freeway I could see the blue Pacific was calm and glistening like a glass table.

I took an off-ramp heading east toward a familiar mountain range. I was looking forward to seeing Mutt and Jeff again. Soon the highway dipped low along a dry river bed and narrowed to the two-lane corridor which wound its way through the foothills.

Thirty minutes later, I drove through a small community nestled in a valley. They'd maintained a Spanish-style ambiance with an arched facade along the main street and bell tower above the post office. A banner announcing a local art show was stretched between the two.

Congestion slowed my progress, but a few miles east of town I pulled in alongside a corner store built to look like a log cabin. It had four umbrella-covered tables outside. I parked, climbed out and headed for the door. Inside, the aroma of coffee was evident. Just as I spotted the cold box against the far wall, a man pushed through the door behind me. I went to the fridge, and after pulling out a diet Coke and a bottle of water I might need for the dogs, I walked back toward the counter. The rough looking stranger stood near the newspaper rack. He picked up a copy of the paper and held it as though reading the headlines, but his dark eyes were on me. I hurried to pay and walked out.

Back in the Explorer, I was waiting for a car to pass before entering the highway when I caught sight of the same guy in my rear view mirror. He stood on the decking in front of the store. I pulled the tab on the can of Coke, took a swallow and studied him. He wore jeans and a black tee-shirt, was overly muscled and had tattoos covering both forearms. His thick brows and mustache matched his long dark hair. An s-shaped scar marred his left cheek. Not someone I'd like to meet in a dark alley.

As if he knew I was watching, he stepped off the deck toward a white pickup truck that had a couple of scratches on the right front fender.

I pulled out and began the climb up a steep grade that meandered around several curves. Before long, I noticed the same truck on a curve below me. It made me uneasy. I didn't know if what I felt was the result of intuition or paranoia because of the recent events, but I pulled off at the first turnout, and let him pass while I finished my drink.

I pulled back onto the road, glad the Explorer had the power to pull several more curves and a steep section before I reached the top of the pass. From there the road leveled off onto a plateau. On the right was a wooded park with picnic tables scattered among the trees. The same truck was parked in the shade. As I rounded the next curve, I glanced in the mirror and saw the pickup start to move. A shiver passed over me, and I stepped on the accelerator. Had he been following me since I left Ortega Bay? Some detective I was, not to notice being tailed. I felt for the PPK under my jacket.

I sped along a straight stretch at a hair-raising speed, slowing only to negotiate a narrow bridge. It was a mile to the turnoff to Francie and Bill's place. Theirs was one of many small ranches in the area. Relief flooded me when I saw the sign announcing "Francie's Folly." I glanced back as I turned in. No pickup in sight. Maybe I *was* paranoid.

All thoughts of the stranger evaporated when I drove into their yard and saw Mutt and Jeff. I stepped out of the SUV and greeted them. They gyrated with glee. After three turns and a yip, my Dobe lunged at me, mopping my face with his big pink tongue. Mutt clawed my pant leg until I picked him up. He wriggled in my arms, too excited to hold still. It took several minutes to calm them.

Francie came out of the house and after a hug, she said, "You look stressed out. Come on in, I'll make some fresh coffee."

I followed her to the kitchen with the dogs at my heels.

She filled the coffee pot at the sink. "The boys are in school. They're sure going to miss these guys. I suspect we'll be shopping for a new pet this weekend." As the coffee began to perk, Francie leaned over to give Jeff's ears an affectionate scratch.

We were soon settled into chairs in the family room with coffee mugs in hand. Mutt jumped into my lap and Jeff flopped at my feet.

"Tell me all the news," Francie said. "What did you find out about your aunt and the murdered woman?"

I told her what I'd learned to date—which wasn't much.

"I bet by the time you get back to Four Creeks, the police will have the culprit in custody."

"I sure hope so. Dad's service will be next week, and then I plan to stay with Madge a bit before starting back to work." I didn't tell her about the other more unsettling aspects of my life. Instead, I changed the subject. "Been biking lately?"

"Not as much as last year. However, Bill and I did a 10K run two weekends ago to raise money for The Diabetes Association."

Francie and I were exact opposites. She was tall, blonde and athletic. I was short, dark haired and hated most exercise. I had to force myself to go to the gym. Bicycling was the exception. We'd met when I joined a bicycling club and had become good friends.

She filled me in on the boys' grades, Bill's new contract, and her decorating plans. Before I left I tried to pay her for caring for my pets but she refused. Francie said I should come back when their apricots were ripe. I told her I would and give myself a bellyache. We both laughed.

"That's a promise, right?"

"You bet."

With the dogs and all their belongings loaded into the back of the SUV beside the office files, I lowered the back windows enough to give them the breeze they liked.

On our way to the main highway, Jeff sniffed my hair a dozen times and finally satisfied, parked by the window in the back seat. Mutt curled up in the passenger seat and went to sleep.

As I wound my way along the back road, my thoughts returned to the man at the store. I speculated as to whether I'd given him the slip, or if I'd overreacted and been mistaken about him. But considering the office burglary, I felt like my uneasiness was justified. Questions kept rotating in my mind. What did the burglar hope to find in our office files? As soon as I'd taken care of matters in Four Creeks, I'd focus on solving that conundrum.

It was past noon when I ascended the hill to Madge's driveway. The sky had cleared from the day before, and fresh snow had accumulated on the mountains. As soon as my feet hit the ground, I stretched out the kinks in my legs.

Much to my amazement, the dog-run in the back yard had been restored to its original appearance. Madge stood in the front doorway, wiping her hands on a dish towel. Her gaze followed mine.

"The plumber will be here tomorrow to fix the water faucet," she said. "I didn't order a shelter because I didn't know what kind your dogs would need."

"That's okay. They don't need one. We're not going to be here that long." I turned and opened the car door for Mutt and Jeff. They jumped out and explored the yard, sniffing and marking the new territory. When they began checking out Madge's shoes and legs, she stood rigid as a board.

"They won't hurt you, Madge."

By her expression, she wasn't convinced.

"They're very obedient and good watchdogs. Sit," I commanded. True to their training, they both sat. "Say hello." Jeff offered his paw. Mutt gave a sharp bark.

Madge looked mildly interested, but I expected a real friendship wouldn't be forthcoming. I allowed them to wander a bit before I introduced them to the kennel.

I went to the rear of the SUV for my luggage. As I handed my overnight case to Madge, she noticed the file boxes in the back. "What's all this?"

"Let's go inside and I'll explain what happened," I said. Mutt and Jeff followed.

She closed the door behind us while I put my bag in the bedroom. Not wanting to sit again so soon, I leaned against the counter and reported what I'd found at the office and about the boxes I had in the back of the SUV.

Madge turned toward the big bay window in the dining room and gazed out at the town below. With a slight shake of her head, she said, "I never understood Wally's attraction for a place so riddled with crime. He had a chance to stay on the ranch after your grandfather died."

"I believe he felt like he was helping people by what he did."

Madge went into the kitchen and opened the refrigerator. "Why would someone want any part of your father's files?"

"I don't know, but I intend to find out." I didn't say any more because I didn't want to worry her with all the speculation I'd been mulling over.

"If it's okay, I'll stack the file boxes in your garage for now. I'll reorganize them and locate the information I need." I gave her an account of my conversation with Dennis Colton. "I'm determined to prove the fee for Dad's expenses is justified."

Madge looked at me with worried eyes. "I think you should leave the whole thing to the police."

"The burglary, yes. But the police won't help me prove the insurance company owes us money."

"Money isn't everything."

I had no answer for that.

A newspaper on the counter caught my attention. It was the *Delta Sun*. Madge had actually bought the newspaper. I opened it to the obituary page, glanced over the columns and spotted Lottie's obit.

The article listed Carlotta Weston as sixty-three, the daughter of Weldon and Carla Woods, born in Four Creeks. She graduated from Four Creeks High School and married Melvin Weston. It went on to say she was preceded in death by her son, Frederick Weston, who was killed during military maneuvers in 1983, and by her husband, Melvin, in 1985.

A graveside service was scheduled the next day at eleven o'clock in Four Creeks Cemetery. Except for specific dates, the obituary didn't tell me anything I didn't already know. It didn't mention any next-of-kin, so I wondered who provided the information.

As I closed the paper, a prominent article caught my eye. "Local Family Man Holds Winning Lottery Ticket," the bold letters said. Lucky stiff. The ticket, worth seven million dollars, was purchased at Avila's Quick Mart in Four Creeks. In a curious twist of fate, the winner was Eddie Lee, the nephew of the store owner, Maximo Avila.

Holy Cow! I imagined the grin on Max Avila's face. There'd be a bonus for selling the ticket, and it meant the problem of Eddie would be solved for him.

I stared at the winning numbers: nine, fourteen, thirty-six, seven, fifteen, and fifty-eight. For a minute, I fantasized about what I'd do with that amount of money.

Madge broke into my reverie. "I bet you're hungry. I have chicken salad sandwiches ready, and I'll heat a can of soup. Vegetable beef okay?"

"That sounds great." I was thinking about Lottie. She'd bought a ticket at Avila's every week. Too bad she never won.

I folded the paper and laid it aside. "I see by the newspaper Lottie Weston's service is tomorrow morning," I said as I slipped out of my jacket. "We can go together."

Madge's eyes widened at the sight of the pistol in my shoulder holster. Her trepidation was obvious.

"I better put this away," I said and hurried to the bedroom where I took it off and stuffed it under the mattress. Between the dogs and the pistol, I was fast becoming an unsettling intrusion into Madge's life.

I returned to the breakfast counter and sat on a stool. "I'll be curious to see who shows up for the funeral service."

"Well, it won't be me. I have no reason to mourn her passing. The police probably still think I killed her."

"It's been almost a week. If that were true, they'd have contacted you again." It was obvious Madge was still worried. I'd have to get in touch with Buzz Walker. Maybe I could get him to tell me something reassuring I could pass on.

Madge placed the sandwiches and soup on the counter and sat beside me. As we ate lunch, her attention kept drifting to where Mutt and Jeff lay on the floor. Always alert, they both raised their heads each time she looked their way. I tried to distract her by describing the patches of wildflowers I'd seen along the highway during the drive. It didn't work.

70

"Has the big one ever bitten anyone?" she asked.

"No," I lied. "But he lets me know if there's someone around he doesn't like." In fact, he'd bite if I gave him the command, but more often than not, his mere presence made it unnecessary.

When we finished lunch, I put the dishes in the sink. "I better unload the SUV. I donned my jacket again. Always eager for a ride, Mutt and Jeff followed me out to the Explorer. I was sure Madge had heaved a sigh of relief when the door closed behind us.

Mutt and Jeff followed me as I hauled the sacks of dog food around the house to the patio in back, and then the box of grooming supplies. Mutt's long fur was going to be a problem. He'd pick up every burr within a mile, and I'd have to brush him every day. I put the dog's beds in the guest room, and then tackled unloading the file boxes and stacked them in Madge's garage.

By the time I finished my back ached. The events of the last two days had drained me of energy. I was eager for a long soak in the tub.

Afterward, I dressed in a comfortable sweat suit and joined Madge in the kitchen. We had a light dinner of a large salad and bread sticks and finished with homemade apple pie. After I fed the dogs, we sank into easy chairs by the TV. One of the channels was running an old movie, but I had a hard time paying attention. My thoughts ran back to Lottie Weston's murder. I hoped the next day I'd hear there'd been a break in the case. Then Madge would have nothing more to worry about.

Chapter 9

I peeked out the window Saturday morning. A thick layer of gray clouds hung over the valley, an appropriate atmosphere for a funeral. I didn't bother with a robe or slippers, but headed for the kitchen with the dogs following at my heels. A fresh pot of coffee was waiting. I poured a cup.

Madge was sitting in her easy chair in front of the TV. CNN was running the news, but the sound had been muted. Her expression was as gloomy as the sky.

I popped a piece of whole wheat bread in the toaster and while waiting, wondered if Madge was contemplating the end of life, or whether she was rummaging through memories of when she and Lottie were young. I decided not to disturb her. Perhaps she'd feel like talking about it later.

After I finished the toast and coffee, I donned jeans and a sweatshirt to take the dogs for their morning outing. Mutt and Jeff were already waiting by the patio door, and when I opened it, they loped several yards ahead of me up the hill in back of Madge's house. Well, Mutt didn't really lope. His was more like a scamper. I trudged behind them and was winded by the time I reached a level spot.

At the crest, I settled on a good-sized rock, gazed through the low-lying haze and thought about Lottie. After what I'd heard about her, who would attend her funeral? Did anyone care that she had died? More to the point, who wanted her dead? Surely not my aunt. Irma? I had doubts. A random act of violence? Also a long-shot. Maybe the funeral gathering would reveal other connections, someone who'd have a motive.

When it was time to get dressed, I whistled, and my pals reluctantly obeyed. I coaxed them to the new pen and gave them each a doggie treat. I didn't look back after I secured the gate. Their sad eyes would make me feel guilty.

After my usual morning routine, I put on the navy-blue business suit I'd brought from home, and chose a light blue turtleneck sweater to go underneath the jacket. Before putting on my shoes, I peeked around the corner and was going to ask Madge if she'd changed her mind, but she wasn't there. I heard the shower running in her bathroom. It was quarter to eleven. I decided she was avoiding the whole subject.

The cemetery was a couple of miles from Madge's house, past the high school and north of town. A white canopy over the gravesite was not hard to spot from the parking lot. It was situated next to a hedge separating the cemetery from the access road. A few people had already gathered. I maneuvered across a thick layer of damp grass and speculated about who had arranged for the service.

I spotted Irma Foster, dressed in a dark gray pantsuit and matching veiled hat. She was talking to a tall bald-headed man whose expression said "mortician." After her scathing remarks about Lottie, why had she bothered to attend?

I was surprised to see the clerk from Fair Buy Market. Hester was wearing chocolate-brown slacks and a striped shirt with the store's logo emblazoned on the shoulder. I nodded to her, but she didn't recognize me. Max Avila was there. His tan coveralls did nothing to camouflage his oversized mid-section. He was probably the only one who genuinely mourned Lottie.

Buzz Walker and a younger man stood like a pair of statues at a discreet distance from the others. They had substituted dark blue suits for their uniforms. Did they think Lottie's killer would show up at her funeral? I nodded in their direction and Buzz nodded in return.

Russ Treadwell and a long-legged man in a black parson's robe strode across the lawn. The robe, open in front, flapped on either side of him as it caught the current of his movement. The pastor seemed to know everyone and shook hands with enthusiasm.

"I'm Pastor Joe," he said as he approached me, hand extended. "I don't believe we've met." It was more a question than a statement. I had the feeling he was about to ask my church affiliation when Russ rescued me with a formal introduction.

Pastor Joe called everyone together at the graveside where a dark green urn sat on a mound of dirt covered with artificial turf. After a brief opening prayer, he expounded on the idea that God loved everyone, including the eccentrics of this world, like Lottie, or words to that effect. As he spoke, I scrutinized the crowd, if you can call eight people a crowd. For a woman who had lived in Four Creeks all her life, it was a paltry turnout. I heard Irma sniffle. The others maintained grim funeral-faces.

Buzz and his partner stood with their hands folded in a "parade rest" stance. I was speculating about Russ Treadwell's presence when the answer came to me. He must have been Lottie's attorney and arranged for the service, all pre-planned no doubt.

A white pickup caught my attention as it crept along the road bordering the cemetery. By the outline of the driver, he was watching us. When I turned my head for a better view, the truck sped away. Was it simple curiosity, or could that person be Lottie's killer? Not all together improbable.

The service lasted all of fifteen minutes. When it ended, I worked my way toward Buzz. The others drifted together, murmuring over Lottie's unfortunate demise. Max was telling the story about the cats again. Hester was the exception. She hurried to a VW Bug parked near the cemetery office.

I saw Buzz motion to his companion and start toward the parking lot. I felt sure he was avoiding me. As Dad would say, time to eat crow. "Buzz," I called. "Wait."

He hesitated, but kept walking, his long legs keeping distance between us. My high heels sunk into the thick grass, making it feel like walking in sand. I was out of breath by the time I caught up. When I did, he stopped and turned toward me, his face deadpan.

"I want to apologize," I said, panting. "I shouldn't have talked to Mrs. Foster without consulting you first. I should have told you what I'd heard. I'm sorry."

His expression didn't change. "Okay." He said it in a way that meant, what are you going to do next to interfere?

"I'll be leaving right after Dad's service. I have quite a mess in Ortega Bay. While I've been here the office was broken into."

Still deadpan, he said, "What do the police say about it, or are you doing your own investigating?"

His sarcasm was not lost on me, but I decided not to take the bait. "It's too soon for answers."

He nodded, then indicating his companion, "I'm sorry. I should introduce you two. Mike Huerta, this is Deena Powers. Deena and I were friends in high school."

Mike had a broad, open face and a warm smile. I pegged him at twenty-five. His dark expressive eyes searched my face as we shook hands, and I sensed nothing much missed his attention, which would make him a good cop.

"I don't think I asked you," Buzz said. "Were you injured in the accident?"

I shrugged. "Only my head."

That got a quick smile out of both of them.

"A concussion. But I'm fine." I didn't want to discuss the intricacies of my health.

Fine lines crinkled around his eyes, like someone who laughed a lot. Those blue eyes... Long ago they'd made my heart skip a beat. I felt awkward, so I launched into the reason I wanted to talk to him.

"Madge wouldn't come with me this morning because she thinks you assume she had something to do with Mrs. Weston's death." I watched his face. "Can you tell me something that would reassure her?"

Mike Huerta's attention flicked between Buzz and me.

Buzz's mouth worked as though he were deliberating. Then he said, "Will you promise you'll give up playing detective?"

I wanted to kick him in the shin, or someplace else more sensitive, but restrained myself. I was having a hard time swallowing those crow feathers. I nodded, and crossed my fingers inside my coat pocket.

"Whoever killed Mrs. Weston moved her body in order to leave her in the canal," Buzz said.

"You mean she was killed someplace else?"

His eyes narrowed. "That's all I'm going to say. You can draw your own conclusion."

A young Hispanic man in blue coveralls approached from the cemetery's main building. He carried a shovel. Buzz motioned in his direction. "He probably wants to get his job done." Buzz and his partner turned to leave.

I nodded in agreement, but was distracted by what Buzz had said. Was he telling me he didn't think Madge was strong enough to move the body, or that she had to have help?

I wolfed down a hot dog from one of the lunch stands near the high school. I didn't have time for anything more elaborate before my appointment with Russ Treadwell.

The offices of Treadwell, Barton and Bates were in a new building on the corner north of the city park. Just before one o'clock I drove past the post office, swung a right at the library and pulled into a parking space in front.

When I stepped into the office and saw no one at the reception desk, I reasoned it must be a social call, sandwiched into Russ' heavy schedule.

At the sound of the outer door closing, he appeared in the doorway of an adjacent room and greeted me with a lawyer's handshake, firm, but not tight. He looked a lot like his father, except he had a more prominent nose. He'd kept his lanky basketball-player physique, and his business suit was tailored to fit his long torso.

"Deena, you haven't changed a bit," he said with an expansive smile.

I knew it wasn't true, but enjoyed hearing it anyway. We exchanged pleasantries and he offered condolences about my father before he ushered me into his private office.

I was more than a little surprised to see Irma already seated there. She was dressed in the same gray slack-suit, but without the hat. Her hair had been trimmed and the roots had received a touch-up. She nodded a greeting as I sat in one of the high-back leather chairs positioned opposite Russ's desk.

He took his seat. "I called you here regarding the estate of Carlotta Weston." He put on a pair of reading glasses before handing each of us a sheaf of papers.

It was a will—Lottie's will. "Curiouser and curiouser" flashed in my mind. I glanced over at Irma. Her eyebrows lifted and she shifted in her seat.

"Notice item three," Russ continued. "Mrs. Weston named our

firm as executor. The first petition will be filed with the court this week, and I've prepared the required advertising for any claims against the estate. I've arranged to have the house appraised as soon as it's cleared by the police."

"I'm really puzzled," I said. "Other than being a classmate of Freddie Weston's, I hardly knew the family."

"You and Mrs. Foster are the heirs of record," Russ replied.

"But why am I an heir?" I asked.

Russ shook his head. "This document was drawn up over a year ago, and Mrs. Weston never mentioned her reasoning. Next," he continued, "item five: she names the two of you as the only people to receive a bequest and eliminates all other claimants."

How was Irma going to explain this inheritance to her friends? Her dislike for Lottie was no secret around town according to Madge's account.

"Her death was such a shock," Irma said. "I mean the way she died, at the hands of a burglar. But finding myself in her will is even more so. We were friends during high school, but since then..."

"Mrs. Weston was an eccentric woman with a mind of her own," Russ said. He turned toward me. "I have to admit, Deena, your bequest is rather odd. Turn to the bottom of the next page."

Irma and I flipped pages. The paragraph stated I was to be awarded a key held by Russell Treadwell, Attorney-at-Law.

I didn't have to worry about windfall wealth, it seemed.

He opened an envelope, fished out a key and handed it to me. "It looks like a key to a bank deposit box."

It was flat, with no distinguishing marks and not like any door key I'd ever seen. "I think you're right."

Russ leaned forward, conveying earnest lawyership. "Mrs. Weston never mentioned a bank account to me, so I have no knowledge of where such a box would be. Until the contents of the box are known, we can't complete the assessment of the size of the estate. Normally, we'd hire an investigator, but in this case, since that's your profession, Deena, I thought perhaps you'd like to make inquiries."

I nodded. What a strange legacy. I was dumbfounded.

"That's not all," Russ continued. "Turn to item six on the next page." Looking at Irma he said, "Mrs. Weston left her house and land to you, Mrs. Foster, but she left the contents of her home to Deena."

Irma opened her mouth as if to protest, but snapped it shut. Her face flushed.

He looked at me. "The court generally considers the personal belongings of someone of modest means to be worth in the neighborhood of five to ten thousand dollars. You need to understand that if anything of substantial value is found in the house, it will have to be added to the estate." Then to Irma he said, "Considering the size and age of the house, there may not be any estate tax due."

My thoughts shifted to the scene in the library between Madge and Lottie. Was this the legacy Lottie was talking about?

Irma piped up. "I drove past it this morning on my way to the funeral. It looks run-down, needs paint. I don't want to sink any money into it. I'd like it sold during probate. It'd be the easiest thing for me."

She turned to me. "And those cats. You'd be wise to get rid of all those cats as soon as possible. Who's feeding them, by the way?"

Russ cleared his throat. "I'm sure the police notified the SPCA, and the cats have been taken care of." He paused. "There'll be a hearing on the petition, and then some time for any creditors to file a claim."

Irma scooted to the edge of her seat. "Surely she can inventory the contents of the house and move everything of any value to storage."

I felt a headache coming on.

"That will be up to the police," Russ said. His gaze swung in my direction. "You'll need to contact them. It'd reduce expenses if you can locate the deposit box, Deena, but if you think it's too much trouble, we could hire someone."

"It may be as simple as locating a receipt in her belongings," I said.

Irma asked about court costs, realtor's fees and Russ's percentage as executor. She seemed well informed about such things.

I stared at the key and felt like Alice tumbling down the rabbit hole.

Chapter 10

My brain was still spinning with amazement and confusion when I rang Irma's door bell. I reasoned that Irma knew more than she'd let on.

"Oh, it's you," she said when she opened the door. She stepped back to let me in and pushed the door closed.

Irma had changed into blue denim pants and a red sweatshirt. The color complimented her blonde hair, but her demeanor was like someone who'd received depressing news. I followed her to the living room where she motioned toward the cushioned sofa. I noticed the aroma of fresh-brewed coffee.

"I was just making a pot of coffee. Would you like a cup?"

"Sure. Thank you." I settled on the couch as she disappeared into the kitchen.

A couple of minutes later Irma returned with a tray containing two mugs of coffee, cream and sugar and a plate of bakery cookies. She placed the tray on the coffee table, then took a position at the opposite end of the couch and angled herself to face me. She pulled a green throw pillow into her lap and combed the fringe with her fingernails. "I didn't know anything about Lottie's will, I swear, not until today. It has me in a stew."

"I know what you mean. I don't understand why I'm involved at *all*."

She tossed the pillow into the side chair and reached for one of the mugs. "The truth is..." She paused and took a sip as though giving extra consideration to what she was about to say. "Lottie and I were sisters, at least, half-sisters anyway." She looked at me as if expecting me to gasp at the disclosure.

I nodded, careful not to act like it was anything other than an interesting bit of information. But inside, I was thinking Four Creeks was beginning to sound like Peyton Place. I took a cup from the tray, sipped and remained silent.

"I learned about it from my mother," Irma continued. "You might say it was a deathbed confession. She was real sick with cancer. One evening when I was feeding her, she said there was something I ought to know. Mama explained that she and Lottie's father had an affair. She said she wasn't proud of it, but it was a fact, and I was the result. I guess Daddy never knew, or never let on." She stared at the coffee cup, and after a pause, took another swallow.

"Daddy was a hard working, but distant man. I loved him so much, I thought I'd die when that tractor rolled over and killed him. He'd been disking along a creek bank and it gave way." Her eyes grew misty. "Mama said she wasn't sorry about the affair, because she wanted a baby and she and Daddy..." She shrugged. "Well, I was an only child.

"After Daddy was killed, Mama took a job in Digg's Packinghouse. Lottie's father was the manager. I think he got her the job. Her paychecks were small, and she was laid off each time the fruit ran out. Her unemployment checks didn't go very far, so I quit school and got a job in the Ben Franklin Store to help out. I suspect my mother and Mr. Woods continued..." She looked straight at me again as if to see that I understood her meaning.

"Every now and then Mama had a little extra money. Sometimes we hardly had enough to eat, and then she'd have twenty dollars. She never said where it came from and I didn't ask. After I learned about the two of them, I understood. I kept her secret. I didn't want anyone to know about it—ever."

Irma took a cookie and passed the plate to me. She popped the cookie in her mouth, a signal her confession was over.

"Do you think Lottie knew?" I asked.

After a swallow of coffee she said, "I think Lottie knew. About me being her sister, I mean. It explains the way she treated me at school. She often sat with me at lunch, even though I was two years younger. I didn't understand why, just thought I was lucky to have a friend like her. But after I quit school, I didn't see much of her."

I took a cookie and considered her sudden openness. In Treadwell's office she'd acted like she could hardly wait to get me out of the picture and sell the house. And what happened to all the resentment she'd expressed about Lottie earlier?

Irma put her cup down. "Ask anything you want."

"You said Lottie and you were friends up until you quit high school. What changed?"

"That's easy. She was good looking, had nice clothes and lots of boyfriends. I worked and had no time for a social life. I got depressed and put on weight. That didn't help. We saw each other less and less— drifted apart.

"I have something to show you." She rose and disappeared down a hall I figured led to the bedrooms. A minute later she returned with an envelope in her hand and sat closer to me. She opened the envelope and withdrew a snapshot. "Lottie left Four Creeks a month or so after graduation. I didn't know where she went. Then this arrived from Las Vegas on my birthday."

She handed me a black-and-white photo of a shapely woman wearing a skimpy sequined costume and a feathered head-dress.

"Wow! What a beauty. Is this Lottie?" I flipped the picture over. A note on the back read, "Happy Birthday, Irma. Look at me now!" It was signed, Lottie. Rita Diamond was written in parenthesis. I handed it back to her. "What did you think about that?"

"Oh, I envied her, of course. It seemed to me she was living the good life, and I was stuck in a dime store working for peanuts."

So Lottie hadn't *always* lived in Four Creeks. Interesting, but it didn't address my main interest. "Do you have any idea why I ended up in her will?"

"There were a lot of things about Lottie turned out to be odd." She put the picture on the coffee table, reached for a pack of cigarettes that lay there and lit one. "As far as her property is concerned, she owed it to me. That's what I think." She blew smoke from the side of her mouth and away from me. Her eyes narrowed. "She stole from me as sure as I'm sitting here." Her tone was hard edged. No more fond reminiscing.

"How's that?"

"Melvin Weston and I were going to get married in June. Lottie waltzed back into Four Creeks in January that year. She showed up at the house one evening. I introduced her to Mel. She said she'd been a dancer in Las Vegas, but quit for health reasons. She looked healthy enough to me. She was dressed flashy like she was something special. The next thing I knew, she and Mel were a steady thing. A month later they got married, and I was left out in the cold."

"But you married Mr. Foster."

"Yeah, it was a bad bargain—for both of us." She nodded and after another puff on the cigarette, she said, "There was that car, a dark blue Buick convertible. They bought it when no one else in town could afford a new car. I always wondered where they got the money. A ranch hand, that's all Mel was. He didn't have that kind of income." She tapped ash into an ashtray on the table. "I married Frank, I guess you could say on the rebound and ended up living on his folk's ranch in the foothills. I didn't see Lottie again for a long time."

Her chin raised and with a defiant expression, she said,

84

"Everything that went wrong in my life leads back to Lottie. I deserve her property. It's justice." She stubbed out the cigarette with vigor, and then turned to me with a false smile. "And now you know why. When can you have the house cleared out so it can be sold?"

Her sudden change of tone surprised me so much I almost stuttered. "I'll have to talk to Lieutenant Walker about it."

Irma rose and stuck out her hand. "Good."

I put my cup on the tray and rose to my feet. It was obvious our conversation was over. She followed me to the door, and when it closed behind me, I heard the lock click.

Irma's openness was a puzzle in spite of what she claimed was the reason. She was a bitter woman, but bitter enough to kill?

I left Irma's and was idling at the stop light on the corner near Fair Buy Market when I noticed a white pickup truck in the parking lot. It looked like the one I'd seen cruise by the cemetery earlier that morning. The light changed to green, and I turned to drive through the main part of town. At the stop sign by the fire department, I noticed the same truck behind me. It stayed on my tail until I turned onto the road leading to Indian Hill and Madge's house. I reminded myself that if I counted, I'd likely see half a dozen white trucks in town, but it bothered me anyway. It was the third time I'd seen a truck of the same make and color with a driver who acted interested in what I was doing.

I pulled into Madge's driveway and noticed her car was gone. Inside, I changed into jeans, sweater and sneakers. By the time I released Mutt and Jeff from the kennel it was sprinkling. While I let them run off energy, I leaned against the fence and considered the disconcerting twist of fate. Why would a woman, someone who didn't know me, leave the contents of her house to me? The reason had to be linked to the argument between her and my aunt. Irma had said Madge and

Lottie had known each other most of their lives. If so, why hadn't I heard about her before? The only thing I could think of was that Madge, like Irma, had some sort of grudge against her, something she didn't want to talk about.

Five minutes later, inside the house, I brushed Mutt's coat, and then located Jeff's stuffed squirrel and spent another ten minutes playing tug of war with him. Mutt tried to join in, demanding his share of attention, but he was no match for his larger companion. A generous amount of ear scratching satisfied both of them, and they stretched out on the bedroom carpet.

I was lying on the bed fingering Lottie's key and daydreaming about a secret fortune I'd find in the deposit box, when I heard kitchen noises and caught the aroma of onions cooking.

When I wandered through to the kitchen, Madge startled. "Oh. I didn't hear you come in. I just made a pot of coffee. Let me pour you a cup." She set a blue mug on the counter and filled it then glanced at the wall clock. "That must have been the longest funeral on record."

"No. Before all the ruckus in Ortega Bay, I ran into Russ Treadwell and he wanted me to come to his office."

"Why was that?"

"To inform me that I'm an heiress. I've inherited a key." I held it up for her to see. "And the contents of Lottie Weston's house. It's the damnedest thing."

I saw her wince. "Good gracious," she muttered under her breath. "It would be just like her to leave you a worthless key. Huh, I doubt there's much of value in that house. I'm surprised she didn't leave it to her cats."

Her comment triggered a mental image of twelve cats sitting around Russ Treadwell's office waiting to hear the will read.

"Irma Foster inherits the house and the land." I went to the stove and peeked under the lid of a simmering kettle. "She seems to be in a big hurry to sell it."

Madge waved the large wooden spoon she held in the direction of the steaming pot. "It's going to be chicken noodle soup."

"Tell me about her."

"The chicken? I got her at the grocery store."

"Irma."

She made a face. "I don't know any more scandal, if that's what you're after."

"What was her relationship with Lottie Weston before she was jilted?"

"We were all friends in high school." Madge opened the refrigerator, picked out a couple of carrots and started washing them at the sink. "Don't let Irma stick you with Lottie's funeral expenses. She pretends to be poor, but she's not. I heard she got a pretty penny for the ranch property when it sold."

If Madge knew Irma and Lottie were sisters, she wasn't about to divulge it. I settled on the counter stool and approached the subject from another angle. "What about Lottie? Tell me more about her

"Now there's another story." Madge finished scrubbing the carrots and turned off the faucet. "She was the town nuisance, especially these last ten years. After Mel died she kept to herself for a while, but then she wrote a letter to the editor of the newspaper about a burned out street light near her house."

Madge chopped the carrots and added them to the kettle. "She got action from the city, and that started a stream of letters from her. She sent a new one every month, complaining about one thing or another: the utility tax, kids on skate boards, weeds in the park. She became a one-woman town improvement committee.

"After that she started going to the city council meetings, and managed to get herself on the agenda to voice her complaints. It was all reported in the paper, so everyone in town knew." Madge went into the pantry and returned with a clove of garlic, reached for a paring knife and peeled it. Madge's voice rose a bit as she diced the garlic with vigor. "And all the while we'd see her on the street looking like she'd just crawled out from under a rock."

I sat there cradling my mug of coffee, trying to reconcile the woman in the sequined costume with the Lottie I was hearing about.

"But Madge, you knew Lottie when you were in high school. She wasn't like that then, was she?"

Madge scraped the chopped garlic into her hand, dropped it in the kettle and adjusted the burner knob. "No, she wasn't."

She washed her hands, then turned as she dried them with a kitchen towel. Her expression changed, as though giving her answer extra consideration.

"Personally, I think Lottie went off her rocker when Freddie was killed." She reached for a coffee mug and poured herself a cup. "I had Freddie in my sixth grade class. He was a bright boy, a little cocky sometimes, but good natured. I never heard anything negative about him even in later years. He was scarcely out of high school when he joined the Army. He didn't even tell his parents what he planned. He came home one day and announced it to his folks. Freddie went through basic training all right, but something happened on maneuvers. I can't remember the details, but he was killed. You'd already left for college. It must have been during the next year. My memory's not so good anymore."

Madge shook her head. "Sad. It was like a cloud hung over the whole town for weeks. The funeral was enormous with full military honors. The American Legion arranged it. It looked like all of Four Creeks was there. He's buried out there beside Mel, and now, his mother.

"I remember you sent me the clipping out of the newspaper, but how was she off her rocker?"

"Well, no one saw her for months. But they sure saw Mel. He started hanging out in the saloon. Maybe he always drank, I don't know. Or maybe Freddie's death was eating at him. One night he was arrested for DUI. He fell asleep at the wheel and ran off the road. Fortunately, he didn't hurt anyone or wreck that Buick. I guess he did his drinking at home afterward. About a year later, he was laid off from the ranch where he worked. Then he could drink full time. At least that's what I suspected."

"Did Lottie work? How did they support themselves?"

"It was a mystery to me. No, Lottie never held a job in Four Creeks. And from the moment Freddie was killed, she never set foot in church again. I expect she blamed God. About a year later Mel died. You'd have thought his liver would have killed him, but no, it was his heart. Before long Lottie started collecting stray cats."

Madge put her coffee mug in the sink, fished a spoon from the kitchen drawer, and picked up a pot holder. She lifted the lid on the soup and spooned out a taste. I watched as she added some salt and then ripped open a package of noodles to add to the mixture.

A cold nose nudged my elbow. "I better feed my pals or they'll be hanging around the table looking for a handout." I rose and led Mutt and Jeff outside. While I poured kibbles for the dogs, I speculated about whether Madge was withholding something. Except for the little telling flinch, she didn't seem surprised about Lottie's legacy to Irma or me. And she didn't offer a reason for it. The answer was probably in Lottie's house.

The next day was Sunday, and I was awakened by Madge making as much noise as possible in the kitchen. I knew she was hoping I'd get up and go to mass with her. There were two things she consistently tried to get me to do when I visited her: go to church and eat cauliflower. I found no fault with God, I simply didn't like church. I found no fault with cauliflower either, except for the smell and the taste.

I snuggled beneath the covers and waited until the house was quiet. A half hour later my furry friends were getting restless. I let them out the patio door, went to the kitchen for a cup of coffee, then returned to keep an eye on them from the warmth inside. I sipped my coffee and watched the fluffy clouds hanging over the mountains change bit-by-bit from pink to pale orange and then fade to white as the sun inched upward.

I let the dogs back inside and was considering how best to use my time when the phone rang. It was Judy.

After a greeting she said, "I've been thinking this would be a good time for me to spend a week with my grandchildren. And my daughter, of course. The baby is having her first birthday party on Friday."

Judy's daughter, Violet, lived in San Diego with her husband and the three young ones.

"I cleaned up all the black dust the police left behind," she continued. "The office repairs are complete, and I've updated all the accounts so everything's ready for tax time. There's not much going on. The only phone call was a survey about which radio station I listen to."

"I can't thank you enough, Judy. And you're right. The timing is perfect for you to have a vacation. I'll be here at least another week, maybe two. Something else has come up." I told her about my peculiar inheritance. "I expect I'll find a bank receipt in Mrs. Weston's belongings and maybe even the reason for the legacy."

"If her deposit box contains a fortune, you won't have to work anymore. You'll be a lady of leisure."

I laughed. "Sounds dreary but I'd give it a try."

She laughed and said goodbye.

I dressed and fixed myself egg and toast. I was eager to search Lottie's house, but no one with the proper authority would be on duty at the police department on Sunday. I could look for Dad's records related to the fire. On the other hand, Jeff and I were long overdue for obedience training practice. Jeff was a pussycat most of the time, but he weighed eighty pounds and had remarkably sharp teeth. An animal like that could be a serious liability unless well trained, and it had been over a month since his last workout.

I was rinsing the dishes to put them in the dishwasher when I heard Madge's car. Once inside, she shrugged out of her coat and said, "I heard the wildflowers are beginning to bloom up the canyon. Seems a bit early."

"I have a favor to ask," I said as I wiped the kitchen counter. "I'd like to take Jeff out for an obedience training session. Could I leave Mutt with you?"

Madge looked down at Mutt whose bright eyes were watching both of us. He knew we were talking about him and sensed something was up. "I guess it'll be all right. How long will you be gone?"

"It depends on how long it takes to refresh Jeff's memory. A few hours anyway. Mutt *will* make a fuss when we leave, but only until I drive out of sight. I'll leave his brush and his leash for you. He loves to be brushed. And you can use the leash when he needs to go out."

I gave Mutt his favorite chew-toy for a distraction, put a leash on Jeff and led him to the Explorer. After loading the box of supplies I'd need, we were on our way to one of the parks in town. We spent the next few hours in happy companionship and training exercises. Jeff, of course, thought it was the best of games. By the time we were finished, I was bushed and longed for a hot shower.

When I stepped through the front door at Madge's, I saw her

sitting in her easy chair with Mutt in her lap. His long coat fairly glistened. I detected a budding friendship. Madge flashed a smile at me over her shoulder. "Come and join us," she said. "The Winter Olympics have started. This year it's in Nagano, Japan."

Chapter 11

Early the next morning, I dressed in a hurry and let the dogs out for their run. Overcast skies had prevented frost from forming during the night, but it was still cold. Shivering as I waited for them on Madge's patio, I called, "Come on, guys, I want to get to the police station before Buzz Walker has a chance to leave." They didn't care. In a dog's world the scent of a wild critter was more important.

I put them in the kennel, and ten minutes later parked in front of Nelson's Insurance Agency. I hustled toward the police station where I found Buzz leaning on the reception desk talking to Elena. He turned and gave me an appraising once-over.

"I'd like to treat you to breakfast," I said. I felt sure he'd eaten much earlier, but after I'd humbled myself sufficiently at Lottie's funeral, he wasn't going to turn me down.

He checked his watch. "All right. I have a little time. The Wildwood Café is only a block from here. We can walk." He turned to Elena. "Tell Mike I'll meet him at nine, and we'll go over the interview."

Buzz held the door for me as we entered the restaurant. The aroma of coffee and cinnamon filled the room. I ordered a small bowl of fruit, toast and coffee. He ordered a bear claw and decaf. We drew our coffee from the carafes on a nearby counter and found a table. Through French doors, a mural of an old wagon and some pine trees could be seen on the next building.

"Four Creeks sure has a lot of murals," I said. "I keep discovering new ones."

Buzz added cream and sugar to his cup. "I've lost count. They attract tourists and that makes the local merchants happy. But you didn't ask me here to talk about murals."

"No, I have something to show you." I pulled Lottie's key from my jeans pocket and held it up between my thumb and finger for him to see.

He slowly stirred his coffee, a quizzical expression on his face. Our food arrived, courtesy of a young woman in a short skirt. I laid the key on the table between us. He took a bite of his bear claw and I tasted the fruit. Between bites, I described the meeting at Treadwell's office the previous day. "It seems like I'm to inherit the contents of Lottie Weston's house and this key."

His eyes narrowed as though analyzing the new development. "Looks like one to a safe deposit box."

"That's what everyone says. Before the estate can be settled, Russ needs to know if her house contains any valuables. I'd like to search it to see if I can find something from a bank that will lead me to the deposit box. Can you arrange that?"

He scratched behind his ear and looked at me. "It's part of the crime scene. A trail of footprints led from the back yard to where she was found. We turned the search of the house over to the Sheriff's Department team."

"But they wouldn't be looking for a bank receipt. Most people keep things like that in a desk."

He swallowed a big gulp of coffee and rose from his chair. "Give me an hour. I'll have to clear it with the chief. Meet me at her house."

"Thanks." I took a deep breath. He was doing me a favor, something that wouldn't happen if Four Creeks were a big city. I was capitalizing on our old friendship.

I killed time by lingering over the breakfast, paid the bill, and then strolled around the main part of town to look at the various murals. It was easy to see why they attracted tourists.

When the proper amount of time had elapsed, I drove to the house I'd driven past the week before and pulled into the driveway. It was bungalow-sized with faded tan siding and a single-car garage attached on the east side. An evaporative cooler protruded from a window on the opposite end.

Since I was early, I fished a lipstick out of my purse, pulled down the visor mirror and checked my reflection. I applied a dab. I doubted Buzz Walker would notice—or care. He had the investigation on his mind. I wondered if he were married. Not that it mattered.

Ten minutes later, he arrived. I stepped out of the Explorer and strolled over to his police cruiser. Buzz rolled down the window. Leaning across, he popped open the glove box and pulled out two pairs of plastic gloves. "You're lucky the house has been released. I'll take you inside, but don't remove anything. If we find bank records, you can copy the information. Here, put these on."

I obliged. He was being a bit officious. I couldn't remove anything without permission from the court anyway.

"I really appreciate this," I said as he got out and we went to the gate. "I know you're busy. This bequest has me baffled."

"I suppose now you have a vested interest in what happened to Mrs. Weston, but mind you, no interfering." He gave me a side-glance.

"Who me?"

The gate squawked in protest as Buzz opened it. Sprigs of weeds had sprouted in the neglected lawn. A narrow sidewalk led to the front step where a roof jutted out to shelter the concrete stoop. Planter boxes hung from braces on either side of the door, each containing limp, frost-damaged angel wing begonias. The window shades were pulled halfway like eyelids about to open.

Gloria Getman

Buzz unlocked the door and gave it a push. As we stepped inside, the stench of cat urine was overwhelming. He started opening windows. "Whew. It wasn't this bad last week."

"How many cats live here?"

"I've been told there were twelve, but we only saw one. The back door was standing open when we arrived. They must have escaped."

I hunted for the source of the odor and found a cat box behind the front door. "I know you didn't want anything removed from the house, but I think this stinky box should be exempt." I pushed it toward the open door with my foot. He lifted it outside.

I glanced around the sparsely furnished living room. A smattering of leftover fingerprint dust could be seen on some of the surfaces. The hardwood floor was bare. A television sat on a wrought iron stand a few feet from the front door and faced a lounge chair. A 1970's pole lamp and an aqua Danish Modern sofa stood against the wall opposite the entrance. Above the couch hung a clock shaped like a black cat. Its tail and eyes moved back and forth at the same cadence. Through the doorway on the right, a kitchen table was visible. A small wood stove filled the corner behind the lounger, and an oak secretary desk stood on the west wall at a safe distance from the stove. Lottie's decorating was strictly utilitarian. It seemed like her cats were a higher priority.

On the far side of the kitchen doorway was a bookcase. Its four shelves were crammed with paperbacks. I moved closer and glanced at the titles. Most were old Harlequins. The top surface displayed cat figurines of various sizes and poses. A bare spot indicated a figurine was missing. I turned and looked at Buzz.

"The only sign of struggle was a broken figurine. The evidence team collected the fragments for evaluation."

While Buzz stood by and watched, I opened the antique desk. A door folded out to provide a space for writing. Beneath were two drawers and to the right of them was a small door to an additional

96

compartment. I opened the main section, pulled a chair from the kitchen and sat.

Inside, several pigeon holes were stuffed with a clutter of grocery receipts, store coupons and newspaper clippings. The clippings were Lottie's letters to the editor Madge had mentioned and reports of city council meetings.

I closed the desk's writing surface and pulled open the first drawer. It contained stationery, pens, cellophane tape and a stack of Christmas cards banded with a faded red ribbon. I untied it and shuffled through them, giving attention to return addresses. Nothing from my aunt. I didn't recognize any of the names, but noted most had 1950s or '60s postmarks. All were discolored by time.

I opened one envelope. A smiling Santa adorned the outside of the card and inside the sender wished "Happy Holidays." A scribbled note reminded Lottie of the Christmas they had spent together. It was signed Cuddles McGee. Enclosed was a black-and-white snapshot of a well-rounded brunette in a tight pullover sweater. Her arms were raised in a cheesecake pose with her hands resting on the back of her head.

I found it interesting that Irma made it sound like Lottie was a viper and yet, she'd kept old greeting cards from thirty or forty years earlier. It seemed like she had a sentimental side. I returned everything to its place.

The bottom drawer held an album of Freddie's grammar school pictures, plus a few envelopes of snapshots. I opened one, shuffled through and saw that most of them were of Freddie at various ages, some in sports garb. No pictures of Mel. Their marriage hadn't sounded like a happy one. Maybe she burned them. I slid the pictures back in the envelope and closed the drawer.

The compartment door was locked. "I have a collection of old style keys in my camera bag. I think one might fit this," I said to Buzz.

He didn't object, so I went out to the car to get them. When I was seated again, I inserted a key. With a click, it opened. Inside was a metal box, business envelope size, four inches deep. A perfect place for a bank receipt. No lock. I held it on my lap and lifted the lid. It contained several envelopes, one quite thick. I shuffled through the lot. Nothing from a bank. Some old property tax bills. The stubs were missing, so I reasoned that she'd paid her taxes.

I felt Buzz's presence in back of my chair. His aftershave was distracting, evoking memories of evenings when we'd parked along the river years back. I banished those thoughts and focused my attention on the sheaf of paper in the fat envelope. I pulled it out and unfolded it.

"This is her old will," I said. It had been handwritten. I scanned the document. Lottie had named Irma Foster as her sole heir. I flipped through to the last page. It was dated the same year as her husband's death. But it was the signature of the witness that surprised me—Margaret Hatcher—my aunt.

Buzz leaned in closer for a better view. "What the devil?"

His surprise matched mine. It was clear the connection between Lottie, Irma and Aunt Madge was more complicated than first evident. Neither Madge nor Irma wanted anyone to think they even *knew* Lottie, and yet there definitely was a relationship. "I need to have another talk with my aunt."

"It doesn't look like you found what you're looking for," Buzz said as he straightened himself.

"Not in this desk. Everything here is ancient history." I closed the box, returned it to its place and locked the compartment door. "I think I'll look in her bedroom. Maybe she kept current stuff in a dresser drawer." As I headed toward the opposite side of the house, Buzz moved toward the back porch.

A short hall led to two doors. The first one I opened was the bathroom. The fixtures were clean, but old and stained with mineral deposits. A thin green chenille bath rug lay on the floor and a faded green shower curtain hung over the tub. The matching towels were well worn. I decided to move on. The next door was locked. "Hey, Buzz. You have the key to this room?"

"I thought you were only interested in the bank papers," he called from the back of the house.

"I am, but I'd also like to get an idea of what I've inherited."

"The key's on the nail."

I looked upward and spotted it, also noticing the attic access in the hall ceiling. On tiptoe, I snagged the key and unlocked the door. The room was stuffy, but without a hint of cats. The furniture was dark pine. A red-and-black bedspread was rumpled, evidence of the police search. Matching curtains were pulled against the light. A picture of a young football player sat on the chest-of-drawers, and above it, on the wall, a banner read Four Creeks High School. Freddie's room. It brought back the memory of our home game and cheering in the grandstands.

I opened the closet. His clothes were there, including an olive drab outfit. The drawers probably held his socks and underwear too. The room had been kept unchanged, like a shrine. I turned to leave. On the wall next to the door hung a picture framed in dark walnut of a smiling Freddie, plainly proud of his military uniform. I imagined Lottie receiving the news. Melancholy swept over me. The air felt thick with pain and grief. I backed out, locked the room and replaced the key.

I needed to shake the sense I'd intruded. I passed through the kitchen where faded green café curtains adorned the window above a chrome and Formica table. Buzz stood on the back porch. He'd opened the screened windows.

I glanced at him, and as if he knew what I was feeling, he said, "Sad, huh."

"Yeah, I've been told it changed their lives completely."

Cat food and kitty litter bags were stacked in the corner. On the floor were several stainless steel pet bowls. It looked like Lottie spared no expense when it came to the care of her feline friends.

"I put out some fresh water and food." Buzz turned and pointed to a shelf above the washer and dryer. "I wish the cat could talk."

Hunched between a container of detergent and a gallon of bleach was a huge black cat with white paws. Its yellow eyes were wide with fear. I guess a man who feels sorry for a terrified cat can't be all tough.

"Not much of interest in the kitchen," he said. "The standard stuff: pots, pans, dishes. Not much food in the refrigerator. Looks like about enough for a week."

"What's in the garage?"

"Only an old Buick convertible. It's a beauty, blue with wire wheels." He stepped out the back door onto the grass. "We checked the empty pigeon pen. The mice can't talk either."

I glanced over the backyard to where a faded red pickup stood, its tires flat and windows broken. Next to it was the empty cage Buzz was talking about. A nearby lean-to sheltered a pile of firewood covered with burlap.

"The investigators took her wheelbarrow," Buzz continued. "A piece of her dress was caught on it. We figured the killer used it to haul her body to the canal." He nodded toward a trampled path in the weeds. "There's a wheel track along with footprints."

The thought of it sickened me. "I'm going to check the dresser in the other bedroom," I said and turned back to the interior.

I walked through the house and stood in the doorway to Lottie's bedroom. A mahogany spool bed dominated the scene. It was pushed tight against the wall leaving barely enough space to walk between it and a chest-of-drawers and mirrored dressing table next to it. The pink chenille spread and bedding had been pulled back. A black handbag sat open on the dressing table along with a bottle of hand lotion, hair brush and comb.

I stepped into the room. To my left was the closet. The door had been removed. I could see why. No room for it to swing. A gallon jar half filled with pennies sat on the closet floor. Her infamous black coat hung above it, probably the same coat I'd heard the gossips in the library talking about. A room-sized Oriental rug didn't quite fit the room. It left a wide border of exposed wood flooring at the foot of the bed and also between the bed and the chest of drawers.

I pulled open the bottom drawer of the chest of drawers and saw a loose snarl of panty hose. I lifted a couple of them with my fingertips. Each had large runs. Why did she save a bunch of old panty hose? Gingerly, I pushed them aside. Underneath I found a large letter envelope. It contained several ten dollar bills, but no bank receipt. I put it back and went to the next drawer. Only clean underwear there.

The drawer above that contained a couple of sweaters with their original tags, a neatly folded nightgown, and a stack of letters, tied with a black ribbon. The postmarks were 1983, all from Freddie.

At first Lottie's sense of order seemed puzzling. She kept her mementos in different places. Then it dawned on me. Lottie must have reread Freddie's old letters before bed at night. I felt heart-sick as I pictured her sitting hunched over in dim light, reading her dead son's letters. I blinked back tears and pushed on.

The contents of the top drawer were most curious. It contained a box of 1950's style costume jewelry, two pair of dark glasses and an enormous heap of discarded lottery tickets. I pushed the drawer closed and went to the dressing table.

Sitting on the bench in front, I opened the shallow drawer and found a layer of loose change. Next, I peeked inside her purse. I poked through the contents and found the usual: wallet, house keys, grocery receipts and store coupons. Her wallet contained a ten and nine ones. No bank receipt. I put the wallet back. Why would someone invade the house and not take her money? If not robbery, what was the motive?

My hopes of finding a bank receipt were dashed. I stood, took a couple steps toward the door and tripped on the corner of the rug. I looked down. A hundred dollar bill peeked out from underneath. "Holy Cow. She sure was careless with her money."

As I heard Buzz close the back door, I leaned over and lifted the edge of the rug. "Hey, Walker, come here. Do you suppose this would be worth killing for?"

He appeared in the doorway. I looked at him, raised my eyebrows and pointed to a layer of dust-covered cash under the rug.

Chapter 12

I stepped around the foot of the bed and lifted another section of the rug. More of Uncle Sam's finest. I looked up at Buzz.

He was stone-faced. "Did you know this money was here?" he asked as he pulled his cell phone from a case on his belt.

"Of course not. How would I know?" I lifted the foot of the bed enough to free the rug next to the wall. More money—most of it hundred dollar bills.

"Stop," Buzz said as he pressed a button on the phone. "This changes everything." He held up his hand as though to silence me. "Elena, contact Mike. Tell him I want him to come over to the Weston's house with several evidence bags." He replaced the phone.

I stared at him. Did he think I was going to grab a handful of cash? "What's the matter? Don't glare at me. I had no idea she hid her money under her rug. I literally stumbled over it."

"Anyone who stands to profit from the death of another automatically becomes a suspect. Right now this money is going into the evidence room. And you're going to have to leave."

I admit it, my mouth hung open. I couldn't imagine he'd think I had anything to do with Lottie's death. "Okay." I started toward the door.

"Hey, don't leave me alone with this cash. You're my witness that I didn't pocket any of it. Wait until the team arrives." His expression softened a bit. "It's not you. I'm disgusted because the sheriff's crime scene people didn't find this last week. But I suppose they were distracted by the bank robbery and hostage situation they had over in

Delta." Buzz rubbed a knuckle along his chin. "If the perp was looking for money, he sure didn't search very hard."

"How did she accumulate this large an amount? That's my question. According to Madge, she never held a job after she married Melvin Weston. One thing's certain, it wasn't from saving on grocery coupons, and I doubt it's lottery winnings. You'd have heard about something like that."

The old photo of Lottie in the sequined costume popped into my head. Maybe she won it in Las Vegas. But any normal person would have bragged and stuck it in the bank.

I heard the crunch of tires on the gravel outside. Mike Huerta entered the house with two officers following him. The guy behind Mike was a square fellow with a drooping Pancho Villa mustache. The second man was tall with wavy brown hair and glasses. He had several clear plastic bags in his hand, and Mike had a camera slung over his shoulder.

Buzz raised the corner of the rug.

Mike shook his head. "Who'd have thought that scroungy old woman would have a stash like this?" He raised the camera and started snapping photos. The others pulled on plastic gloves as they commented on the find.

"We'll have to get this bed out of the way first," Buzz said as he stepped back into the doorway. He was distracted, giving directions to his crew to dismantle the bed. I decided I'd keep quiet and hang around until he booted me out. I was curious about how much money Lottie had hidden. I stood near the front door while the officers hauled the mattress and box springs into the living room and stacked them on the floor. The bed frame followed.

When they rolled back the rug, one of them whistled. A number of comments emanated from the men as they surveyed the scene. Then they went to work gathering the money and shaking off the loose dirt.

The bills were splayed out, fan-like on Lottie's mattress. Mike took pictures to document the numbers, then a generous stack was deposited in an evidence bag. Each bag was sealed, the contents and date recorded on the outside, plus signatures. I watched from behind Buzz and promptly recognized the bills as vintage currency due to the red treasury seal.

A year earlier I'd helped an elderly woman who'd discovered a canvas bag of cash buried in the dirt floor of her partially burned barn. She imagined that it dated back to stagecoach days and hired me to find out its current value to collectors. I learned a great deal about U.S. money while doing the research.

As they were about to bag the last collection, I tugged on Walker's sleeve. He swiveled around. "Are you still here?"

"Uh, yes. I thought I should mention those bills are old, printed before 1968."

"It doesn't matter. They're still evidence."

"Could be a clue as to their origin. May I look at one?"

He shrugged. "Hand me one of those," he said to Mike. "I don't see the significance, but here."

My focus caught on the inscription on the treasury seal. I pointed it out to him. "In 1968 the wording on the seal was changed from Latin to English. I'd say her treasure has been under the rug since before then."

"And?"

"If she's been living off this, she must have cashed these someplace, maybe with a coin dealer. Considering her lifestyle, most banks would notice breaking a bill of this type."

He plucked it from my hand and placed it in the bag.

"I wonder if there could be more hidden somewhere else." I raised my eyebrows and pointed toward the access in the hall ceiling. "Like in the attic?"

"I remember seeing a ladder leaning against the shed out back," Mike said with a hint of anticipation.

By his expression, Buzz was less than enthusiastic about my idea. He ran his hand across the back of his neck, and after a thoughtful pause, sent Mike to bring in the ladder.

With the ladder positioned beneath the trap door, Buzz gave a wave of his hand, sending the mustached officer up. We gathered nearby as his man pushed back the door. A fine layer of dust filtered down. He pulled a flashlight from his belt, flashed the beam around the attic's interior and looked down at us. "There's a couple of things up here."

"Can you reach them?" I asked.

He leaned forward and I heard one of them being dragged.

"Mike, give him a hand," Buzz said.

The edge of a plastic bin-like container came into view. Mike climbed a few steps and supported the weight as it was lifted over the edge. Buzz helped ease it to the floor.

The name Weston was stamped in black on the top. It wasn't locked. Buzz opened it. A musty odor escaped. A couple of pairs of Army fatigues with baggy leg pockets were on top. Below were several caps and a pair of boots. An envelope of photos was tucked in a corner. I pulled it out. Inside, the first snapshot was of a group of smiling young men, arms draped around each other's shoulders. They looked like they were having a good time. A barracks building stood in the background. Basic training, most likely.

"This must be Freddie's stuff the Army sent home after his death," I said.

Buzz nodded and closed the lid as soon as I replaced the pictures. He sent his man up the ladder again, and a large dark brown suitcase was passed down. It was locked.

Buzz extracted a devise from his pocket, popped the lock, and lifted the cover. Everyone gawked. It held several pairs of sequined tights in various colors along with matching caps and several scraps of feathers dyed to match.

"I meant to tell you earlier," I said. "Irma told me Lottie spent a couple years as a Las Vegas show girl before she married Melvin Weston."

"Is that so?" Buzz pushed aside the clothing and beneath was a snapshot envelope with a Las Vegas Rexall Drug store label. A date stamped on the outside read 1957, and the owner's name was Rita Diamond.

It was the same name that was on the back of the first photo Irma had shown me. I reached for the envelope, shook out several black-and-white photos and shuffled through them. Buzz leaned over my shoulder. Most were shots of the same woman Irma had identified as Lottie. She was on a stage, in costume, sometimes solo and sometimes with another woman. In another picture, the two women were sitting around a table with a couple of men, all smiles, with a third man in the background. There were a couple of prints of Lottie and one of the men in an amorous pose. The guy had dark, slicked-back hair and thick eyebrows.

"I'd lay odds Mel never saw these pictures," I said. The bottom photograph was of the same fellow sitting alone, showing a toothy grin. I flipped it over and on the back were the initials, B.B.

Did Mr. B.B. have something to do with the cash under the rug?

I spread the photos in my hand like playing cards. "I'd like to take these pictures to show to Irma Foster and find out if she knows who these people are."

"No. I do the questioning, remember?" He held out his hand.

"Of course," I said without moving. "But I think I've gained her confidence." It was a stretch. "She's likely to be more candid with me than with a cop. And it'd be a waste of your time if these photos mean nothing."

His eyes narrowed.

"I won't be interfering. I'd be helping. I'll call you this afternoon and report what she said."

"I have a better idea," he said. He cocked his head to one side and regarded me with steely blue eyes. "You show Mrs. Foster the pictures, and meet me at the Wildwood Café at twelve-thirty. You can return the pictures and report to me over lunch."

All conversation in the room stopped like everyone was waiting for my answer. I had a strong sense the directive was not Walker's usual mode of operation.

I didn't hesitate. "Okay. It's a deal."

I was about to leave when I noticed one of the lottery tickets had fallen beneath the dresser. I stepped into the bedroom, picked it off the floor and glanced at the numbers—nine, fourteen, thirty-six, seven, fifteen and fifty-eight. I opened the drawer to replace it, chose another and glanced at the numbers. They were the same. I picked another one and another. They were all the same.

"Hey, Walker, look here."

"What is it this time, a sock full of rubies?" He came in and stood beside me.

"No. Look. Every lottery ticket has the same numbers. There are dozens, all with the same numbers."

He shrugged. "Lots of people do that. They think the odds are their picks will win eventually."

"Can I take one of these? The numbers might mean something."

"I think you've been reading too many detective stories." He gave my forearm a light touch and grinned. "Sure."

Chapter 13

I climbed into the Explorer and sat a few moments. The bank receipt I'd been hoping to find wasn't in Lottie's house. I'd have to go from bank to bank and inquire. To do that, I'd need a letter from Russ Treadwell. In the meantime, I couldn't help speculating about the new-found cache and the ghosts of Lottie's past life. I set my course for Irma's house.

Five minutes later, I pulled into her driveway and rang her doorbell. A moment passed before I heard the door unlock. It opened a crack.

"Oh, it's you again." She let the door swing open and shook her head. "I can't seem to get rid of you. Come on in. What do you want this time?"

I felt about as welcome as an invasion of fleas. "Sorry to bother you, but I have some pictures I found in Lottie's house. I hope you can identify the people in them."

"Okay," she said with a sigh of resignation. "But let's sit on the patio. It's not as cold out there today."

I followed her through the patio door. The long open porch stretched the width of the house. Vines clung to the corner posts. Pansies and snapdragons bordering a strip of lawn were struggling to gain a foothold. Beyond the grass, a tree stretched its bare branches.

As soon as we settled into cushioned wicker chairs, Irma fished a cigarette package and lighter out of the pocket of the flowered smock she was wearing.

I'd decided not to mention the cash under Lottie's rug. Her

reaction when she learned I'd inherited the contents of the house, as though she wanted to protest, made me wonder if she might have already known about the money. Perhaps Lottie had told her about it years before. Or maybe she was the other woman in the pictures.

She lit a cigarette as I pulled the photo envelope from my purse. I handed her the pictures one at a time. The first was similar to what she showed me the day before. She took it with her free hand and nodded. "That's Lottie all right." She handed it back.

The next picture was of Lottie and the other woman. Irma studied the picture, pressed her lips together, and shook her head. "That's Lottie, but the other one doesn't look like anyone I know." She returned it without further comment.

"This one has the initials B.B. on the back." I passed it to her.

Irma glanced at the photo, flipped it over and back to the front again. "Sorry, I can't help you." She gave it back to me and took another drag on her cigarette.

When I held out the last picture—the one of the two couples at the table—she gave a quick glance and shook her head.

With a half-smile she said, "You might show those pictures to your aunt. I'll bet she'd find them interesting."

"I found a hand written will in Lottie's desk," I said. "It's dated shortly after her husband's death and witnessed by my aunt. Were you aware of that?"

Her expression flattened, and she shifted in the chair. "Certainly not. I don't keep track of everything that goes on in this town."

"There's something I want to ask you. Don't take offense." I pulled a notebook from my purse.

"What?"

"Where were you the night Lottie was killed?"

Her back stiffened and she gave me an indignant look. "Why, at Bible study, of course. I go to Bible study every Saturday evening at

Peggy Stallings' place in Sandy Cove. We're studying Jonah. You know, the prophet who was swallowed by a whale."

"Uh huh. What time?"

She tapped an ash into the tray on the table. "We start at seven and I'm home by nine."

"And after that?"

Her eyes narrowed. "I was at home in bed watching television. You can't possibly think I had anything to do with Lottie's death. Why, she was my own sister."

I didn't answer her. "Give the pictures some thought. Something might come to you later." I glanced at my watch and rose.

"Not likely." She snuffed out her smoke, popped out of her chair and followed me to the door. "Do you think someone from Lottie's past killed her?"

"Nothing can be ruled out."

Lottie was an enigma and each bit of information was like one more bread crumb along the trail, but leading nowhere. I left Irma making fussy noises and went to the Explorer, no more enlightened than before.

In an investigation you talk to anyone who knows even the least bit about the subject. If you poke around long enough, after a while a pattern develops. It wasn't the case with Lottie. Ever since I'd arrived in Four Creeks, it had been more like a kaleidoscope. Every day the colors shifted and the picture was different. I couldn't grasp a pattern. Who knew about the cash under the rug? Was that the reason for the murder? But then, what about the argument between my aunt and Lottie? Nothing made sense. What was the common denominator?

I found myself back on Main Street and was formulating my next move, when I noticed a white pickup a block away headed in my direction. It turned into an alley. It looked like the truck I'd seen the day before, but by the time I passed the alleyway, it was out of sight.

I thought about following, but if someone saw me snooping around, I'd have a hard time explaining my actions. I decided against it. I couldn't be certain the guy in the truck was following me. But if he *was*, it might have something to do with Lottie's murder. The next time I saw the truck I'd stop and confront him about it. Or maybe I'd be clever, tell him he resembled an old classmate and find out who he was that way. I glanced at my watch. Time to meet Buzz.

The café was busy when I arrived. A line of people were waiting to order at the counter. I stood aside and studied the menu while I waited for Buzz. He came in at exactly twelve-thirty. He always *was* a stickler for promptness, something else we'd argued about back in the day. Several heads turned as we moved to the counter together. We'd probably be the subject of afternoon speculation, one of the joys of small town life.

I ordered a cup of broccoli soup, a tuna sandwich and coffee. He chose a club sandwich, macaroni salad and a Coke. We filled our glasses at the fountain and found a small table in a corner near a window. While waiting for our lunch, I told him Irma denied knowing anyone in the snapshots, other than Lottie. "She said I ought to show the pictures to Madge—which I'll do—and also ask her how she happened to witness Lottie's will. But I'll wait until after Dad's memorial service."

"I don't see how any of it is going to help you find the receipt for the safe deposit box," Buzz said as our orders arrived.

"It's not." I dipped my spoon into the soup. "But I can't help feeling Irma and my aunt are being evasive when it comes to Lottie. Look, Buzz, tell me the truth with no cop-speak. Are you close to making an arrest for Lottie's murder?"

After a long pause, while he poked the macaroni salad with his fork, he gave a deep sigh. "No. We've canvassed her neighborhood, and no one saw or heard anything that night. You and Irma are the only ones to gain anything and both of you check out. We're no closer than we were last week."

"In that case, what difference would it make if I ask questions of some other people? By now everyone in town knows about Lottie and Madge's argument and that I'm a private investigator. It's logical I'd ask questions on my aunt's behalf. I might unearth a bit of information or make someone uncomfortable. Then you'd have more to go on. Besides, there must be someone who knows where Lottie did her banking, if she ever did. It'd serve two purposes."

He didn't say anything, bit into his sandwich and chewed slowly, as if considering my proposal.

"Dad's service is tomorrow," I continued my argument. "I need to find the deposit box and its contents so I can get back to Ortega Bay. The probate of his estate will take months and in the meantime, I need to earn some money for my hospital bill. There's an insurance company that owes us for work Dad did before the accident." I told him about Dennis Colton, his lie, plus the missing file and audiotape.

"I can't give my permission for you to go snooping around," he finally said, "because if I did, and you *did* irritate the wrong person, you might get hurt. But I won't stand in your way, *if* you'll agree to tell me who you're going to contact beforehand."

"Agreed," I said. "And another thing. I'd like to find Mr. B.B., the man in the photos."

Buzz gave a chuckle.

"I know it's a stretch, but the only thing of value in Lottie's house was the money under the rug. What if it's his money and she took it? It's been a long time since she was in Vegas, but maybe he's been out of the country or in jail or something. He might have come here looking for it."

"Your theory sounds like something right out of the movies."

We ate our lunch in silence for several minutes. I took a bite of my sandwich and gazed out the window. The sun was peeking through the overcast sky.

"About your concussion." His attention fixed on my face. "How long ago was the accident?"

I hesitated. Did he think I was addle-brained?

"Oh, I'm sorry," he said. "Do you mind talking about it?"

"I guess not. It happened the first week of January. Dad had finished the case I was telling you about, and we decided to relax for the weekend at a friend's cabin near Pine Mountain. I was driving and hit black ice. We went over an embankment and the car rolled. At least that's what the accident investigator concluded. I don't remember much. The seat belt and airbag saved me. I got away with only a concussion and cuts from broken glass." I looked into my coffee cup and took the last swallow. "Dad wasn't so lucky."

"And you blame yourself."

"I suppose."

"Ice can be treacherous for anyone."

"Maybe if he'd been driving it wouldn't have happened, or..." A blurry image of a man's face came to me for a few seconds along with a faint dizziness. I squeezed my eyes shut and shook my head to clear it.

"You okay?" Buzz asked.

"Yeah, every now and then a bit of memory returns. It's weird." I took the last bite of my sandwich and tried to retrieve the image, but it was gone.

Buzz put his hand on my shoulder. "It's only natural. I probably shouldn't have asked."

I felt my reserve start to crumble. I was close to tears and didn't know why. I'd cried buckets in the hospital and thought I was past that stage. I focused on my empty soup bowl until the moment passed.

Buzz seemed to sense my discomfort and finished his lunch in silence. He drained his glass of Coke. "Well, the mystery of Lottie's fortune calls." He placed his napkin on the table. "I better get back to work."

I rubbed my hands together in mock greediness. "Am I going to be a rich heiress?"

He laughed and raised his eyebrows. "If you prove your theory, who knows." He rose and pushed his chair in.

I did the same and we went out the door together. As we paused on the sidewalk outside, he said, "I won't be able to attend your father's service. I have a court summons. I'm sorry."

"That's okay. Madge was the one who insisted on it. Dad never cared for funerals."

He followed me to the Explorer and opened the door. His mother had raised him right. I got in, closed the door and waited until he waved as he pulled his police cruiser away from the curb.

Chapter 14

I figured the best thing to do about unraveling the puzzle of the key was to talk to Russ Treadwell. I was on my way to his office when I spotted Mike Huerta sitting at a picnic table outside Bob's Hot Dog Stand. I pulled over to the curb, climbed out and went to talk to him.

As I scooted onto the bench opposite, he said, "Imagine. That old lady had all that cash and never spent it. I can think of a lot of things I'd do, if I had ten grand."

"Is that how much there was?"

"Looks like it."

In Lottie's day, it would have been enough to buy a house. For a few seconds I fantasized about how I'd spend it, when and if, it were mine. Replacing my mangled Cherokee was high on the list. Odds were it was about to go into a crusher. I envisioned a big down payment on a red sports car. I glanced in Mike's direction. He must have guessed my thoughts because he gave me a knowing smile.

"About Mrs. Weston," I said. "You know about any of her acquaintances in town?"

"Nah. I didn't know much about her, except I'd see her most Thursdays, if I was on duty. When I patrol I make a point of watching for patterns around the businesses. Like when the lights are on or off, blinds up or down, the times the different places open and close. That way, if something's different, I know to check it out. Most shifts, it's a quiet town."

"On Thursday, you say. Where did you see her?"

"Oh, I might see her walking along the street, or going into Fair

Buy Market. Once I went into Avila's Quick Mart for a soda and saw her in there."

"Ever see her go into any banks?"

"Nope. Looks to me like she didn't trust banks."

"I think I'll go talk to the folks at Fair Buy Market. I saw one of the checkers at her funeral service. She might know something that would help me find her deposit box. You know the name of the manager?"

"Clark Weir."

"And the clerk. The frizzy-haired blonde?"

"You mean Hester? She's the only blonde there."

"That's her."

His expression changed. His brow creased. "You better be careful, Miss Powers. Buzz, er, Lieutenant Walker might not like you questioning folks."

I put my finger to my lips and gave him my most engaging smile. "It's okay. I'll tell him about it tomorrow."

"I dunno," he said with a tilt of his head.

"Thanks for the information." I winked and headed to the SUV.

A parking place right in front of the market opened up as I turned in. I parked and headed inside. When I didn't find Hester at the check-out, I asked the middle-aged clerk to call the store manager.

While I waited, I paced the floor. A couple of minutes later Clark Weir approached me with a smile. It was the kind used for customers when you think you're facing some inane complaint. He was, by my estimate, in his mid-forties, with thinning gray hair. He was dressed in dark slacks, short-sleeved, striped shirt and tie.

I introduced myself. "I'm looking for one of your cashiers. I think her name is Hester. She's tall, slender, has blue eyes and frizzy blonde hair."

His smile faded. "What do you want with Hester? If you're unhappy with the store, you need to talk to me."

I pulled my ID from my purse and held it out for him to read.

"A private investigator," he said with a touch of awe in his voice. He'd probably never met one before. "Is Hester in some sort of trouble? I need to know if she is. I have store security to consider."

"It doesn't have anything to do with the store. I'm talking to everyone who was acquainted with Mrs. Weston and might know her movements the week before she died."

"Oh, yeah, I read about her in the paper." His shoulders instantly relaxed. "It's Hester McKay you're looking for. She's a good employee, always on time, never sick."

"I want to ask her about Mrs. Weston. I'm hoping she'll remember when Mrs. Weston last came into the store."

"She might. You could call her. She's in the phone book. She lives on Elm Street. Drives a gray VW. She's divorced, I think. No kids. Maybe that's the reason."

"What?"

"No kids. The reason she's on time and never sick, I mean." He smiled. "She's real nice to the customers. Never a complaint."

I returned his smile, thanked him and bought a package of peanuts on the way out.

I set my course for the center of town to find Elm Street. The houses in that neighborhood, mostly rentals I suspected, were cottages with narrow lots and backyards separated by an alley. Many had neat lawns and flower beds even though the paint might be faded or peeling.

A gray VW Bug was parked in front of a once-white house. I parked behind the bug, climbed out, and dodged a pile of dog doo-doo left on the sidewalk in front of the house. As I climbed the concrete steps, a pair of shoulder-high nandina brushed my jeans, giving the impression it was not the most commonly used entrance.

I reached inside the screen door and knocked. A few seconds passed, and I was beginning to think I'd missed her. I tried a second time and heard footsteps approaching. The lock clicked, the door opened, and Hester's face appeared in the gap. Her frizzy hair was flattened on one side. Perhaps I'd disturbed an afternoon nap.

"I'm Deena Powers." I handed her my card. "I've been asked to gather information about Mrs. Weston, the woman who was killed last week. I believe she was a customer of Fair Buy Market."

She studied my card for several seconds, but didn't move to open the door. "I don't know nothing about her."

A door closed in the rear of the house, heavy, like a back door. Her eyes flicked sideways at the sound.

It occurred to me she'd been entertaining on her day off. Hardly any of *my business*. "I'm checking with people she might have come in contact with that week," I said.

She pulled open the door. "You can come in, but I don't have anything to tell."

Hester had on a loose fitting gray jersey with long sleeves and knit cuffs, an outfit that could be used for exercise or serve as pjs. She was barefoot. She motioned me to a faded orange sofa that dominated a 12 by 12 front room while she perched on the arm of the matching overstuffed chair.

"When was the last time you saw Mrs. Weston in the store?"

"Probably Thursday afternoon. She always came in that day."

"Always?" I pulled a notebook and pen from my purse.

"Yes, generally." She ran her thumb and index finger along the hem of her knit top, smoothing it.

"Only on Thursday? Never Tuesday or Wednesday?"

"It was her habit. She bought a bunch of cat food once a week."

"And you waited on her that day?"

"I guess so. She always picked my aisle even if my line was the longest."

"Was there anything unusual about her that you noticed?"

She gave a snort. "She was always unusual. The way she dressed, I mean. But no different that day than any other."

"Did you notice who she talked to?"

"She hardly ever talked to anybody in the store. She wasn't chatty, just put the cat food in her cart and took off."

"Is that all she purchased?"

"No. She'd get a few other things, but she bought *a lot* of cat food. Always bought the same stuff though, pretty much, cat food, bread, and hamburger." She shrugged. "Always paid with a twenty and wanted her change in one dollar bills. I noticed because sometimes my ones got low."

I nodded and jotted notes. If she was using the money from under the rug, where did she cash those C-notes?

"Oh, and she used a lot of coupons," Hester said.

"Coupons? What kind?"

"You know, store coupons, for the cat food."

I recalled the coupons I'd seen in her house. "Other than in the store, did you see Mrs. Weston at other times?"

"You mean around town?"

"Yes. Did you ever see her talking to other people in town?"

Hester paused, thoughtful. "Only once, a month or so back. I saw her by the railroad tracks talking to an older man I didn't know."

I made a note. "You work every weekday?"

"No. I usually have Tuesday or Wednesday off and every other weekend—except this week. I had a three-day weekend."

"What time do you get off work?"

Her brow creased a bit. "Depends on whether I'm on days or evenings. I sometimes work Friday evening. If it's days, at three. If evenings, about nine-thirty. What's that got to do with anything?"

"Do you work evenings on weekends?"

"No, not usually, unless someone is sick. Why?" Her tone became guarded.

"I'm interviewing everyone who had contact with Mrs. Weston and asking the same sort of questions. Were you working the weekend she was killed?"

"Yes. I think so." Her eyes narrowed.

"After work, where did you go?"

"Home." She stood. "Hey, I ain't answering any more questions." She moved to the door and jerked it open. "Get outa here. I don't know nothing about how ol' Mrs. Weston got her head bashed in. Leave."

I did, thanking her. I wasn't likely to get more information, even if I pressed. It was curious that she knew about Lottie's head trauma, but perhaps it was in the newspaper. I didn't think it was, but then, I didn't have as much confidence in my memory banks since the accident.

Chapter 15

Interviewing Hester had led me nowhere, so I turned my attention to my next stop, Russ Treadwell's office. I couldn't go waltzing into a bank and ask to look for any deposit box the key would open.

Russ' secretary, Marsha Trout, greeted me with a warm smile. Behind the glasses, her bright, blue eyes told me nothing much passed her attention. She buzzed Russ on an intercom and waved me into his office.

Russ stepped around his desk to offer his hand. I could see he'd been hard at work. His shirt sleeves were rolled up, and his desk had several manila folders spread across it.

I explained the lack of results from my search at Lottie's house. "If a receipt for a deposit box exists, I didn't find it. I think I'll need a word from you to gain cooperation from the banks."

"You're absolutely right. I'll have Marsha type a cover letter and we'll have the appropriate documents ready for you by tomorrow afternoon. With a letter and your key, you shouldn't have any trouble."

I told him I'd stop by after Dad's service, thanked him and gave Marsha a smile as I left.

When I turned the key in the SUV, I glanced at the gas gauge. I hadn't refilled the tank since my return from Ortega Bay on Friday. The fuel was getting low. I headed for Avila's Quick Mart. Perhaps I'd have a chance to talk to Mr. Avila again at the same time.

When I entered, I recognized Eddie from when I'd seen him with Hester in Fair Buy Market. He was replenishing the cigarette supply.

"Excuse me. Is Mr. Avila around?"

He turned and jerked a thumb toward the back of the store. Avila sat at a desk behind a windowed partition that separated an office from the main room.

I frowned.

"I'll buzz him for you." Eddie reached under the edge of the counter. Avila turned toward us with the telephone receiver held to his ear and waved an index finger.

"He's lining up interviews for help," Eddie said.

"Business must be good."

He shook his head and poked a cigarette package into the last empty space. "I'm quitting, gonna blow this town." He dropped the empty carton into a waste container and grinned, revealing an uneven line of teeth. "I won the lottery."

"I read it in the newspaper. Congratulations. So you're planning to leave?"

"Soon as I get my first check."

"What's the matter with Four Creeks?"

He frowned. "No jobs that pay decent. Weather's lousy. Rotten winter fog. I'm going someplace where the sun shines all the time."

"The paper said you're a family man."

"Yeah, I got a wife and kid."

He didn't sound very happy about it.

Max Avila approached from the back of the store. "How may I help you?" He smiled. "Oh yes, I remember. You're the lady detective from down south. I have your card here someplace." He made a pretense at finding it, looking under some loose papers on the counter.

"I've been asked to check with people who knew Mrs. Weston to determine her movements the week before she died."

"Sure. Makes sense," Avila responded.

"You said she always came in on Thursdays. Did you talk to Mrs.

Weston that day?"

Eddie interrupted. "Uncle Max? Can I take a break?"

"Wait. I'm sorry, Miss Powers. I should introduce you. This is my nephew, Eddie Lee." He turned to his clerk. "This here's Miss Powers. She's a private investigator. Stick around. She might want to talk to you." Avila turned back to my question.

I watched as Eddie's eye movements flicked from his uncle to the rear of the building.

"I've thought about it," Avila said. "I wasn't here. My wife was sick with a terrible cough, and I went to the drug store to pick up a prescription. I missed Lottie that day. Eddie would've waited on her." He turned toward Eddie, but Eddie was gone. I'd seen him edge toward the back door and slip out.

Avila went slack-jawed and his face flushed. "That kid," he said with annoyance. "I'm sorry Miss Powers. Eddie's got a short-timer's fever. He won the lottery and plans to leave Four Creeks." He took a deep breath and gave a sigh of exasperation. "Hasn't been able to keep a job since his father died. I'm afraid my sister-in-law spoiled him. Not enough discipline. He's been sort of restless.

"It's all right. I'll catch up with him." I couldn't decide if Eddie wanted to avoid me, or if his goal was to skip out on work.

"You say the word and I'll find him for you, anytime."

I shook my head. "Now, about Mrs. Weston. Did she ever talk about other businesses she patronized? Or mention her bank in conversation?"

"Can't say as she did. Mostly we talked about our pets."

"Did she ever complain about any trouble with her neighbors?"

He shook his head. "No, but she did complain about the condition of the road in front of her house. She said the shoulder of the road was rutted from the rain, and she thought the city ought to do something about it."

A man in dirty blue jeans, red plaid shirt and a hard hat entered the store. He took a six-pack of beer from the cooler and placed it on the counter. Mr. Avila moved to total the purchase while the man dug in his pocket.

After the man left, I laid a twenty dollar bill on the counter for the gasoline. "Winning the lottery was a lucky break for Eddie. And for you. I guess there'll be a bonus."

"Yes, indeed." His broad smile returned.

"Where does Eddie plan to go when he leaves Four Creeks?"

"He talks about a lot of places, San Diego, Las Vegas." He shrugged. "His wife might know better. Let me give you their address. You can probably catch him there." He scribbled on a piece of note paper and handed it to me.

"Thanks." I went out the door and slipped the note into my jacket pocket as I strode toward the Explorer. I didn't need the address. I already knew where they lived. Right across the road from Lottie.

It was almost 2:30 when I arrived at Eddie's house. A young woman jerked open the door as I raised my hand to knock. Her dark hair was disheveled, her eyelids red and she held a squalling infant. Her eyes widened in surprise when she saw me on her doorstep.

"Oh. I was hoping you were Eddie," she said.

"Maria Lee?"

"Yes." She jiggled the baby and stared at me expectantly. The child continued to yowl. Maria's face was drawn with fatigue, but she was still a twenty-something beauty. By my guess, the baby she held was less than a year old.

"Sarah won't stop crying. She's real sick. I called my husband, but he hasn't come home. I don't know what to do." The large pupils of her velvety brown eyes exposed her worry.

My own experience with illness was limited to my pets, but I understood her concern. The baby's cheeks were flushed. I reached out and put my hand on her forehead. "She has a fever," I said. "If I were you, I'd take her to the doctor."

"I called. They said I could bring her in right away, but Eddie's got the car. He said he'd come get us. That was an hour ago."

It wasn't part of my plan, but there she stood with a screaming kid. What was I to do? "Come on, I'll take you." I told her my name and showed her my ID. The flicker of a question crossed her face and was gone. She grabbed her purse and followed me to the car. A mother will do anything for the sake of her child.

The vehicle's movement temporarily comforted the baby. She quieted to a whimper, and I briefly explained the reason for my visit. "I was hoping to find Eddie at home. I missed him at the Quick Mart. I wanted to ask him about the last time Mrs. Weston came into the store."

"I heard what happened," Maria said. "The police came and asked questions. I didn't know her. I've seen her a time or two and heard people talk about her, but that's all."

"When you saw her, where was she?"

"Maybe walking along the road toward town or in her yard. Turn left here." She indicated the street next to the junior high school.

"You never saw her go into a store, or anything like that?"

"No. I don't get out much. Only when Eddie takes me."

"Well, that should change now that you and Eddie won the lottery."

"Eddie won the lottery. He's like a caged lion since he found out. He wants to move away from Four Creeks. I want to stay near my family. Frankly, Miss Powers, since Sarah was born, I hardly know him. He acts distracted all the time. He used to come home after work, but now, if he comes home at all, he eats and leaves. Comes back late.

He's got a friend over by the bowling alley. Name's Bud something—Benson or Henson. At least that's what he says." She heaved a sigh. "Oh, turn here."

I saw the clinic parking lot and pulled into an open spot near the door. As we climbed out, Sarah started to fuss again.

"I really appreciate your bringing us here, Miss Powers."

I held the door for her and followed her into the office. "What make of car does Eddie drive?"

"A Honda Civic." She moved to the receptionist's window, propped the baby on her hip and signed her name on the clip board and then turned to me. "My mother gets off work at four. I can call her for a ride home. I sure thank you."

The infant set to wailing in earnest. Maria glanced around at the row of chairs. Except for one next to the door, all of them were occupied. I gave her my card and left.

It was hard to believe that Lottie Weston, with the money she had under her rug, never went into other stores. She was the strangest character.

I retraced the route and turned onto Main Street, thinking I'd drive around the bowling alley and look for a mailbox with the name Benson or Henson on it. As I passed Elm Street and the alley behind Hester's house, a bit of color caught my attention. I pulled over and backed up for a better look, figuring I could safely bet my next jelly doughnut that Eddie's blue Civic was parked behind Hester's house.

That evening I sat at the kitchen counter with the phone directory and made a list of all the banks in the county, their addresses and phone numbers. I was determined to begin visiting each one the next afternoon after Dad's memorial service.

Madge was cleaning up the dinner dishes in silence. I sensed her gloom and figured it was related to the upcoming funeral.

"Madge, you're too quiet," I said from my perch on the bar stool. "Do you want to talk about it?"

She sighed. "I was wondering. Do you think your father still believed in God?"

I didn't know what to say. I'd heard Dad call on God many times, but not in the way she had in mind. "Dad never talked about things like that. I guess he thought the subject was private and personal."

"I've been praying for his soul. I pray that he didn't turn his back on his childhood catechism altogether. I know it's hard to hang onto your faith when you see so much of the seamy side of life like he did." She wiped the last sauce pan, put it in the cupboard and pushed the button to start the dishwasher. "I wish I'd been there at the end." Her voice was barely a whisper.

"Me too." But I wasn't. And I didn't know if he regained consciousness before he passed. I couldn't reassure her.

"I think I'll go to bed a little early tonight," she said without looking at me.

Dad's service was scheduled for the next morning. I knew she wasn't planning on sleeping. She'd be on her knees at the bedside, rosary in hand, trying to pray Dad into heaven.

Chapter 16

That night I had another nightmare, identical to the others. Jeff must have sensed my discomfort, because he put his nose next to my ear and snorted until I woke. I rolled over and gave him a reassuring pat. A headache was beginning to dig in its claws. I slid out of bed and tiptoed across the cold floor to the bathroom for a dose of Advil. I crawled back in bed and had dozed off when I heard the shower start in Madge's bathroom. It was still early, but I knew Madge was getting ready for Dad's service.

Jeff rose to his feet and tilted his head, listening. I reached over and scratched his ear to let him know barking wasn't necessary. The movement woke Mutt and he started performing his jumping ritual, begging to be allowed onto the bed. I obliged.

I wanted to linger under the covers, but I could see Jeff was getting restless, a sure sign that nature called. I crawled out of bed and dressed in sweats. We slipped out the patio door, and I let the dogs run. The air was damp and chilly, the sky overcast again. I hiked up the hill and sat for a few minutes on what I was beginning to consider "my rock." Broad green hills spread out before me with the snow blanketed Sierra in the background. Spring was still weeks away. I hated to leave the peaceful spot to face saying goodbye to Dad. But before long the cold penetrated my clothes, so I gave in and called the dogs.

Madge had seemed pleased when I agreed to delay Dad's service until after the newspaper published a notice. I was hoping for a brief, painless ceremony, but when I saw her face set in grim resignation, I knew it wasn't going to be that way. She was dressed in black with hat and gloves to match. I put on the business suit I'd brought from home and set my jaw.

We met Reverend Hamilton in the parking lot at the cemetery and shook hands as we introduced ourselves. I had already given him Dad's background over the phone the previous evening: his service in Korea, the years with the two police departments and finally Powers Investigations. When he'd asked about my mother, I explained that she died from cancer when I was seven.

Mr. Van Dyke, the mortician, had arrived earlier. Chairs were already arranged under a green canopy and faced the small mahogany box that held Dad's ashes. The sight of it nearly cracked my composure.

A group of Madge's friends from the local chapter of the Women of Colonial Heritage had gathered, and she introduced them to me. Madge and I took our seats in the front row. I was concentrating on the toes of my shoes when I heard male voices. Four gray-haired men approached.

The tallest man stuck out his hand and leaned forward. In a subdued tone, he said, "You must be Wally's daughter. I'm Art Washburn. I went to school with your father."

I took his hand, nodded and thanked him for coming. He stepped over to speak to Madge.

"Bill Boxford," the next man said. He was shorter and heavier than the first. He patted my hand and told me he'd also been a classmate of Dad's. The other two men were farmers, both dressed in jeans and plaid jackets. They'd known Dad during his ranching days when Grandpa Powers had been sick.

"Your Dad was a good neighbor," one of them told me. "He was always there to lend a spare part if a piece of machinery broke. He was someone you could count on."

The other man nodded in agreement. "You're sure right about that, Fred. I got Valley Fever that summer and Wally took over the haying for me."

The four men clustered in a circle, obviously well acquainted. As they chatted amongst themselves, I heard that my father had helped each one in some significant way. I glanced at Madge who had an I-told-you-so look in her eyes.

"If you'll all take a seat, we'll begin," Reverend Hamilton said.

The minister had just started his welcome greeting when a stoop-shouldered elderly man struggled across the expanse of grass in the group's direction. He wore a black suit coat. It was unbuttoned and oversized to the point of being comical. It hung almost to his knees. Underneath, his jeans were suspended on narrow hips, leaving the cuffs to drag the ground. His labored gait caught everyone's attention.

Mr. Van Dyke noticed, turned and rushed in his direction, meeting him at a distance from the gathering. He took him by the arm. "Go on now, Jonesy. You don't belong here," Van Dyke said in a gentle, but firm voice.

"I do too," he protested. The little man jerked his arm away from Van Dyke's grasp. "I wanna pay my respects to Wally."

"But you don't understand. This is a private service. Be a good man. Go on about your business." Van Dyke blocked the man's path with an outstretched arm.

The old fellow took a feeble swing at the mortician and tried to maneuver around him. "You lying sack 'o shit. You think I can't see." His voice echoed in the morning air. "That there's Art Washburn and Billie Boxford. I know 'em both. This ain't no private affair, and I got just as much right here as anybody else."

I started to rise and felt Madge's hand on my arm. She was

frowning, but I couldn't help it. If the old man wanted to attend my father's service, it was okay with me. No need to make a scene. I moved to intercede.

"It's all right, Mr. Van Dyke. Let him be," I said when I drew close.

"Thank ya, Miss Deena," Jonesy said. "You don't know me, but your daddy and I were pals when we was just lads out on your grandpa's ranch." He stumbled along through the grass and finally stood clutching one of the posts supporting the canopy.

Van Dyke and I took our places and Reverend Hamilton continued the service. While he read Dad's life accomplishments, my mind wandered. I thought about how hard it is to think of your parents as regular people, like anyone else. Maybe I'd reached an age old enough to recognize it. Most people are flawed in some way. If that weren't true, Dad and I wouldn't have had a business.

Later, I couldn't recall a word the minister had said beyond the twenty-third Psalm, but when it was over, I noticed Jonesy wiping his nose on the long, black sleeve of his coat.

Dad's four friends shook hands with everyone except Jonesy, and headed for their cars. As Madge and I started to leave, Jonesy took hold of my arm. Madge's eyebrows nearly disappeared under her hat.

"I wanna tell ya something," he said.

I paused, gazed at his matted hair and caught his sour aroma.

"Your daddy was the best friend a boy could ever have. When my pa went on a drunk, he was mean. He'd whip me, sometimes real bad and fer no reason I could figure out. This one time I was all bloodied, and when he passed out, I run to your grandpa's hay barn. I hid there, waiting for Pa to sober up. Your daddy found me, patched up my bloody ear and even brought me some food. That's how I met 'im. I was just a little feller, six or so. I'll never forget." He shook his head the way old men do when they don't know what else to say. Tears cut paths through the dirt on his face, the pain of that long-ago time in his eyes.

I swallowed hard.

"I'd be proud to help ya, Miss Deena, if I ever can," he said with a nod, turned and stumbled toward the gate.

Madge hadn't waited to hear what Jonesy had to say. She was still pinch-faced when I climbed into the car.

"That crazy old coot," Madge said as she started her car. "I know you're going to ask. His name is Harlan Jones. He's homeless and wanders the countryside like a stray cat. No one knows where he goes at night. I see him now and then digging in a trash bin. That's probably where he found the coat."

"He said he was a friend of Dad's."

Madge snorted. "If he was, I never knew about it."

"He seems harmless."

"That's about the only good thing you can say about him. He's too old to do anybody harm." She paused. "I hope."

I was grateful to Harlan Jones for surprising us and distracting me from thinking about death: Dad's, Aunt Madge's and my own. That's what people are supposed to think about at funerals, mortality—mostly their own.

As Madge pulled away from the curb, I glanced back at where my father's little brown box sat on a mound of earth, and the finality of his death hit me. It was like a door had slammed on my past life. I felt tears form, and my breath caught in my chest. I turned my face away, knowing I'd have to chart my own course from that day on.

Chapter 17

Later, after refreshments at the home of one of Madge's friends, I spent an hour walking my dogs and reflecting on my current situation. In the end, I decided taking one day at a time was the best option. I couldn't change the past. I put the dogs in their pen and drove to Treadwell's office to obtain the copies of the letter of introduction and associated documents.

My next stop was the Four Creeks branch of Bank of America. By city standards it was a small bank, but when I entered I could see that everything about the interior was up to date. I was soon seated across the desk from Melody Mitchell, Customer Service Associate, a serious looking woman, probably ten years my junior.

I pointed to her nameplate on the desk. "Melody. What a pretty name."

She smiled and straightened in her chair. I guess she needed a compliment. I handed her the letter and my card as I introduced myself and explained my situation. She read the letter slowly and glanced over the remaining documents. When she finished, I showed her Lottie's key.

"It shouldn't take more than a few minutes to answer your question," she said. Her fingers clicked around the computer keyboard, changing screens at a mind-numbing pace. She was right. In less than two minutes, she shook her head.

"Carlotta Weston is not in any of our data bases. I'm sorry." She handed the papers back to me. "Good hunting."

I thanked her, returned to the car and crossed that bank off my list.

On my way to find the next bank, I passed by the alley behind Elm Street and caught sight of a familiar blue Civic. I still wanted to talk to Eddie, but obviously I couldn't go banging on the door. I don't know why I cared about his philandering tendencies. Maybe it was my innate curiosity. I pulled to the curb and dug for my binoculars in the bag where I carry the tools of my trade. With them, I had no trouble reading the license plate on the car.

As I jotted down the number, out of the corner of my eye, I saw a black and white car pull to the curb in front of me, blocking my departure. I swiveled to see Buzz Walker emerge. He was wearing a dark blue suit, white shirt, and a gray-and-blue striped tie. His pants were sharply creased.

I rolled down the driver's side window as he approached.

"What are you doing skulking around?" he asked with a smile.

"Actually, you're exactly right." I handed him the binoculars. "Look at the blue car in the alley."

He focused. "Yeah, it's a Civic. 7BDA867. So what?"

"It belongs to Eddie Lee, Max Avila's nephew. It's parked behind Hester McKay's house. She's the clerk at Fair Buy."

"I see." He sighed. "Adultery may be shameful, but it's not a crime. Eddie's a wild kid. Doesn't surprise me." He handed the binoculars back to me. "I've been in court all day, and I'd like a good meal and better company. How about we go out to dinner? Do you like Mexican cuisine? There's a new place, just opened. I've heard the food's terrific."

It was past three o'clock. It would give me a chance to ask about progress with the investigation, and also help me break out of the gloom I felt after Dad's funeral. "Suits me."

"Great. I'll pick you up at five."

"Better make it six o'clock. I want to check out the other bank in town, and I'll have to feed the boys too."

His smile disappeared. "Boys?"

"My dogs, Mutt and Jeff."

"Oh." He nodded and grinned, obviously relieved. "Six o'clock it is." He moved toward his cruiser. When he was out of sight, his comment about "better company" brought a question to mind. What about a wife? He gave no indication he was married. It didn't matter. It was information I was after.

My visit to Grower's Bank and Trust was similar to the first. The woman at the desk was pleasant though she was unable to find any record of Lottie in her files. Everything about Lottie was elusive and frustrating, and I caught myself grumbling out loud on the way to Madge's.

As soon as I climbed out of the car, I hurried to release Mutt and Jeff from the pen. They followed me inside. Madge was in the kitchen with a package of chicken in her hand. She looked tired. Even though the service for Dad was her idea, it must have been just as emotionally draining as it was for me.

When I told her about my dinner invitation from Buzz, she said, "Good. I'll warm up the casserole from last night." Her comment was the first hint that I was making more work for her.

After taking the dogs out for a run and feeding them, I stepped into a hot shower. The daytime temperature hadn't reached sixty degrees and I felt chilled. The hot water was luxuriant and restored my spirits after the stressful day. After I dried myself off, I turned to the mirror, glad my hair was only shoulder length instead of the long mane I'd worn for many years. It made getting ready to go out much easier. A quick blow-dry, a flip at the ends with a curling iron, and I was done. Makeup took longer.

The evening would be chilly. I slipped a smoke-blue sweater over my head and slid into a pair of matching slacks. I tied a red-and-gray scarf loosely around my neck, then checked my reflection in the mirror. Was that a gray hair? I leaned closer. The sight of an invader made me shudder. I plucked it out. Vanity, vanity.

The castle guards set to barking, announcing Buzz's arrival. I slipped on my dress shoes, grabbed my coat and went to meet him. Much to my surprise, he was driving a silver Porsche, an older '86 model. How did he manage that on a policeman's salary?

When I opened the door, Jeff pushed between me and the door frame, shot out and circled the car a couple of times before he stood facing the driver's side. He was trying his best to scare off the intruder and doing a good job. I spent several minutes reassuring him and Buzz. Finally, after much sniffing and friendly talk from Buzz, Jeff decided the stranger might pass muster, though he was still suspicious. I coaxed the dogs into the kennel with pieces of chewy rawhide while Buzz paid his respects to Madge. Then we climbed into the Porsche and wound our way down the hill toward town.

We entered Hugo's through brightly painted arches. The aroma of tortillas and refried beans stirred hunger pangs. A waitress seated us in a booth. A string of decals, red and green chilies, encircled the room at eye level, and a Mexican-style lantern hung over each table. Music, with a sultry voice I couldn't understand, played in the background.

Buzz ordered a beer, and I asked for a Margarita. We munched on tortilla chips while waiting for our orders. When the waitress brought our drinks, Buzz took a swallow of his beer and asked, "Have you had any luck finding the deposit box?"

"Not yet." I described my visits to the two banks in town. "I made a list of every bank in the county. The one in Creekside is next."

Our dinners arrived. My burrito was enormous. He'd ordered an enchilada combo and for a several minutes we ate with enthusiasm.

After another swallow of his beer, Buzz leaned forward on his elbows. "We faxed a list of the numbers from those bills to the feds. An answer may take some time. Couldn't lift any fingerprints, but that was to be expected. I've been considering the possibility of a connection between the money and the pictures you found."

My attention sharpened. Guess my idea wasn't so crazy after all. My tendency to say something sarcastic was squelched by the eagerness on his face.

"I have a friend in Merced," he continued, "a guy who was in the academy with me. His dad worked for the Las Vegas PD back in the late '50s. He might remember Mrs. Weston's friends. I don't have time to go to Merced, and the chief wouldn't let me anyway. Officially, I can't encourage you to go talk to him, but since I'm not wearing my badge tonight..." He leaned back. "It might be a waste of your time."

"No, no. I like the idea. I could ask him if there was a big robbery around that time. What's your friend's name?"

"Bernard Bertram. We called him Bert because he didn't like Bernard. I met his dad at graduation, but didn't catch his first name. I'll call Bert tonight. He's a great guy, started with the Oakland PD when I did. We both bailed out about the same time. He went into business, and I came back to Four Creeks."

"Bailed?" I worked on my burrito as I listened.

"In a manner of speaking. It's a long story. After about seven years there, I was fed up with department politics and big city crime. I took a look at the schools and drugs and decided I didn't want to raise my daughter in that situation."

"You have a daughter? I didn't know you were even married." Of course he'd have married. What did I expect, he'd be sitting around pining for me?

"That's history," he said with a dismissive gesture. "My folks died within a year of each other. I inherited the ranch, so I moved my family back home. Becky, my daughter, loved it. Irene soon hated it. She had a good career getting off the ground in the Bay Area as a fashion designer. At first we thought she could work here and travel back and forth to promote her designs."

He swallowed a forkful of beans and continued. "It didn't work out. She said the design business was as much who you knew as it was talent. She needed to be there to take advantage of the three-cocktail lunches and make the right contacts. I didn't want to leave Four Creeks. She found an apartment and came home on the weekends. That lasted about six months. We'd drifted apart." He sighed, stared at his plate a few seconds, and then scooped the last bite of enchilada into his mouth.

"What about your daughter?"

"I convinced Irene that Becky would be better off in a country school. She stayed with me until junior high, but she spent school vacations and summers with her mother. It was hard on her. She missed her mother. The summer she turned thirteen, she decided country life was too tame. She'd made some new friends, daughters of a colleague of Irene's. I didn't want her in Oakland public schools, so we put her in the same private school where her friends attended."

"You must have felt lost without her."

"Sure did. That's when I started giving riding lessons to kids. Becky came home during school holidays and summers for the first two years, but when she entered high school the summer visits grew shorter and shorter. Last year she stayed a week. She has a boyfriend." He forced a smile. "She graduates in June. Honor student. Wants to be a plant geneticist."

"You must be proud."

"Yeah, but I feel like Tevye, singing *Sunrise, Sunset*. Where have the years gone?" He finished his beer and said, "Enough of my life, tell me about you."

"I suppose you heard I married right out of college."

He nodded, signaled the waitress and ordered coffee for us.

"I thought I wanted to teach like Aunt Madge, but then changed my mind and turned to law. That's how I met Rick." I gave him a thumbnail sketch of my failed marriage to Rick Hansen. I left out my more recent encounters with men. He didn't ask. I was grateful. I told him about my various jobs: proof reading law books for a publisher, working for a legal aid society and finally as a clerk in Dell Fisk's office.

Buzz was a good listener. I paused as the waitress delivered the coffee and cleared away our empty plates.

"I more or less stumbled into my current career. Dad had coronary bypass surgery in '93, and I took a leave of absence to look after him. When his doctor cleared him to go back to work, Dad suggested I help him at the office. He didn't say it, but I think he still didn't feel well. It worked out because Dell had hired someone else to fill my position by then.

"Dad put me on the payroll, and at first I did mostly research, land records and such. It was the part he disliked. I didn't mind it. In fact, I like reading musty old records. But after a few months, I wanted to branch out and decided I should be licensed. Dad said I didn't have enough experience since I'd never done police work. I hit the books. Gradually, he had me doing interviews and much later, surveillance. He was a tough coach. After I put in the required hours to qualify for a California license, he gave the nod, and I took the test. Finally, I had my own cases."

"And now you're on your own," Buzz commented.

"Yeah." The prospect gave me a shiver. I was relieved when the waitress interrupted with the check. My pride wouldn't let me admit how uncertain I felt about being *on my own*.

We rose to leave. "This is a nice place," I said as he helped me into my coat. "And the food is perfectly spiced."

Buzz smiled down at me, put his arm around my shoulder and gave me a brief squeeze. "We'll have to do it again before you leave."

Chapter 18

We were silent during the drive to Madge's house, but it didn't matter. It was a comfortable silence between old friends who didn't need to speak.

After we parked in Madge's driveway, he opened the door on my side and extended his hand to help me out. "I'd like to show you the ranch."

"I'd like to see it, but there's a little matter of an elusive deposit box that's getting priority attention."

We ambled toward the front door. "The dinner was delicious. Thank you. Want to come in?"

He glanced at his watch. "No. My mother always said I should leave a party while I was still having a good time." He leaned over and his lips brushed my cheek. "And I've certainly had a good time."

His closeness and the scent of his aftershave sent my pulse into a gallop. It's a good thing the porch light was dim, because I felt my face flush. I had a sudden urge to throw my arms around his neck, but suppressed it.

He returned to the car and paused as he opened the door. "I'll call Bert tonight and get the address for you."

"Call me and I'll drive up there tomorrow."

He climbed in and closed the door. When he backed around, the tail lights cast a rosy glow over me. He paused at the outlet of the driveway, stuck his head out the window and looked back. "By the way, the Porsche isn't mine." I heard him chuckle. It figured. He wasn't the Porsche type. He was more the pickup-and-horse-trailer type.

I watched until the car reached the stop sign under the street light at the bottom of the hill. His hand appeared above the top of the car. He waved.

Maybe I'd been a damn fool to hold back. Maybe I should've grabbed him and kissed him. Shyness was not my style. On the other hand, though Buzz and I had a history, we were collaborating and that's all. I had to keep focused. I couldn't afford an involvement.

I released the dogs from the kennel and headed for the bathroom. Afterward, I sat on the edge of the bed and kicked off my shoes. Mutt looked at me with his beady brown eyes, begging to be picked up. I took him on my lap and stroked his velvety ears.

It had been over ten years since the end of my marriage to Rick Hansen. In reality, I hadn't dated much since the divorce. There'd been a brief encounter with an airline pilot, but between his work and mine at the publishing firm, we couldn't maintain connections. Next was Brad, who was charming, but a jerk. I'd hardly finished my salad on our first date when I figured out his agenda. He was a party guy looking for a party girl.

Dell introduced me to a lawyer at the *Black and Blue Ball* in Santa Barbara. The relationship didn't last long. He was looking for a trophy wife. I didn't fit the bill, nor did I care to.

I met a building contractor when we had some remodeling done at the office. He was too busy creating an empire to have any permanent tendencies. Mark McCarthy was handsome and had a great sense of humor. I was counting my lucky stars until Dad found out he was married.

I'll probably always miss Rick. I met Rick Hansen in my senior year at UCSF. We clicked right away, married too soon and moved to Minneapolis where his family lived. He went into law practice with his dad. I hated the winters and couldn't stand his sisters. Plus, I didn't fit the corporate wife picture. I stuck it out for a year and a half before I begged him to try California. He gave in and we moved to Thousand Oaks. He found a position as a junior partner in a local firm. He was relegated to all the low profile cases. He detested it and figured he'd never get to practice the type of law he really wanted—criminal law.

Love doesn't conquer all. It was painful, but we agreed it wasn't going to work. He went back to his father and I went to mine, licking my wounds all the way. Since there were no children, Dad suggested I reclaim the Powers name.

Enough ruminating old history, I told myself. I shifted my thoughts to Madge. It was time to ask her some questions. I put Mutt in his bed and pulled the envelopes from my purse. It contained the pictures I'd shown Irma. Jeff, who'd settled himself on his blanket in the corner, raised his head when I left the room, but didn't follow.

I found Madge sitting in her favorite chair in front of the television. She was wearing blue pajamas and matching lounging robe. An old movie with a young Jimmy Stewart on horseback played on the screen. A gentle gurgling sound came from a small shallow fountain on the coffee table.

She glanced up and lowered the sound of the TV. "How was your dinner?" By her tone, it was only a polite inquiry.

"It was good." I slid into a cushioned chair. "I need to talk to you. I found a copy of Lottie's old will in a desk at her house. It's dated right after her husband died. I was surprised to see you were the witness on the document. Want to tell me how that happened?"

"Oh, it's not as mysterious as you might think. Lottie caught me coming out of church one Sunday. The homily that day was on the virtue of charity. She met me on the sidewalk and asked if I'd witness her signature. I felt sorry for her—losing both Freddie and Mel in such a short space of time. She had the will with her, so we went to the parking lot, and I signed it there on the hood of my car. I didn't think much about it. It was some hand-written thing she'd made up. She didn't even unfold it."

Her explanation seemed reasonable. "I also found some snapshots. Looks like they date back to the '50s. I showed them to Irma and asked her if she knew any of the people. She said I should show them to you, that you'd be interested in them."

I pulled the photos out of the envelope and held them out to her. She straightened in her chair and took them from my hand, then leaned to catch the light from the table lamp.

"That must be Lottie," she said about the top one and laid it aside. She glanced through the rest, and laid each one on top of the first. "Huh. Irma probably wanted to rub it in," she said with disdain.

"What do you mean?"

"Lottie was a real beauty at that age. The people in those pictures were all young and good looking. I used to look like that too—when I was young. She wants to remind me I'm not young and appealing any longer. But then, neither is she, so the joke's on her."

"You don't recognize any of these people?"

Madge picked up the pictures again and shuffled through them. "My memory's on the skids. Sometimes when I look at old pictures I took myself, the faces look familiar, but I can't remember the names. I guess it's part of getting old." She passed them back to me with a sigh.

Madge's explanation was plausible. If she was withholding what she knew, she deserved an Academy Award. I believed her. I started to rise.

"Why don't you sit back and watch TV with me? Seems like you're not here much. I was hoping we could spend some time together."

"I'm sorry." I settled against the soft back of the chair. "The mystery of the key has complicated things. That, and the records for Dad's last investigation. I need to locate them if I ever hope to get the people at the insurance company to pay for his work."

Madge reached over and patted my arm. "I know. I don't blame you."

After forty-five minutes of watching Jimmy Stewart chase the bad guy, I couldn't concentrate any longer. I rose, excused myself and returned to the bedroom. I put on my sneakers and took the dogs out for their last run of the day.

I leaned against one of the posts supporting the patio. It wasn't late, but I was tired, confused and uneasy about several things. Buzz's sudden about-face in his dealings with me was unsettling. And my reaction was *not* what I expected. On top of that, every conversation I'd had in the last week left me with the sense that something was missing. But maybe it didn't matter. Everyone is entitled to a few secrets. I'd find the deposit box, collect Dad's money from Tri-Counties and see what the future brought my way. I yawned. "Come on fellas. The varmints will still be around tomorrow. And I don't mean only the four legged kind."

Chapter 19

I sped along a two lane road, maneuvering the curves and concentrating on the pavement ahead. A sharp left curve appeared. In the rear-view mirror I saw a pickup truck following close behind. It started to pass. The crazy fool! My heart raced as I edged over to make room. Anger and fear flooded me when I heard our fenders touch and my passenger side tires on the soft shoulder of the road. Who was this madman? I looked his direction and saw him grin. I heard someone shout, "Watch out!" I slammed on the brakes, but it was too late, the car was skidding and . . .

The phone rang. I woke, briefly disoriented, with my insides quivering. I jerked back the covers and lurched to the desk where the telephone continued to jangle. The illuminated numbers on the clock read 7:30. Daylight filtered through the bedroom curtain. I'd slept longer than I'd planned, and a dull ache gripped my head.

"Hello," I croaked into the receiver, still trying to quiet my frazzled nerves.

"You sound awful. Have you caught cold?" It was Buzz.

"No. The phone woke me."

"Oh." He paused. "I have the address in Merced for you."

As he dictated, I scribbled directions on a notepad.

"Bert's dad's name is Lawrence, but everyone calls him Larry. He said his dad loves visitors and he'll be expecting you."

"Good. I'll get going as soon as I can. I appreciate the arrangements. Right now, I need a cup of coffee."

"Wait. My mare is due to foal soon, probably this weekend.

Would you like me to call you when she does?"

"You mean to watch?"

"Yeah, it's quite a show."

"I'll bet you've been up since five."

"Sure. Are you always so grouchy in the morning?"

"Let's just say the dogs are hiding under the bed. I'll talk to you later." I replaced the receiver, slid my feet into slippers and fumbled for a robe. My head throbbed and coffee was my goal of the moment. The dogs, sensing my state of mind, followed me to the kitchen at a respectful distance.

Madge was seated at the dining room table with the newspaper. She laid it aside when I entered. "Good morning."

Unlike me, she was bright-eyed and cheerful sounding. I took the coffee mug she'd left on the counter for me and poured a cup of salvation.

She voiced her quick assessment. "Another headache?"

I nodded as I took the first sip.

"You ought to see your doctor again."

"He can't do anything for them. Only tell me the same thing, that they'll go away eventually."

"Then take the medicine he gave you."

"I can't do that and drive, and I have to go to Merced this morning. There's a man Buzz Walker located who worked for the Las Vegas police during the '50s. I'll show him those pictures and see if he knows any reason Lottie's murder could be connected to those people."

Madge didn't comment.

I topped off my cup and started for the patio door. "But first, the boys need to go out."

The crisp morning air was like an elixir. I breathed deep and shuffled toward the back of Madge's property. "Don't go far, guys.

148

I'm not dressed for it." I leaned against the back of the dog pen while they sniffed out their territorial marks.

I reconsidered the nightmare. It was the first time the driver's face had appeared in the dream. I wanted to hang onto the picture, but it had faded too fast. I sensed I'd seen that face somewhere before. And who was shouting? Was it Dad? Was my memory returning? If it was, and my dream was reliable, there was a good reason I didn't make the curve. The second set of tire tracks at the scene bothered me. Maybe I should call Ben Fraser, but then I had no proof. It was only a bad dream.

By nine o'clock I was showered, dressed and heading north on Highway 99. My headache had subsided, and I was feeling hopeful about the trip. Road construction and a concrete divider installation slowed traffic to a crawl for nearly a mile near Ceres. I took the Tuolumne off-ramp in Merced and drove west to a collection of housing tracts.

Buzz's directions were perfect. Lawrence Bertram lived in a gray stucco house with a red brick facade. A large walnut tree was strategically positioned in back to provide shade from the hot summer sun.

The door was open a crack. I pressed the doorbell and heard a deep gravelly voice say, "Come in."

I stepped inside and saw an elderly man sitting in an overstuffed chair with a portable wheelchair waiting nearby. Buzz had neglected to tell me one important detail about Mr. Bertram.

I covered my surprise, stepped forward and extended my hand as I introduced myself. He offered a big smile, his hand engulfing mine. A dark blue tee-shirt stretched over muscular shoulders and gray slacks covered his spindly legs.

"My mother taught me to rise when a lady entered, but unfortunately, I'm unable," he said as he motioned me to a nearby flowered loveseat.

I sat and admired the silk flowers and framed photos in the cheerfully decorated room. Other than a big-screen television, sparse furnishings rested on the bare hardwood flooring.

"My, you're a pretty woman. I've always liked chestnut-brown hair." His steely blue eyes sparkled.

I felt flattered and embarrassed and concluded he didn't have much company outside of his family. He inquired about Buzz, his family and the ranch. I tried to answer his questions.

"I dug out a picture of Bert and Buzz to show you." He handed me a snapshot. "It was taken at their graduation from the academy."

Buzz didn't look much different back then, maybe a little thinner.

"He was a good cop," Mr. Bertram said. "Bet he still is." Finally, he said the magic words. "How can I help you?"

I explained Lottie's sad demise and my theory that the money under the bed might have come from Las Vegas at an earlier time. "The big question in all this is whether or not the cash has anything to do with her death." I pulled the old photos from my bag and handed them to him. "We found these with her belongings. I'm hoping you can identify the people."

He shuffled through them, squinting at each picture. A pair of glasses lay on the table. I handed them to him, and he flashed me a sheepish grin.

With his glasses on, he studied each photo again and shook his head. "I was there from January of 1955 to November of 1957 when I was shot. I've been like this ever since." He motioned to his legs. "Las Vegas was a small place then. The casino owner's kept their friends in line most of the time, but late one night Saar Motella decided to settle an old score with a guy from Chicago who'd shown up in town. It was a coincidence that I was in the way when the bullets started to fly. I caught a slug in my back and ended up in the hospital for six months. Heck of a thing to happen to a guy with a wife and a baby on the way. When Bert decided to go to the police academy, I tried to talk him out of it. It didn't work, but after some experience, he decided I was right."

He sorted through the pictures again, stopping at the photo of the two couples at a table. "I don't remember her, but him..." He pointed to the man sitting next to Lottie.

"We've identified her as Lottie Woods. His initials were B.B." I showed him the photo with the initials on the back.

"Baker," he announced. "Bingo Baker. Yeah, I remember now. He worked at Durango's. Dan Durango was a small time operator out on the edge of town with gambling, plus some other unsavory ventures. I always wondered if that was his real name."

While he talked, I pulled a notepad from my bag and scribbled notes. "How did you know Baker?"

"I didn't exactly know him. I only knew his reputation. Our job was to make the customers feel safe. We were mostly show. Like I said, the casino owner's had the control. I didn't like the job, and Betty and I were planning to leave when I got hurt. I received a small pension, hardly enough to raise a family. Betty's folks loaned us money to move back to California. She found a job teaching here in Merced." He removed his glasses and rubbed his eyes with a thumb and finger. "But you're not here to listen to my sad tale.

"Baker was an odd guy. Too quiet. Crafty." He paused. "This other gal, I think her name was Cutesy or Cuddles or something like that." He pointed to the second woman in the foursome."

"Cuddles McGee?"

"Yeah, that's it. She was quite a rounder. A night or two before I got shot, she was out walking along the strip, somewhat tipsy. I saw her sway and offered to drive her home. She was a talker, tried to tell me about some big score about to be pulled off. Considering her condition, I didn't pay much attention to it. When I dropped her off, she tried to give me a twenty dollar bill. Of course, I refused and told her to keep me informed. She laughed and said if everything went as planned, I'd never hear about it."

"Did you hear anything?"

"Only rumors from the guys who came to see me in the hospital. They'd heard some counts were short at Durango's place. It was never reported officially. Some figured Baker took it and went to Mexico because he vanished about that time. They never saw him again. There were others who thought he'd been given cement shoes." He shook his head. "Dirty business, corruption and all. I'm probably lucky I got shot and got out of there."

Mr. Bertram pushed himself up straight. "I'm sorry. I have so few visitors, I forget my manners. There's a pot of coffee in the kitchen. Help yourself."

I declined. "What about Cuddles? Did you hear anything more about her?"

"Naw. I was out of touch after I got out of the hospital. All I could think of was how I was going to make a living for my family. I went back to school in '59 and became a C.P.A. You can do that from a wheelchair. Did okay. Had my own business for many years. I still have a few clients. Sorry I couldn't be more help."

"You *have* helped, and I appreciate your time and your memory. Perhaps the money under Lottie's rug came from Baker. I wonder where he is now."

"Seems like an awful long time has passed for someone to start looking for the money now. Baker, if he's still alive, would be older than me. But if you could find out what happened to Durango, he might know something, if he's not dead. He was a bad dude." He shuffled through the photos again. "You know, this woman you call Lottie? I think they called her Rita something."

"Rita Diamond?"

"That's right. She was a dancer." He paused and pressed his lips together for a second. "You know, I think Baker's first name was Ted or Fred. But he was known as Bingo. I can't put a name on the other guy in the picture at all, but the fuzzy man standing in back might be Durango." He apologized again as he handed the pictures back to me.

I thanked him and rose to leave.

"You tell ole Buzz to come see us. I'll bet he's bald by now." He chuckled.

"I'll tell him you said that. He'll want to show you it's not true." I shook his hand and let myself out.

Chapter 20

It was after two o'clock when I reached the Four Creeks police station. Buzz wasn't there. I left him a note with Elena asking him to call as soon as he returned, and then drove to Avila's Quick Mart to refill my gas tank. As I approached the door, I saw Max Avila through the glass, his face florid and twisted in anger. The rumble of his shouting was like distant thunder. There was little doubt that the target was the person with his back to me—Eddie Lee. As soon as Avila saw me, he turned and disappeared from view. Eddie too.

Walking in, I saw Eddie behind the counter. I flashed him a congenial grin as if I hadn't heard a thing. "Hi, Eddie. I'll take twenty dollars worth of gas from number two pump."

He nodded without looking at me and took the money I laid on the counter.

"How's the baby?" I asked.

"Teething," he growled. "Dang kid cries all the time. Kept me awake most of the night." He jabbed the cash register buttons for emphasis.

"Gee, that's too bad." You didn't need to be psychic to figure out what Avila was shouting about. Eddie had been late for work. And it probably wasn't the first time.

"Say, I never did get a chance to ask you about Mrs. Weston. Do you remember the last day she came in here?"

"I don't remember nothing," he said in a sullen tone.

"It wasn't so long ago. Surely you remember Mrs. Weston."

He still didn't look at me, but pulled a dust cloth from under the counter. "Yeah, she was that weird old lady who came in and talked to my uncle about cats. What about it?" He turned his back and started moving small boxed items around on a shelf behind the counter, giving each one a swipe.

"Do you remember anything unusual about that day? Did she act anxious or worried? Anything like that?"

He didn't turn around. "My uncle always waited on her."

"He said he wasn't here, said you were on duty."

"Maybe I was, but I don't remember nothing unusual."

It was obvious Eddie had no interest in his uncle's customers. To him, it was just a job until he had the money to leave Four Creeks. I wasn't getting anywhere.

"I think I'd like a candy bar. Which one was Mrs. Weston's favorite?"

Eddie dropped the dust cloth.

"I guess I'll take the chocolate in the brown wrapper." I dug some change out of my purse to pay as Eddie turned to hand it to me.

"When I saw you last, you said you were going to move to someplace sunny. How are your plans coming along?"

"The lottery people are taking their own sweet time." He looked me in the eye for the first time. "There's lots of regulations, information I have to provide the bank for the *Infernal* Revenue. They gotta get their cut. Soon as I get the money, I'm gone."

"You have a destination in mind?"

"Not yet."

I pulled one of my business cards from my purse and handed it to him. "In the meantime, if you think of anything important about Mrs. Weston, give me a call."

He took the card and nodded, but I expected he'd file it in the trash basket.

I started for the door, paused and turned back. "By the way, did Mrs. Weston buy a lottery ticket that day?"

He flinched, ever so slightly. "I don't remember."

"Mmm, okay. See you later." I left and pumped my gas. Maybe Eddie really didn't remember anything about Lottie, or more likely, didn't care. But he was shifty, always evasive and it bothered me. From his exchange with Hester in the market the previous week, I'd reasoned he planned to leave town with her and abandon his wife and baby. A louse of the first order.

I twisted the gas cap tight after filling the tank and climbed into the Explorer. Anyway, Eddie wasn't my problem. I had more urgent considerations at the moment, like letting Buzz know what I'd learned from Larry Bertram.

Madge must have been watching for me, because when I pulled into the driveway, she was standing in the doorway. "Avis Walker's on the line."

As I dashed to the phone in the kitchen, I noticed the aroma of fresh baked bread. "I guess I just missed you," I said into the receiver.

"By five minutes. What'd you find out?"

I filled him in on the new information. "Can you trace Dan Durango and Fred or Ted Baker through your computer system? Maybe one of them crossed with the law."

"The state keeps archives. If I can't, I'll call to Sacramento. Nevada will take longer."

"Try Cuddles McGee too. If she was mixed up in the theft, she might have a record too."

"Slim chance without an authentic first name, but I'll see. Talk to you later."

I turned to see Madge with a dish cloth in her hand. She'd heard everything I'd said to Buzz. The look in her eyes was something new—almost wary.

"Did you have lunch?" she asked.

I glanced at the kitchen clock. "I'll have a piece of that bread that smells so good, along with some of your homemade strawberry jam."

She sliced off the heel of a loaf, laid it on a plate and handed it to me. It was still warm. I covered it with jam and sunk in my teeth. Between bites, I filled her in on how Mr. Bertram had been shot and what he remembered about his last month in Vegas.

While I spoke Madge bent forward and scrubbed an invisible spot on the counter. She didn't look up until I mentioned Cuddles McGee. "All that was forty years ago. I doubt he'll find records that old."

"I sure hope so because I'm counting on it. Now I have to wait and see what Buzz turns up. I'm not good at waiting. But it'll give me time to tackle the stack of office files in your garage." I popped the last bite of bread into my mouth. "That really hit the spot." I headed for the bedroom where I changed into jeans and sweat shirt before going outside.

I let Mutt and Jeff out of the kennel with a warning. "You guys behave and don't wander off. I have work to do." They circled the yard, and after marking their usual spots, followed me to the garage. I raised the door and took a deep breath.

Madge had a stepstool she used to reach the high shelves. I pulled it over to the stack of file boxes to use as a seat. The dogs sniffed around and then flopped on the cold concrete nearby. With a box of loose papers and folders at my feet, I sorted. Many of the names reminded me of recent investigations Dad and I had worked on together. I felt a pang of nostalgia.

An hour later, I had them in order and arranged in the boxes. But like the files I'd left in Judy's bedroom, I hadn't found anything related to the Tri-Counties case. I leaned my elbows on my knees and speculated about what would be in the folder I sought. Besides the initial contract, there'd be the fire investigator's report and any notes Dad had made, plus transcribed interviews. I'd be hard put to prove my claim without them. The only other help I'd get would be from a taped interview. I knew my father's habits. He always had Judy transcribe them for a permanent record. That way he could reuse the tape. But she said she hadn't transcribed anything related to the case.

Mentally, I revisited the break-in at the office. The thief took the camera. That made sense if he figured it contained photos of evidence. An audiotape might have had an incriminating interview on it. I turned my attention to Dad's cassette tapes piled in a cardboard carton. I pulled the box next to the stool, plucked out each one, studied the dates and matched it to a corresponding client folder. In the end, I came up empty handed. None of them had a recent date. I'd spent all that time without finding what I needed. I decided it wasn't a total loss. The absence of anything related to the possible arson case was telling.

A picture of the real reason for the break-in formed. The scoundrel was probably looking for anything that had to do with the fire investigation. And judging from the fact he crushed Dad's tape recorder, I figured he didn't find the related recording either. I'd have to get another copy of the fire investigator's report and figure out who had a stake in the investigation.

Again, Dennis Colton's lie came to mind. If my conclusion were correct, my issue was more than his trying to refuse payment for Dad's expenses, it was fraud. But how was he involved?

If the burglar didn't find the audiotape, where was it? Where would my father put something like that? An idea flashed, and I rushed to the Explorer. I pushed the eject button on the tape deck. No reaction. To be sure, I pushed open the little door and peeked inside. Empty. Rats! The glove box was next. I shuffled through a collection of Dad's favorite music. Zilch.

I went back to the garage and stood thinking. Where else? In his coat pocket? Or could it have been in the tape deck in my car? My *wrecked* car. Dad had taken it for servicing before the trip to the mountains. He might have played it back to himself and forgot it there. No, he wouldn't have forgotten it. Not something important and confidential. If he played the tape for me, I'd lost the memory. But why would he do that? Enough time had passed that my car could have been smashed and melted down. I had to call the wrecking yard right away.

The dogs jumped to their feet. I'd been concentrating so hard I hadn't heard a car drive up. I whirled around. Buzz appeared in the doorway.

"Sorry to interrupt," he said. "But I thought you'd want to know. I received an answer to one of the inquiries." He held a sheet of paper in his hand. "It took a couple of calls and a computer search to make sure I'd found the right person. A man by the name of Frederick Baker was paroled a year ago." He pointed to the address on the page. "He's listed at an address in Ortega Bay."

"You're a miracle worker," I said. "But listen, I have to call the wrecking yard where my car was taken." I hurried back to the Explorer. Buzz followed, looking perplexed. I opened the door and pulled the Ortega County phone book from beneath the seat. Flipping through the Yellow Pages, I located the number, used my cell phone and soon heard a male voice say, "Marshall's Wrecking."

I identified myself and asked if my car was still in one piece. He put me on hold. I turned to Buzz. "I'm hoping Dad's audiotape is in the tape deck of my wrecked car."

He shook his head, not understanding what I was talking about.

The man returned to the line. "Most of the salvageable parts have been stripped off, but it hasn't gone to the crusher yet."

"Can you put it on hold until I get down there?"

"Hey, Lady, we own this wreck now, remember? You got the insurance money."

I *wish*, but that was not the issue. "Please. I need to find out if there's an audiotape in the tape deck. It would be a recording my father made before he was killed in the accident. It's really important."

"Well," he hesitated. "If that's all you want, tell you what I'll do. I'll send my kid out to check. If there's a tape there, I'll have him bring it to the office for you. Call me back in fifteen minutes." He hung up.

Time stretched like bubblegum. I turned my attention to Buzz. "This has nothing to do with Lottie." I reminded him about Tri-Counties Indemnity giving me the run-around. "If it's not in the car…" I shook my head. "It could have been in what he was wearing when they took him to the hospital. No telling what happen to those things."

I took the paper from Buzz and read the address. "How do we know this is the right guy?"

"It was the best match."

"When I go south to get the tape, assuming Mr. Marshall finds it, I can check out the address." I glanced at my watch. "If this is Bingo Baker, he's been in circulation long enough to figure out where Lottie's been living. He could have arrived here looking for his money and killed her."

Buzz shook his head with vigor. "You stay out of it. I'll call Ortega Bay PD and let them visit this Baker. If he's the person we think he is, and if he killed her, he wouldn't hesitate to kill you too."

Buzz's jaw was set. Even after all those years, his expression evoked a memory of the argument we once had about marriage. I'd become smarter since then. I didn't protest.

"You're probably right." I punched in the number for Marshall's

Wrecking. The same voice answered. "You were right," he said. "The kid found the tape. I'll have it in an envelope waiting for you."

"I'll be there first thing in the morning." I disconnected and turned to Buzz. "Maybe now I can get my problem with the insurance company settled."

He glanced at his watch. "It's almost four. I have some paper work to catch up on. Could I interest you in another round of Mexican food?"

"Sure. I'm finished with these records. I'll meet you there. Six o'clock?"

He nodded and strode to where his cruiser was parked.

I stacked the file boxes, called the dogs and closed the garage door before heading inside. I'd recognized the street name in Baker's address. It was in the same area as my old grammar school. I'd find Bingo Baker before the PD located him.

Chapter 21

A little over an hour later, I was standing in a local drug store searching the vitamin shelf for Madge's favorite brand. She'd asked me to pick up a bottle for her on my way to meet Buzz. I finally spotted the silver and white label, grabbed it and went to the checkout. As I pushed through the exit, the light was fading in the west and a chill breeze warned of an incoming storm front.

I had my mind on an enchilada combo when a couple of blocks from my destination, I spotted Harlan Jones struggling to climb out of a ditch alongside the road. His face was ashen.

I pulled over, jumped out and hurried over to him. "Here, let me give you a hand." I reached out.

He extended his right hand in response while holding his left arm close to his chest. "I think my arm's broken."

"Did you fall?" I asked as I hauled him out of the leaves and mud.

"No. He pushed me. Crazy kid. What's wrong with kids these days?"

Once he was on solid ground he straightened with effort. He was wearing an oil-blotched tee-shirt and tattered jeans with cuffs that were too short. I decided he must have dressed up for Dad's funeral.

"Who pushed you?"

"That one. The one from the mini-mart. Stole my shoes."

I stared at his bare feet. I figured he must be talking about Eddie Lee, but why would he take Jonesy's shoes?

"I think you're right about your arm," I said when I saw his misshapen wrist. "Come on, I'll take you to the hospital."

I gave him a boost into the Explorer. "Are you talking about Mr. Avila's nephew?"

"Yes, damn him. He was standing in the doorway when I came around the corner from the trash bin. Found a pair of real nice shoes there last week. They was muddy, and I had to stuff paper in the toes to make 'em fit, but I didn't care. Soon as he saw me, he hollered, and I run across the road. Next thing, he's chasing me. I went fer the culvert, figuring to hide there. I run hard as I could, but he caught up before I could get inside. He pushed me down and pulled off my shoes. I kep' askin' him why he done that, but he jus'called me a stupid old man and kicked me."

"That's awful! What he did is called assault and battery. We'll report him to the police."

"Oh no, Miss Deena. Please don't do that. If you do, he'll come after me fer sure."

"No he won't. He'd get in more trouble."

"He's mean, that one." His voice dropped to a whisper. "He'd kill me."

"But the hospital will report it, even if we don't. It's the law."

Jonesy was silent, holding his arm and grimacing with every bump in the road. I felt sorry for the old fellow in spite of the fact that his fragrance made my eyes water. I let a few miles pass under the wheels of the car before I spoke again.

"Jonesy? Can I ask you a question?"

He nodded, but didn't look in my direction.

"Where do you sleep?"

"Oh, here and there."

"No, really. You must have some place you call home."

"I go where I please. I find a spot where no one will bother me, and I don't bother nobody. Depends on the weather. Maybe an old barn, empty shed or dry culvert."

"You must have had a home sometime."

"After my pa died, I was on my own. He drank hisself to death, I guess. The most home I ever knew was in the Army."

"Why didn't you make a career of it?"

"Got wounded in Korea. Shell landed beside me. Messed up my leg. They didn't want me no more."

I took the off-ramp leading to the hospital in Delta and swung a right to pull in next to the emergency room door.

"Wait here." I went inside and asked for a wheelchair. A young woman in maroon scrubs followed me out with the chair, positioned it next to the car and opened the passenger side door. I saw her recoil when she caught a whiff of Jonesy. She shot me a scorching look.

I held open the door to the entrance and once inside she positioned the wheelchair next to the glassed-in reception desk. She set the brake and disappeared behind a door that closed with a thud.

We were second in line, so I used the opportunity to dig out my cell phone to call Buzz to let him know I wouldn't be able to meet him for dinner. I dialed Four Creeks P.D. When he came on the line, I told him where I was and about the attack on Jonesy.

"The hospital staff will notify Delta P.D. They'll send someone to get a statement from him."

"He may not tell them much. He's afraid of Eddie Lee and thinks there will be repercussions if the assault is reported."

"In that case, I'll talk to him myself. Let me know what happens, but call me at home. I have to feed the horses." He gave me his home number.

"Sorry about dinner."

"It's okay. Some other time." He ended the call.

When the clerk was free, I pushed Jonesy's wheelchair into

position. She asked a series of predictable questions and stiffened when I admitted Jonesy had no address, phone number or insurance.

She skewered me with a frosty look. "So you're telling me he's indigent."

Her perfume, though more pleasant than Jonesy's, was pungent. My stomach rebelled—maybe because of the combination of scents confusing my olfactory receptors—or maybe because I told her I'd be responsible for the bill and signed on the dotted line.

She leaned over the desk and gingerly snapped an ID bracelet on Jonesy's wrist. "Have a seat. Someone will come to get him soon."

I turned to survey the waiting room. On a string of chairs, welded together so no one could steal them, sat a line of tired looking people. A dark-skinned woman with gray hair leaned her elbows on her knees and held a handkerchief over her face. A younger woman had her hand in a wad of gauze. Her brow furrowed with worry as she leaned forward, whispering to the older woman.

A grandmotherly-looking woman held a squirming toddler and spoke firmly to two school-aged boys who crawled under the chairs. The TV that hung from the ceiling was alternating between extolling the wonders of the hospital's perinatal unit and showing the happy faces of men awaiting heart surgery. I maneuvered the wheelchair out of the way and leaned against the wall. Jonesy closed his eyes.

After what felt like an hour, the door to the inner sanctum opened, and a young man in green scrubs called out Jonesy's name. We responded.

"I'll let you know when you can come in," he said to me as he wheeled the old man through the door. Jonesy gave me the same look as my Dobe when I take him to the vet.

I settled back for what I expected to be a long wait. But fifteen minutes later, the door opened again. A young woman in a blue smock and white jeans propped the door with the toe of her shoe and motioned to me.

Once I was inside, she leaned against the wall. "We haven't gotten an x-ray as yet, but there's little doubt Mr. Jones' wrist is fractured. He'll need an orthopedist for follow-up. His blood pressure was dangerously high, so we had to treat it with some I.V. medication right away. We also gave him a little something for pain. The doctor is going to admit him overnight under Dr. Westerly's care to be sure his blood pressure is stable before discharge."

"That's good to hear," I told her, "because I don't know where he'd go with a fresh cast after release."

She led me to a brightly lit room where Jonesy lay on a gurney, eyes closed, his broken wrist propped on a pillow with an ice pack over the fracture. An I.V. bag hung on a pole, the tubing trailing down to his right arm. I paused at the sight. The stubborn, independent old fellow looked even smaller and more elf-like against the white sheets. I moved to his side. "Feeling better?" I asked.

He squinted at me with one eye. "Doc said my blood pressure was too high. They want to keep me here."

"I think it's a good idea."

"I don't like places like this. They hide your clothes so you can't get away."

"It's only one night. They'll take care of your arm and fix your blood pressure too." I perched on a stool to wait.

A tall man with a radiology badge on his shirt swept into the room waving a paper he compared with Jonesy's wristband, then flashed a smile in my direction. "Time to get a picture of that arm, Mr. Jones," he said with overly cheerful tone. He released a lever under the gurney. "He'll be back in a jiffy."

His cheeriness was something I suspected he'd learned in a customer relations class. But as he pushed the gurney into the hall, I saw his eyebrows raise and his eyes widen when he caught Jonesy's fragrance.

His wrist was officially declared fractured when he returned to the room. I took a deep breath, resigned to another wait until he'd be admitted.

Jonesy squirmed on the gurney trying to find a comfortable position. All at once his eyes opened wide and then instantly snapped shut.

I turned to see a dark-haired man in a police uniform in the doorway, report book and pen at the ready. He stepped over to where Jonesy lay. His badge and name tag were shiny, and I pegged him for a newly minted academy graduate. "Mr. Jones, I'm Officer Montoya." He extended his hand.

Jonesy didn't respond. He scrunched his eyes tight shut and jutted his jaw, his lips disappearing into a thin line.

"I understand you were a victim of an assault," Montoya continued. "Tell me about it."

No response.

I touched Jonesy's shoulder. "Tell him what happened."

The pinch-faced elf was silent.

"Mr. Jones. I want to help you. If you'll tell me what happened, we'll hold the perpetrator accountable."

His words had no effect.

I shrugged and gave Officer Montoya an *I don't know what to do* look. "He's afraid. That's why he won't talk to you."

"He's not afraid of me, is he?"

"No. He's afraid of the person who hurt him, afraid if it's reported, the guy will do worse."

The officer snapped his notebook closed and pocketed the pen. "In that case, there's not much I can do." He plucked a business card out of his shirt pocket and handed it to me with a shrug. "If he changes his mind, call me."

As he disappeared, I wondered if his lack of real concern was because the incident happened out of his jurisdiction or because Jonesy was a homeless old man.

The next person to enter the room introduced himself as Dr. Tillman. He gave Jonesy an artificial smile and announced he was going to fix his arm. As he donned an apron, I was invited to leave. I stood out in the corridor and watched a wall clock tick off the minutes.

After Jonesy's broken arm was encased in a plaster cast, another young fellow in blue scrubs arrived. He released the brake on the gurney and moved a groggy-looking Harlan Jones out and down the hall. I tagged along as he was transported to a hospital bed on the second floor. When he was settled in bed, I went in to say goodbye.

"I have to go to Ortega Bay in the morning, but I'll stop by to check on you before I leave."

"I'll probably be dead," Jonesy mumbled.

Chapter 22

It was dark when I reached Aunt Madge's and released Mutt and Jeff. They tore back and forth around my legs, nipping each other before taking off. As I stood waiting for them and soaking up the silence, Eddie Lee invaded my thoughts. What was it with him that he'd go around kicking old men? Was he really the menace Harlan Jones thought? And why take the old man's shoes? His behavior really angered me. I was certain he didn't *need* them. I'd have to buy Jonesy a new pair before he was released from the hospital.

I allowed the dogs a few more minutes, and then fed them before going inside the house. When I entered, the scent of enchiladas reminded me I'd missed dinner.

Madge was sitting in her easy chair watching TV.

"Were there any leftovers? I asked.

"Why yes, but I thought you were having dinner with Lieutenant Walker."

I handed her the sack from the drugstore. "That was the plan, but it got interrupted. I've been at Delta Hospital for the last four hours." I related Eddie's attack on Jonesy, his injury and admission to the hospital. When I saw Madge grimace, I knew she didn't approve of my getting involved with Jones' problems.

"Well, I couldn't just leave him sitting in the ditch with a broken arm."

"I guess not." She rose from her chair. "I'll warm a plate of food for you. It'll only take a few minutes." She went into the kitchen.

By the time I'd changed into my comfortable jeans and T-shirt, my stomach was growling like a hungry hound. When I appeared in the dining area, Madge added a scoop of green beans to a plate of enchiladas and slid it in my direction across the counter. I sat on one of the stools and ate in silence for a couple of minutes, then asked, "What do you know about Eddie Lee's background?"

She shrugged as she set two coffee mugs on the counter and filled them. "His mother is Vietnamese. His father was American, a veteran who couldn't keep a job after the Vietnam War, probably because of his drinking." She sipped her coffee and her brow tightened.

"And?"

"He was a troubled man. One day his wife found him in the garage. He'd put a bullet in his head."

I shuddered. "How old was Eddie?"

"About fourteen. He started acting out, setting fires in school trashcans—things like that. Eddie was a handful for his mother. Later he sneaked into a neighbor's house and helped himself to some valuables. And then one night, when he barely knew how to drive, he took his mother's car for a joy-ride. Came down Miller's grade too fast, ran the stop sign and broadsided an older couple by the name of Larsen. They died from the injuries."

"Was he charged?"

"He was still a juvenile. I think he spent some time with the California Youth Authority."

"His uncle described him as restless," I commented. "It wouldn't be the word I'd use. There's something I don't understand. Max Avila said Eddie was his brother's son, but Eddie's last name is Lee."

"That's because Max Avila and Eddie's father, Travis, had different fathers. Max's father died when he was little and his mother remarried. Travis was younger by six or seven years."

The family certainly had a lot of tragedy, but that was no excuse for Eddie's behavior. I finished the last bite of enchilada, rose from my chair and took my plate and silverware to the kitchen sink.

"That was so good. Your enchiladas are always terrific." I refilled our coffee cups and returned to my seat. "Tell me what you know about Harlan Jones."

She rolled her eyes toward heaven. "He's been around here as long as I can remember, and homeless most of the time."

"Why's that?"

"His father was an alcoholic. The bank foreclosed on the property his father owned, and when Harlan was discharged from the army someone else owned it."

"Did he ever hold a job?"

"Yes, for a while, but he got hurt. He worked as a ranch hand and was trampled by a bull—back injury. The farmer paid the hospital bill, but he couldn't do the same type of work anymore."

"Surely there was other family."

Madge shook her head. "His mother died when he was young. I never knew of any siblings."

I finished my coffee. "I better call Buzz. I promised a report on what happened at the hospital." I figured he'd be finished caring for his horses. I went to the bedroom, sat at the little desk and used the number he'd given me.

On the seventh ring, a low muffled voice said, "Hello."

"I'm sorry. I must have caught you in the shower. I can call back."

"No, no. Wait. Give me a minute."

A clunk and silence. I had a mental picture of him dashing around, trying to get dry enough to put on his pants. I waited.

"It's okay. I was drying off. I'm glad you called. What happened with Jones?"

"His blood pressure was so high they had to keep him overnight. He's not happy to be in a hospital." I described Officer Montoya's visit.

"I'll go over there in plainclothes tomorrow. He'll be less intimidated."

I shared an abbreviated version of what Madge had told me about Eddie Lee.

"Your aunt is right. The suicide devastated his wife. During the war she'd seen too many scenes like the one she found in the garage. It pushed her over the edge. I talked to her after the accident Eddie caused. She blamed herself, said she'd been on tranquilizers and not much of a mother to him."

"Sounds like he virtually lost both parents."

"Yeah. His dad was one of the five hundred plus POWs released in '73. He never adjusted. There were rumors he was not only using, but dealing street drugs. But we never established enough hard evidence for an arrest."

"Do you suppose Eddie was involved?"

"Doubtful. You remember Mike Huerta?"

I nodded to myself.

"When his sister, Maria, started dating Eddie, he kept tabs on him. I thought Mike would go nuts about three years ago when Maria announced she and Eddie were getting married. Mike's been diligent, but still unable to catch Eddie doing anything illegal."

"Any thoughts about the shoes?"

"That's a real puzzler, but I'll locate Eddie tomorrow and find out."

We said our goodbyes, and I went to see if Madge needed help in the kitchen. With everything that had happened, I'd forgotten to tell her about the money under Lottie's rug, or that I'd be going to Ortega Bay the next day.

It had rained a little during the night, but the sky was clear by morning, and as soon as the dogs were in the kennel, I left for the hospital to check on Jones.

When I stepped into his room, I hardly recognized him. His face was clean, his hair combed, and he was sitting with his legs dangling over the edge of the bed eating breakfast. A big grin brightened his face when he saw me standing in the doorway.

"You're all slicked up this morning," I said as I moved to the bedside.

His sharp blue-gray eyes shone. "The food's great." He bit into a strip of bacon. His tray was loaded with juice, coffee, scrambled eggs, bacon, and a stack of pancakes. Someone must have thought he looked like he needed a decent meal.

"How's your arm? Did it hurt much last night?" His left arm with the cast rested in a sling.

" Nah. I've had worse." His attention shot to the doorway behind me.

I turned to see a slender black woman wearing a pale green dress, white lab coat and dreadlocks. She carried herself with an air of quiet efficiency. A chart was cradled in her left arm. Her gaze fastened on me. "Miss Powers?"

I nodded.

She stepped into the room, withdrew a business card from her pocket and handed it to me. It read, *Kit Harris, MSW, Social Services.*

"I understand you're responsible for our patient." Her tone was pleasant but serious.

One good deed and I was trapped like a fly in a spider web.

"Mr. Jones will be ready to for discharge this evening if his blood pressure stays in good control today. Will you be picking him up?"

He obviously was in no shape to fend for himself on the streets. He'd need medication for his blood pressure, and unless someone supervised, he probably wouldn't take it. Or when he ran out, he'd have no money for the prescription.

She stared at me, waiting for an answer, and I hadn't a clue as to what to do.

Jonesy must have sensed my dilemma. "Don't you worry 'bout me, Miss Deena. I'll be jus' fine. This here cast's no problem. I've had lots worse trouble with my leg." He slurped his coffee and forked the last mouthful of scrambled eggs between his uneven teeth.

"I have to drive to Ortega Bay today, but I'll be back this evening."

"You'll need to stop by the office downstairs before you leave to give them billing information." She entered a note in the chart.

Did she *really* think I'd skip out and never return? Jonesy's mention of his leg gave me an idea. "Mr. Jones is a veteran. Surely he's eligible for help from the VA."

Her face brightened. "Most certainly. You can take him to Valley Center VA Hospital for follow-up care. A doctor there will have to certify his need. If you'll come with me to my office, I'll give you referral information."

I turned to Jonesy, whose face held a faint scowl. I didn't have time to sort out his misgivings. "I'll be back by before dark to get you. You can stay at my aunt's. She has a spare room. Later we'll find another place for you."

His shoulders slumped. "I been doing just fine up to now."

I tweaked his cheek. "And you'll do even better in the future."

I followed the social worker to her office where she handed me a paper with the VA hospital's letterhead. "This is a list of the documents you'll need when you take Mr. Jones for care. He'll need his cast checked in a few days. I'll have a copy of his chart waiting at the nurse's station for you to take along."

The first item on the list was a military discharge document. A

174

man who travels around with all his worldly belongings in a ratty backpack doesn't worry about such things. I doubted Jonesy even knew what had happened to it.

I thanked Ms. Harris, and as I hurried to the Explorer, fished my cell phone from my purse. I poked in the number I dreaded calling.

"Madge? I hope you don't mind. I'm bringing someone home to stay for a few days."

Chapter 23

On the way south my thoughts kept coming back to Eddie Lee. In detective work, you look for patterns, and put all together, I found the pattern of Eddie's behavior alarming. Besides what he did to Jonesy, he was evasive about any question I asked regarding Lottie Weston. What *was* his problem? I determined I'd share my thoughts with Buzz.

A few miles from Ortega Bay, I changed my focus and debated with myself whether to contact Fred Baker before or after I picked up Dad's audiotape. If Buzz had already spoken to the Ortega Bay PD, they might get to Baker first. A visit from the police would surely throw cold water on my efforts to get information. On the other hand, bureaucracies rarely moved fast. I opted for a stop at Marshall's Wrecking Yard and vowed I'd make it quick.

The office building was a little more than a twelve-by-twelve shack. Its construction, corrugated metal and wooden planks, looked like the materials had been scrounged from discards.

I entered and identified myself to the chunky woman behind a battered desk. She was wearing a black, long-sleeved velour top, and it appeared to me she'd gained weight since its purchase. I surveyed the cluttered desk while I explained the reason for my visit.

She rummaged through the disorder. "Ah, now I remember," she said as she hoisted herself from the creaking swivel chair. "He put it on top of the file cabinet."

I stifled a giggle at the sight of her short, cheetah-print skirt and black stockings. A wide elastic belt cinched her waist accentuating her most prominent feature. She bent to move an office stool, giving her audience a remarkable view, and stepped up on it to reach into a basket. The imitation snakeskin high heels were an added touch. She returned to the desk and handed over the tape. I thanked her and departed, concluding her attire would entertain her customers, whom I suspected were mostly men.

Although anxious to hear what was on Dad's tape, I held off. There'd be plenty of time to review it on the drive back to Four Creeks. I made a pit stop at a fast-food restaurant and bought a sandwich before setting my course for the older section of the city.

Garden Street was about a mile from Ortega Avenue Grammar School. I had no trouble finding it since I'd seen the street sign many times as a child. Garden was two-blocks long and dead-ended at the bottom of a high bluff. The houses in that part of town dated back to the '20s. Most were stucco with composition roofs and established landscaping on narrow lots. Not the cookie-cutter houses you see in newer neighborhoods. Many of these modest homes were a bit shabby, but they had character.

Relieved not to see a police car anywhere along the street, I scanned for house numbers, many of which were missing. But mailboxes hung near the entrances with names and numbers, albeit faded. Baker's sister, Helen something. What was it?

I pulled to the curb to search for the information Buzz had given me. As I did, a white pickup sped by. I figured I'd annoyed the driver with my dawdling. He made a u-turn at the dead-end and shot past me going in the opposite direction. Idiot!

I found the note I was seeking. Peltier was the name. I fished my binoculars from the bottom of my bag, in case I'd need them to read the mailbox labels. Before pulling out, I glanced in the rear view mirror and noticed the white truck had parked at the end of the block. He'd probably been annoyed when he overshot his destination, I reasoned.

I continued my search, checking visible numbers and decided the crème-colored stucco house with the Spanish tile roof had to be the place. I parked, stepped out and went to the door.

When the bell brought no response, I knocked on the screen door frame. I heard footsteps. A round-faced woman with silver-gray hair answered the door. Her age, I guessed at around sixty-five.

"Helen Peltier?" I asked through the screen.

"Yes?"

I introduced myself and held up my ID for her to read. "Is Frederick Baker your brother?"

She stiffened, her eyes narrowing. "Why? I don't want trouble."

I took that to mean yes. "I need to speak with him. Do you know where he could be reached?"

A male voice came from somewhere in the back of the house. "Who is it, Helen?"

"Some lady detective wants to talk to you," she called over her shoulder.

"Hell, invite her in," the voice said. "I could use some company besides you and the cat."

She unlocked the screen, and I stepped into a small living room crowded with worn overstuffed furniture.

"Down the hall, on the left," she indicated with a tilt of her head.

A long-haired, black-and-white cat jumped from the back of the couch, stretched and nimbly sauntered in front of me into the hall. At the first doorway it turned and disappeared into the kitchen. With a few more steps, I stood in the doorway of a bedroom. A small fenced yard edged with poinsettias could be seen through casement windows.

"Come on in. I don't get many visitors, so I'm glad to see anyone, especially a lady." The man was sitting in an easy chair in front of a portable television.

I stepped forward and introduced myself. One look and I knew Bingo Baker hadn't murdered Lottie. His hands were gnarled and twisted with arthritis. Even through his pant legs, I could see his swollen knees. His oversized belly suggested an enlarged liver. He definitely was not a well man and not likely to leave the house, much less travel to Four Creeks.

Mentally, I scrambled. I'd rehearsed what I planned to say to him during the trip. I had to revise my approach in a hurry.

He motioned to a ladder-back chair where a blue, terrycloth robe was draped. "Toss that on the bed and sit down." His voice had the raw quality of a two-pack-a-day smoker. The room held the faint odor of Ben Gay mixed with cigarette smoke.

I handed him my card before I moved the robe to sit. He fumbled in his shirt pocket for his glasses, as he squinted at me and then at the card.

"A lady detective." He shook his head. "I thought they were only on TV."

"Mr. Baker . . ."

He interrupted. "Call me Fred, please."

"Okay, Fred. I'm here because of a friend of yours from a long time ago. Her name was Carlotta Weston. You might have known her as Carlotta Woods."

He scratched his ear, his expression quizzical. "I don't think so."

"You might remember her from when you lived in Las Vegas."

His eyes widened. "How did you know I was in Vegas?"

I fished the picture of Lottie, Baker, Cuddles McGee and the two other men from my purse. "This was found in Mrs. Weston's belongings after her death." I handed him the snapshot.

He studied it in silence.

"I believe that's you on the left."

He nodded. "Damn. I haven't seen this photo in over forty years."

"Isn't that Carlotta Woods next to you?"

"Was that her real name? I never knew. She was Rita Diamond to me."

"The other woman is Cuddles McGee, right?"

He fixed me with his gaze and nodded.

"Who are the other men?"

"I did my time. I don't want to dig through all that garbage again." The glint in his eyes was off-putting.

A sudden gust of wind outside made the Poinsettia leaves dance. My thoughts spun. What if he refused to talk to me?

"Perhaps I'd better explain." I related the story of Lottie's murder and how the pictures and greeting cards were found. I didn't mention the cash, considering the possibility he could have engineered a search for the money.

His expression was deadpan as he listened and stared at the photo.

"I came here hoping you could tell me about that period in her life." I paused. "How long did you know her?"

He was silent. I was on a fishing expedition and he knew it.

I caught a movement in the doorway out of the corner of my eye and turned my head.

It was his sister. She stood with one hand on her hip, leaning against the door casing. "You might as well tell her. She'll dig around and find out anyway."

He pulled a white handkerchief from his pants pocket and wiped his nose, back and forth, like old men do. He shot her a sideways glance. "Bring us some coffee."

Shifting his weight, he focused on me. "I met her in Reno. She'd been dealing cards in a club there to pay her way through college. She was real good looking and a smart kid. I saw that right off." He handed the photo back to me. "We had some good times, and I talked her into relocating to Vegas. Got her and her friend jobs in Durango's Dugout. It was a casino on the outskirts of town. I started working there as a bouncer and worked my way up in the organization." He paused as he had a coughing fit into the handkerchief, then continued.

"At first Rita was dealing cards, but after a few weeks she landed a spot as a dancer. Durango put pressure on her to hang out after the late show and be available for any interested high flier. She liked the money, but not the men. She came to me for help, and we got to be a steady thing."

His sister entered, put a green mug on the table beside his chair and handed me a cup and saucer. She took a sugar bowl from the top of the dresser and offered it to me. I declined. She put two spoonfuls into Fred's mug, stirred it and afterward assisted him. With some awkwardness, he wrapped both hands around the mug. When he had a firm grasp, he nodded and she let go. She gathered the robe, shoved a pair of slippers under the bed with her foot and left us alone.

After a sip, I glanced around for a place to put my cup. I wanted my hands free to get a notepad out of my purse. He noticed my dilemma and pushed a couple of magazines off his table onto the floor. A practical man. He nodded in the direction of the bare spot.

I leaned forward, deposited my burden, and pointed to the picture I'd laid on the table. "Who is the other guy?"

"Some fellow named Murray. He didn't stay long."

"And the man standing in back?"

His eyebrows knitted together. "That's Durango, the SOB," he said with a growl. "If it weren't for him, I'd have never gone to jail."

"How's that?"

"Rita begged me to take her away, but I didn't have enough to bankroll us. I told her we'd go to Mexico, but we had to have enough money to last. We worked out a plan. I said 'Give it three months.' By then I worked in the "cage" and helped with the count at midnight. I was able to miscount and pocket some. They didn't have all the electronic surveillance available nowadays. But I wasn't able to collect enough. She figured out a scheme of her own to swipe chips from her customers and cash them in. She sewed the money into her clothes, costumes, coats, even her hats. We had close to twenty grand stashed when Durango's pit boss got suspicious. I could feel the tension. He had his men watching us.

His shoulders slumped and he stared out the window. By the faraway stare, I knew he wasn't gazing at the flowers.

Almost a minute passed before he spoke. "I felt eyes on me even when he wasn't breathing down my neck. I had a real creepy feeling he was about to spring a trap, so late one night I put Rita on a Greyhound bus to L.A. We had it planned to meet in San Diego in three weeks. She carried the money."

"What ever happened to her friend, Cuddles?"

He shrugged. "Don't know. She cleaned out her stuff and left about the same time. I never heard where she went. She wasn't cut out for that kind of life. Too prissy. Cuddles was choosey about the men she went with. Durango was only interested in the money she made. I think one of the guys got rough with her. One night I overheard some heated words between her and Durango. The next morning she was gone.

"Durango was pissed when he found out she'd skipped." He swirled the coffee in his cup. "But Rita was his headliner, so he *really* boiled over when *she* disappeared. I told him I'd find her, search the city and bring her back. I drove around town, stopped at her apartment and a few nightspots. He had me followed. When I finally lost the tail, I knew I couldn't go back, or I'd end up buried out in the desert. I left Vegas with just the clothes on my back."

Chapter 24

After a big gulp of coffee, Baker continued his story. "I took a road straight south and drove all night. Thinking I was in the clear after I crossed the border into California, I stopped for breakfast at a diner I spotted in Needles. I'd just swallowed the first bite when I saw Durango's car cruise by. He was smarter than I thought. I left my food and caught the fastest road out of there, figuring if I made it to the city I'd lose myself in L.A. traffic." He paused for another swallow of coffee. His eyes took on a weariness as though the mere telling was taxing.

"A week later I was asleep in a hotel when two of his men, Malloy and Dirk, hauled me out of bed."

I scribbled those names on my notepad and hoped for more details later. "How did they know where to find you?"

"I made mistakes, called people I shouldn't have. Durango had the same connections, only tighter than mine."

"You think he threatened them?"

"His presence would have been threatening enough."

"Go on."

"They tied my hands and drove me to a secluded place by the L.A. River. Durango was there and wanted his cash. I told him I didn't know where it was. Strictly speaking, that was true. His goons worked me over, then shoved me in the trunk of the car. I figured he wouldn't kill me as long as he thought I could lead him to the money." He slouched, his body sinking in his chair.

"We were on the road a long time, and I thought he was taking me back to Vegas. I was wrong. It was daylight when they stopped and opened the trunk. I saw an old ramshackle building and miles of empty desert in every direction."

"You had no idea where you were?"

"No, not until later. They hauled me into the building and tied me to a four-by-four in the middle of the room. Durango asked questions while Dirk and Malloy took turns pounding on me. I blacked out." He paused, started to reach for a pack of cigarettes on the table, but withdrew his hand.

"How long were you unconscious?"

"Not sure, but it must have been past noon when I came to. The room was warming up. I heard Durango talking to Nick Malloy about getting some food and water. I had caked blood on my lips, and I was so parched my tongue stuck to my teeth." He drank from his mug as if he could quench the long-ago dryness.

"One eye was swollen shut and the other just about. When I heard the door close, I figured Nick had left. I played possum and worked on the knots. I heard snoring and figured Dirk was asleep on a bedroll, no doubt tuckered out from his morning's exertion. Durango had settled himself on the floor next to the door with a .38 by his knee. He clutched a portable radio to his ear and kept one eye on me. About an hour later, he kicked Dirk awake and gave him the gun, said he was going out to take a leak and told him to watch me. By then I'd loosened the knots and was ready to make my move." He twisted in his chair and put the mug on the table.

He made a fist and rubbed it into the palm of his other hand. His eyes narrowed and he hunched forward. "Dirk was one of those short fellows who think they have to be cruel to make up for their size. He'd given me lumps I can almost feel yet. I jumped him. I guess it was the adrenaline. I smacked his head against the four-by-four until he was silent. I had the pistol and was ready for Durango."

He took a deep breath and shot a dark uncertain glance in my direction. "I fired before he got the door open and dragged him inside. Durango was dead. When Malloy returned, I put him out of commission too. I took the car and headed for San Diego. I figured I'd go over the border, heal my wounds and wait until the date I was to meet Rita. Then we'd head to Mexico for good, maybe even to South America.

"I'd given her my sister's address in El Centro. When the time came she wasn't there. I thought maybe she was scared 'cause it was in all the papers about the killing—pictures too. I waited for days, then kept on the move and checked back with Helen every few weeks."

"She never came?"

He shook his head. "Months later boredom drove me to a bar one night. A little game was going on in the back room and I joined in. There was a raid. The cops swept up everyone in the building. I was arguing my innocence when they figured out I was the guy in the newspaper. I pleaded self-defense at the trial, but it didn't work. I didn't have the cash for a decent lawyer. I got fifteen to life. I never did find out what happened to Rita or the money."

He paused, studying my face as if wanting a reaction. "So here I am," he said, "more or less imprisoned in this room." He held out his gnarled hands, palms up.

I sat quiet for a minute, absorbing everything he'd told me, sorting facts from what might be fiction.

"Helen," he called.

His sister appeared in the doorway.

"Take these away." He indicated the coffee service.

She moved to the table.

I passed her my cup and saucer. "Did Rita ever try to contact you?" I asked Helen.

Gloria Getman

"Not once," she said, stone faced. She retrieved the dishes and left.

I turned my attention back to him. "One other thing. My sources indicated you've only been out of prison a year. A long sentence for second degree murder. Something else must have happened."

He looked at his feet. "Yeah. I was not an ideal inmate. A little matter of attacking a hard-ass guard. I got a raw deal in court and took it out on everyone. Five years here, five years there. It all adds up."

He *was* glossing over his record, but I didn't comment. I was certain he hadn't killed Lottie. Who else had a motive? Someone who knew about the money? "What ever happened to Malloy and Dirk?"

He pressed the heel of his hand on the arm of the chair to shift his weight. "I'd like to tell you they were suffering in an extremely hot, dry place." He grinned. "Malloy survived the bullet hole I put in him and went on to get killed in a shoot-out in Chicago. The prison grapevine is good, though sometimes slow. I heard Dirk came to cross-purposes with the Feds in a counterfeit deal and ended up in a Federal prison. I don't know where."

"You remember his given name?"

"When I worked for Durango, we called him several names behind his back, Dirty Dirk for one, but his name was really Charles. It was him that fed the cops a cock-and-bull story about what happened out there. It was them against me. Maybe there was some payola too. I don't know."

I made a note to check records on whereabouts of Charles Dirk and stood to take my leave. I extended my hand. He put his crooked fingers in it. They were cold, in spite of the sunshine that had warmed the room.

"I'm sorry I couldn't be more help," he said. "Won't you stay for lunch? Like I said, I don't get any visitors. I can get Helen to make us some sandwiches." He turned his head in the direction of the door.

186

"Helen," he called.

"No. No, thank you. I have a long drive back. Actually, you have been helpful. You've eliminated suspects, including yourself."

He shook his head. "I have to admit, there were times, early on, when I could've wrung her neck. But not now."

I said goodbye and turned to where Helen waited. She led the way and opened the front door. I was about to thank her for her hospitality when I noticed her blue eyes were giving me a glare as cold as ice cubes.

"You didn't ask me if I killed her," she said with one corner of her mouth turned up in a sneer. "I blame her for the years my brother spent in prison. She suckered him."

The possibility of someone confessing to a murder without prompting was zero. She was taunting me, so I asked, "Where were you a week ago last Saturday night?"

Her expression changed, startled by my unexpected response. I watched her eyes and detected her thoughts scrambling. "Uh, I was here with Fred, of course. He needs constant care since he was released. I even have to help him dress."

"Then why did you say that?"

Her face drooped. "Because it makes me mad to see what prison life did to him. He was young and handsome when he went in. Now he's a sick old man and it's all her fault. I wish I'd had the opportunity. I would've killed her."

I handed her my business card. "Listen, what I'm doing may help both of you. Bring closure, as they say. If he starts reminiscing after I'm gone, he may remember something I need to know. Should that happen, call me collect."

She scowled at the card as if she thought I was lying. I stepped out the door and the screen banged behind me. "If I don't hear from you,

Gloria Getman

I'll be in touch when the investigation is over."

Chapter 25

As I walked to my car, I glanced at my watch. Two o'clock. No time to stop to see if Judy had returned from visiting her grandchildren. I had to get back to pick up Jonesy before dark. As I wound through the afternoon traffic, I called Judy on my cell to say hello, but there was no answer.

Back on the freeway, I mulled over everything I'd learned. The origin of the money Lottie hid under her rug was clear. Fred Baker was ruled out as her killer, but if Charles Dirk was out of prison, he might be a likely suspect. He'd had plenty of idle time to scheme, and if he had connections in the outside world, might have figured out the whereabouts of Durango's gambling proceeds. He'd have a strong motive. I'd ask Buzz for another records search.

After a few miles, my thoughts returned to Dad's audiotape. I fished it out of my purse, slipped it in the cassette player and switched it on. His voice filled the vehicle, clear and strong, giving the date and followed his standard report format.

At the sound of my father's voice, tears blurred the road before me. I stopped the tape. A knot in my chest forced me to turn off the highway at the next exit. I pulled over and parked by a tree. Leaning against the steering wheel, I struggled to gain control.

After my mother died, Dad wouldn't talk about her. He went back to something that made him feel better, the gambling. Was I acting like him, merely pretending to move on with my life? Maybe so. When my marriage failed he counseled me to toughen up, that life was too short to waste. I wondered if I'd ever be tough enough.

A rapid knocking on the driver's side window startled me. I jerked my head up to see a stranger's face level with mine, saying something I couldn't understand. I lowered the window a crack.

"Hey, lady, are you all right? I saw you drifting on the highway and figured I should check on you." He had a ruddy, rough complexion and pale, blue-gray eyes. The baseball cap he wore had a Laker's logo.

"I'm okay, really," I told him. "Thanks for stopping."

"You sure?" He straightened and smiled, showing a gap between his two front teeth.

I nodded.

"Be careful when you pull out. This shoulder is soft. You could get stuck." He turned and walked away.

He seemed like a concerned passer-by, but his sudden appearance left me ill-at-ease. I glanced in the rear view mirror at a black Buick sedan. As he swung a U-turn back toward the freeway, I got a glimpse of the license plate, but caught only three digits.

I mentally shook myself as if rattling all the thoughts and emotions into proper perspectives. The tape would have to wait until later. I needed to keep my mind on the road. There always seemed to be some sort of highway improvement project going on between the coast and I-5.

I was headed north on Highway 5 and driving at a comfortable speed, when I noticed a white pickup truck behind me in the passing lane. I felt a prickle on the back of my neck. A car pulled between us and I couldn't see the license plate. Thinking of the times I'd suspected I was being followed, I took the next off-ramp at a shopping center and pulled into a gas station.

After topping off the tank, I plunked a few quarters into a machine for an orange soda. I put the tape recording back in my purse and found a radio station playing an upbeat tune. As I sipped the soda and forced myself to relax, a news break warned of a rainstorm out of the Gulf of Alaska that would drench all of California. If I didn't get on my way, I'd be driving in the rain.

It wasn't until I was plugging along in the far right lane that I saw the same white truck behind me again. That fact convinced me it was no coincidence. He must have pulled off somewhere and waited for me. I slowed my speed and hoped he'd move closer at some point. If I could get a good look at the license plate, then I could ask Buzz to find out who owned the truck. But he pulled back several cars behind. Maybe I could ditch him at Frazier Park. When I reached the turn-off there, I circled around and reentered the highway.

No such luck. Before I reached Lebec, I saw the truck again. How'd he do that? Then it came to me. The man who'd stopped earlier must have put a tracking device under my SUV. I pulled off the highway at a rest station, parked, climbed out and I ran my hand along the underside of the SUV on the driver's side. I was right. I found one of those cheap GPS trackers. I glanced around and saw a septic tank pumper pulling in. I ran over to it and stuck the tracker on the back of the cab. As I pulled back onto the freeway, I couldn't help but smile and wondered where the septic pumper would lead him.

As an extra precaution, when I entered Bakersfield, I left the freeway at Rosedale and detoured by way of Calloway Avenue, a street I knew only because I'd visited a college classmate who once lived near there. The area had grown with an expanded shopping center and a new golf course. I took my time and decided I'd stay off the freeway and follow an alternate route. I didn't see my shadow again. It worked, or so I thought.

It took several minutes to find a parking space at Delta hospital. I had to be rude and steal one I knew another driver was poised to enter.

I squeezed into the elevator next to a woman in purple leggings who needed a new brand of deodorant. I was glad the hospital didn't have more than three floors.

When I entered the room where I'd left Jonesy that morning, the bed was stripped of linen. Thinking his room had been changed, I went to the desk where a clerk, who looked like a Barbie doll in pink smock, was busy tapping on computer keys, a pencil clenched between her teeth.

"Excuse me. I'm looking for Harlan Jones."

She shook her head and kept her eyes on the screen.

I waited a couple of beats. "Excuse me."

She held up one hand, traffic-cop style, made three more taps on the keys with a flourish and turned my way. "Mr. Jones went AMA about two o'clock."

"You let him go?"

She gave me a vexed expression. "Look, we didn't let him go. He disappeared—sneaked out. We sent Security looking for him, but he was gone. You can't imagine the hassle it is when someone leaves like that." Her blonde ponytail swished back and forth for emphasis.

I turned my back and leaned against the counter. I put my fingers over my mouth, puffing out my cheeks and stifled a curse. Where would the old guy go? I faced her again. "Did he have a visitor today?"

Her blue eyes widened. "Why yes. Two, in fact. I was told a man in a blue suit was here this morning, and then, right after lunch, a younger guy, tall with straight black hair."

My watch indicated it was almost five o'clock. How much ground could Jonesy cover in three hours?

I returned to the Explorer. On my way to Four Creeks wind gusts buffeted the trees along the road. Rain was on the way, and Jonesy would be out there in it with a new plaster cast.

I was inclined to search for him, but my better judgment told me the best option was to contact the PD and ask the police keep a lookout for him. I figured the visitor in the blue suit was Buzz and had a strong hunch the other person was Eddie Lee. But why? Certainly not to apologize, I was sure of that.

When I arrived at the police department, Elena told me Detective Walker was busy with a phone call. I sat and noticed the cobweb still hung above the door.

A moment later Buzz appeared in the doorway. He wasn't smiling and looked perturbed.

"What?" I asked.

He turned and gestured for me to follow. In his office, he pointed to the chair opposite his desk. He deposited himself in his swivel chair and leaned forward with both hands flat on the desk in front of him. His mouth was a thin line.

"What?" I asked again.

His eyes narrowed. "You contacted Fred Baker before the Ortega Bay PD. That's interfering with police business. You know better."

From his expression, it was going to take some major weaseling to escape his wrath. "I figured he'd be less intimidated by a woman."

"You should have told me your intentions. Captain Acosta called and threatened to send a bill for wasting his department's time. He said Baker's sister glared at his men like a mother tiger and wouldn't let them in. She showed his men your card. Acosta wanted to know if I wanted to file a complaint."

I took a page from Dad's book—do what you have to do and apologize later. I'd stepped on too many toes. It was weasel-time.

"I'm sorry, Buzz. I should have called you. After I left the wrecking yard, I decided to check out the Baker residence since I was in the neighborhood anyway. I knew the area since he lives only a few blocks from my old grammar school. I couldn't resist." I crossed my fingers inside my coat pocket. "I didn't mean any harm."

He scowled, rearranged a few papers on his desk and scratched his forehead. "I don't appreciate being left in the dark. I want to know everything that went on down there."

"I'll tell you everything, but there's another problem. Harlan Jones has disappeared."

"What do you mean, disappeared? I saw him in the hospital this morning."

"He had another visitor this afternoon after you left and now he's gone—walked out."

"You think it was Eddie Lee?"

I nodded. "It's my best guess."

"I tried to locate Eddie this afternoon. He wasn't home. I talked to his wife and then his uncle at the store. Neither knew where he was."

"Probably at the hospital intimidating Harlan Jones. Did you explain to his uncle why you needed to see him?"

"Only that I wanted to talk to Eddie about an incident. Since Jones wouldn't cooperate, I couldn't class it as a complaint. I spent the better part of half an hour with him and got nothing for my effort. He stared at me like a scared rabbit. If he won't press charges, there's nothing we can do."

"I told you he was frightened. First you, then Eddie Lee. I'm sure that's why he didn't wait for me. I planned to have him stay with Madge and me until better arrangements could be made." I stood and moved to the door. "I'm going to drive around a little. Maybe I'll spot him."

"Wait." He followed me into the hallway. "I still want to know what you learned from Baker."

"It'll be dark soon. We better talk later."

Buzz glanced at his watch. "All right, meet me at The Golden

Wok at 6:30. You can explain over dinner."

"I'll be there," I said over my shoulder.

Dark clouds hovered, and I figured it'd be raining soon. Where would Jonesy hole up on a rainy night? A dry culvert, an old barn or an empty shed, that's what he'd told me. The image of him huddled in a culvert in the rain made me shudder.

I started my search on the north side of town, stopped every place I saw a large culvert and scanned the countryside for old barns, or an empty house. As I turned onto Orchard Drive, Lottie's place came to mind.

A few minutes later I pulled over in front of her house. Yellow crime scene tape still lay limp on the ground. Daylight had been lost under the cloud cover. I grabbed a flashlight out of the glove box, got out of the car and paused at the gate to survey the location for any noticeable change. Then I checked the front door even though I knew it would be locked. Circling the house, I pointed the beam through a window. From what I could tell, the contents were no different from when I'd seen them last.

Lottie's empty pigeon pen was a spot Jonesy might choose. I'd have to check it out. While wading through knee-deep weeds in her back yard, I remembered the path trampled by the police and about the wheel barrow and the footprints. Once again, I wondered if Jonesy's shoes were somehow connected.

As I approached the pen, the patch of gravel that lay at the threshold crunched under my feet. Then it seemed like I heard movement inside. "Harlan Jones, are you in there?" Slivers of my flashlight beam filtered through cracks in the siding. I paused and listened.

"Come on out. I'll take you home for the night. You can sleep in a nice warm bed." No response. "Oh, rats. I don't know why you have to be so blasted stubborn." I jerked the door open wide and sent a beam of light inside. Mice scurried across the floor. An involuntary shiver spread between my shoulder blades and up the back of my neck. I stepped back. The odor of bird droppings and mouse urine was potent. But it was no time to be squeamish. I held my breath, leaned forward and swept the interior with my light. A step stool and gardening tools crowded one corner. An empty sleeping bag, dirty and probably infested with fleas, was bunched against the opposite wall. Otherwise the building was empty.

I imagined nasty little critters gathering on my ankles and crawling under my pant legs. I stepped back, stomped my feet, hoping to rattle off any hitchhikers, and headed to the Explorer. I'd run out of ideas. My spirits were deflated, and the holster under my jacket was rubbing a raw spot. I shrugged out of the jacket, put the pistol and holster in the glove compartment, locked it and turned the key in the ignition.

Before I reached Madge's place a fine mist covered the windshield. No doubt it soon would be raining in earnest. I tried to convince myself that worrying about Jonesy was useless. He'd survived a good number of years without my help.

Chapter 26

When I entered the house, I saw Madge sitting in her easy chair. Jeff rose from a position at her feet, stretched and ambled over to greet me. Mutt was in Madge's lap, and she had his dog brush in her hand. By the looks of his slick and shiny coat, she'd been brushing him, something I'd neglected lately. She must have seen my look of surprise.

"I wasn't sure when you'd get back," she said. "It's starting to sprinkle, and I couldn't bear to see them out there in the rain." Madge waved the brush in the direction of the kitchen. "There's ham and scalloped potatoes in a casserole to warm up."

"Thanks, but I'm meeting Buzz Walker for dinner at The Golden Wok." As I knelt to stroke each dog, I gave her a brief sketch of my session with Baker. Madge didn't say anything while I described Baker's physical condition and how he'd ended up in jail.

When I finished she said, "Sounds like it was a crazy scheme. He's lucky he didn't get killed."

Then I told her about Jonesy's disappearance from the hospital. I figured she was relieved he wouldn't be sleeping in one of her beds.

"That old coot is as crafty as a coyote," she said. "Don't worry, he'll turn up when you least expect it."

I fed the dogs and while I dressed for dinner, I made a decision.

The windshield wipers sloshed aside sheets of rain on my way to The Golden Wok. I parked in front and raised the hood of my all-weather jacket before making a dash for the door.

Gloria Getman

Inside, opposite the entrance, a six-foot fish tank displayed a number of shiny, golden fish drifting in lazy circles. In the Chinese restaurateur's rule book, an aquarium must be one of the requirements. I glanced around the room. The walls were covered with textured maroon wallpaper and a fake bamboo tree touched the ceiling in one corner. Oriental music played in the background.

I hung my coat on a hook by the door, nodded to the waitress who greeted me, and slid into a booth where I could see the entrance. I didn't wait long. Buzz came in, shook his way out of a black rain jacket and hung it on the coat hook beside mine. I waved.

"Hope I didn't keep you waiting long," he said as he sat opposite me.

"Not at all."

The waitress came to the table, delivered menus, plus a teapot and teacups.

He flipped open the menu. "I'm starving. How about you?" He pointed to dinner number two. "It's always good."

We picked our entrees and poured the tea.

After a comment about the weather forecast, he asked, "Did you have any luck locating Jones?"

"No. He doesn't want to be found. It bothers me, but I can't *make* him accept my help."

Buzz leaned back. I felt his gaze burrow into me. "I'm ready for the Baker report you promised." His expression was serious.

I took a sip of the hot tea before relating my story. "I picked up my father's audiotape at the wrecking yard, and then decided to look for Baker's place." I told him about Fred Baker's condition, the story of the embezzlement and his version of how he landed in jail.

As I finished the account, our dinners arrived, and though he wasn't smiling, his face had relaxed. "An old jail bird like that. You can discount about half of his story." He leaned forward and fixed his attention on the plate of Almond Chicken before him.

The aroma of fried wonton and soy sauce was tantalizing. It had been a long time since the sandwich I'd eaten in Ortega Bay. After a few bites to quell my hunger, I said, "It's a stretch to think Lottie's nest egg had anything to do with her death, but I'd sure like to know the whereabouts of Charles Dirk. If he figured out Baker's connection to Lottie, he could have waited until he was out of prison to look for Durango's money."

"I'll see what I can find out about him, but I think it's a waste of time."

For several minutes we concentrated on our meal. When I'd consumed the last spoonful of my Almond Chicken, I said, "There's another angle I think we should consider."

He poured tea into my cup, set the teapot down and stared at me intently.

"And that's Eddie Lee," I continued. "Three things about him bother me. First, he won the lottery by buying a ticket from his uncle's store, a little suspicious considering Lottie always bought her tickets there. She chose the same numbers every week. He could have recognized them as winners when the newspaper reported it? And that would have motivated him to go into her house with the idea of stealing her winning ticket. He didn't even have to know about the money under her rug."

Buzz nodded. "Mike and I discussed that. And it's a possibility. But where's the proof?"

"The numbers were the same as hers. I compared the ticket I took from her house with the numbers in the newspaper. They are *exactly* the same."

"I agree, but he could claim he found it on the sidewalk—that she lost it. She's not here to tell us otherwise. It's not proof he killed her."

"Okay, another thing. I figure the only reason he took Jonesy's shoes was because they were his, and he was wearing them the night of the murder. I figure he tossed them in the trash bin where Jonesy found them."

Buzz nodded again. "I thought of that too. And it's a valid idea. But again, there's no proof. We don't even have the shoes to compare with the shoe prints from her backyard."

I was getting peeved. If he'd thought of everything, why wasn't he looking for evidence?

I continued my argument. "Then there's the fact he lives across the road from her house. He could easily go back and forth without being seen, especially at night. Motive, method and opportunity. The weapon might still be in his backyard. Locating it before he disposes of it is critical."

Buzz shook his head. "I wish it were that easy. Without some concrete proof, we have no probable cause to get a warrant to search his place." He gave me a wistful smile. "However, that's good thinking on your part, and I'll ask him some tough questions—when I find him."

I folded my arms and glared at him across the table. "I suppose you let me go off on a wild goose chase with the Baker angle to get me out of the way?"

"Not at all. Your theory was as good as any. Eddie Lee is someone we've been watching. He's spending a lot of time at Hester McKay's, as you noticed. And it seems like there might be something else going on over there besides lovemaking."

"Like what?"

"I can't say yet, but we're keeping a close eye on their activities." Buzz opened the cellophane package containing his fortune cookie and broke off a piece.

"Would it have anything to do with the white pickup truck I saw in her garage?"

He'd opened his mouth to pop in the cookie, but halted. "Just when were you looking in her garage?"

"I saw it there the day we searched Lottie's house. In fact, I think whoever drives it may be following me."

Buzz slumped against the back of his seat. "And how long were you going to wait to tell me this?"

"I wasn't sure at first. I thought it was due to my suspicious nature." I explained each incident. "I suppose I'm jumpy because of the burglary, but I don't think so."

"That does it." Buzz laid the cookie aside and leaned forward. "You have to promise me something." He reached across the table and covered my hand with his.

I stared at his hand and then at his face.

"Deena, listen to me. You shouldn't go off by yourself like you did yesterday. You didn't know what you'd find when you located Fred Baker. He might have been a burly gangster instead of a crippled old man. One day your luck will run out." His eyes conveyed concern, not macho, not stay in the kitchen, little woman, but genuine concern. It unnerved me.

"Hey, as they used to say in the old movies, I'm packing heat. Remember?" The truth was I hated to carry a handgun, even though I was licensed for it. I could hit a target as well as any man, but the notion of actually shooting someone made my stomach turn.

"Yes, so do cops. But even they work with a partner. They don't go out to investigate alone, man or woman."

My instinct was to be defensive, explain that I was experienced and trained by the best, my dad. I knew all the precautions. But he was right. The world was more dangerous every day.

He was studying my face. "Promise me something. When you go

to interview like that again, tell someone where you're going, if not me, *somebody*. At least do that."

I grinned at him. "That way you'll know where to look for the body."

He didn't smile. "Promise me."

"Okay. I promise."

"I'm serious. Give me your hands."

I held my hands out to him, and he took the left one in his.

"Now, raise your right hand and promise."

I did as he asked. I couldn't cross my fingers this time and he knew it. He knew me too well. Across the table, he gave me a satisfied smile.

It was my turn to be serious. "Buzz, I want to give you something."

His eyebrows raised and he tilted his head. It reminded me of my Dobe when he's unsure of what I want.

I opened my purse and placed the audiotape on the table. "I want you to take this. It's Dad's audiotape. I started to listen to it, but I couldn't finish. The sound of his voice..."

Buzz's expression softened, his eyes kind, the way I remembered.

"I want you to listen to the tape. You'll know if there's anything there that might incriminate anyone. If there isn't, then you can give it back to me and maybe someday I'll be able to listen to his voice again. Right now, it's too soon."

Buzz took the tape and gave a nod. "Sure. I can do that." For a second, I imagined I saw mist in his eyes.

When the waitress came with the bill, Buzz put the tape in his shirt pocket and we moved to the counter to settle up. We donned our coats and stepped out onto the sidewalk. The rain had stopped, and the only clouds were bunched over the Sierra. The air smelled fresh. I took a deep breath and looked skyward. The stars shone like they'd been washed clean too. Buzz stood beside me. We gazed at the stars for a moment. "When this is all over, what are your plans?" he asked.

"You think it's close to being over?"

We walked to the Explorer and he opened the door for me. "You'll find the deposit box and your part will be finished. I was hoping you'd hang around for a while afterward. Maybe we could get to know each other again. Do some things not related to work."

"I'll think about it." It was the only answer I could give him.

Chapter 27

It was dark and close to eight o'clock when I pulled into Madge's driveway and saw the front door was standing open. No one was in sight, not even the dogs. Something was wrong.

I felt a surge of adrenaline as I reached for the PPK in the glove compartment. I slipped in the clip as quietly as I could and eased open the car door. Crouching, I moved toward the house, hesitating at the first thinly curtained window I came to. I spotted the hind quarters of my big dog lying on the floor near the door. I scanned the room. No movement. I listened. Silence.

The wet grass softened my footsteps as I dashed from one window to the next, finding no one in view, until I reached the back door. It was open too, and Madge lay on the kitchen floor. Blood matted her gray hair. The kitchen phone receiver dangled on its cord.

I glanced around the room, then stepped in and knelt beside her. She was chalk-white and her breathing was shallow. Droplets of blood were splattered beneath her head. Placing the pistol on the counter, I grabbed the phone and dialed 911. After a quick report, I knelt beside her again. I raised one of her eyelids. Her pupil responded to the florescent light above. "Oh, Madge, who did this awful thing?"

Sirens could be heard in the distance as I crossed the dining room to check on Jeff. Blood oozed from a jagged gash at the base of his ear. I felt sure he'd tried to ward off the intruder.

"Good boy," I crooned. He whimpered at the sound of my voice. I patted his side and returned to Madge.

A police car pulled into the drive, followed by an ambulance. Two officers entered with guns drawn. The first was a tall, trim man with graying temples, a florid complexion and a take charge demeanor. The second one was younger and shorter. Excitement shone in his eyes. I didn't recognize either of them.

"I'm Sergeant Gillford," the tall fellow said in a low tone, his gaze focused on Madge.

"The bastard's gone," I said. "I looked through all the windows and didn't see anyone until I found her here."

He motioned to the other officer. "Go ahead, Bob." The other man disappeared through the hall doorway. He'd be opening closets searching for someone hiding there.

"Where did that come from?" Gillford asked, nodding toward my pistol on the kitchen counter.

"It's mine," I said and met his gaze. "I'm licensed to carry." He nodded, but I sensed he wasn't pleased with a civilian carrying a loaded gun no matter what the circumstances. He holstered his weapon, picked up my pistol, popped the clip and emptied the chamber. He put the bullets in one pocket of his jacket and the pistol in the other. His gaze swept right and left, taking in the whole room and back to Madge, then knelt on one knee beside her.

"She's still breathing," I told him.

I heard the second officer announce, "Clear."

Men from the ambulance approached the door with a gurney. Gillford rose and waved them in. He produced a cell phone and pushed buttons with one hand. "We need a photographer and evidence people here," he said and related the address.

I stood and moved out of the way. I focused on the sandy-haired EMT as he swiftly checked Madge's blood pressure while his partner applied a wad of gauze to Madge's wound. A stretchy type of stocking cap was placed over the gauze to hold it in place.

"Except for the laceration on her head, I don't find any other obvious injuries," the sandy-haired fellow told me. He pulled a penlight from his pocket and checked Madge's pupils, then stabilized her head and neck while a brace was maneuvered into place. I bit my knuckle as they shifted Madge onto a rigid board, secured her with straps and lifted her onto their gurney.

"The bedrooms have been ransacked," Gillford's partner reported. "I'm Officer Manning," he said to me. "We'll need you to look things over and tell us what's missing, but first I have to show you something."

Buzz appeared in the doorway, still dressed as he had been at dinner. Astonishment flooded his face as the gurney with Madge passed him on the way to the ambulance. "Good God."

At the sight of her, strapped to a stretcher and white as the sheet covering her, I started to tremble. Madge was my only living kin. First my dad and now her. Who would I be without them?

Buzz's gaze lit on me, and in the next instant he'd folded me in his arms, holding me close. I have to admit it felt good. I needed the comfort he poured over me at that moment.

When he released me, he questioned his officers about what they'd found. The photographer had arrived at the same time. Buzz pointed this way and that, directing his work. The man, a hefty gray-haired fellow with a deeply-lined face, gave Buzz a look of annoyance.

"Miss Powers, come with me." Officer Manning took my elbow and guided me to the bedroom. "This first bedroom is the worst. The other, not so much, like maybe the goon was interrupted."

I gasped when I saw the room. Every drawer had been dumped on the floor. The bedding had been stripped and the mattress shoved against the wall. Thank goodness I'd had my pistol in the SUV. The clothing in the closet had been pushed aside, the contents of the shelves as well.

"Who would do such a thing?" Even as I said it, I knew. Madge's purse was on the kitchen counter, undisturbed. It wasn't valuables the burglar was after. It was something else. The scene at the office in Ortega Bay returned to me.

"Look here." Manning knelt and pointed his flashlight under the bed.

I knelt and looked underneath. Huddled against the wall at the head of the bed was my Chihuahua. He was trembling.

"Mutt!" In a flash, he was in my arms, licking my face and whimpering. Blood droplets were stuck to his fur. "You poor, scared pup." He stuck his head under my arm, as if hiding from the horrible scene. I felt him all over, but found no sign of injury.

I returned to the living room with Mutt in my arms to find Buzz bending over Jeff, speaking in soothing tones like he would to a child. He stood as I approached. "He was trying to get up, but his equilibrium is screwed up."

I knelt and put my hand on Jeff. "The bedroom's been ransacked. I want to go to the hospital to be with Madge, but he needs care too."

"I'll drive you," Buzz said. "We'll take the dogs along. I'll drop you off at the ER and take the big guy to the animal emergency hospital." He nodded in the direction of his men. "They know what to do here."

I was too upset to offer any other suggestion.

Buzz suggested we make a makeshift stretcher out of a beach towel. Buzz moved Jeff onto it, no easy task since he weighed nearly eighty pounds. Jeff raised himself with his front legs, his head weaving from side to side. I coaxed him down while Buzz prepared the Explorer, then we carried him to the rear of the SUV and settled him inside.

I scooped up Mutt and was ready to climb in the car when Officer

Gillford walked up to me and handed over my pistol and bullets. "Lock these up someplace," he said.

"Thanks. I will." I climbed in and secured the weapon in the glove box as Buzz took the driver's seat.

Buzz talked about what would be done to investigate as we drove toward the hospital. I barely heard him. A sense of dread held my attention. All I could think about was Madge's ashen face. It was my fault. If I hadn't been staying at her house, she'd be baking cookies for the garden club bake sale. I remembered the tracking device that had been attached to the Explorer. Maybe if I'd taken that more seriously, given it more attention, Madge's assault could have been prevented.

We pulled into a space near the emergency room entrance. I turned to Buzz. "I really appreciate what you're doing for us."

"No problem. Your dogs are part of your family."

I was sure he felt the same way about *his* animals. I put Mutt on the seat, slipped out and carefully closed the door. As the Explorer started to pull away, I saw Mutt, his paws on the window. Buzz reached for him, and held the little guy against his chest as he maneuvered the SUV into the street.

Chapter 28

I turned toward the dim entrance of River Delta Hospital ER, passing a clutch of young men, all puffing cigarettes. Automatic doors whooshed open, revealing people in various states of injury and illness. They filled the molded plastic chairs strung along the walls of the waiting room. With an air of resigned patience, they leaned this way or that, resting elbows on knees or slumped with their legs extended.

Behind the glassed-in cubicle, a gray-haired woman in a blue smock hunched over a pile of papers. I approached and after a moment of being ignored, tapped on the glass. Her head jerked up. Tired brown eyes crinkled at the corners as she slid back the barrier. She didn't exactly smile, but her round Irish face was a welcoming one.

"I'm Deena Powers. My aunt was brought in by ambulance with a head injury."

"Oh, yes. I'm glad you're here. I need some information." She pointed to the chair in front of the window. "Mrs. Hatcher is being examined. Someone will let you know when you can see her."

I perched on the edge of the chair. "Did she regain consciousness?"

The crinkles disappeared. "I don't know."

I spent the next several minutes trying to remember details of Aunt Madge's personal information. I'd forgotten to bring her purse. It probably contained all those precious numbers hospitals require. In the end, I had to promise to return with the details as soon as I could.

When our exchange was over, I glanced around and saw a man

standing behind me. His hand was wrapped in a blood-stained cloth. I stood and moved away. I found the cleanest chair available and sat, accepting my own resigned patience. The butterflies in my stomach ceased fluttering, leaving me feeling tired and anxious.

A magazine might have helped as a distraction. However, the single copy of *Newsweek* was being shredded by a happy toddler sitting on the floor. His grandmotherly companion stared absently at a TV hanging from the ceiling in the corner of the room. On the screen, Ninja Turtles wrestled with evil doers.

The sweep hand of a wall clock ticked off the seconds. Smokers drifted in and out of the door, trailed by the odor of their addiction. I fervently wished Buzz would return. I longed for news about my dog, my aunt and the investigation. The minutes dragged.

The only thing I could think about was the invasion of Madge's house. Anyone that violent would be back. But when? I glanced at my handbag. My pistol was in the Explorer. Maybe I should wear it all the time.

I tried to imagine what had happened. The front door was open, and to me it meant the culprit must have rung the bell and Madge simply answered it. I figured as soon as Madge saw a weapon, she ran for the phone. Jeff must have sensed her fear, or reacted to the man's hostile moves. My dog probably stood between her and the attacker. Maybe Jeff bit the guy. I liked that idea. After disabling my dog, he went for Madge, who never had a chance to make the distress call. Then he had time to search. I ran through the scenario again. I'd tell Buzz the guy might have a dog bite.

At long last the interior door opened. A tall thin woman dressed in green hospital scrubs appeared, a clipboard in her hand. "Mrs. Powers?"

I bounded out of the chair like my feet were on springs. "Yes."

"Your aunt is back from the CT scan. You may see her now."

I followed her long strides inside and toward a curtained cubicle. "Her vitals are stable, but she isn't responding yet," she informed me.

"Why not?" The second the words were out, I knew it was a stupid question. He'd hit her hard, maybe hard enough she'd never regain consciousness. The butterflies in my stomach stirred to life.

"The doctor will talk to you in a few minutes. We'll be admitting her to the Neurological Unit as soon as the bed is ready." As she left me, she patted my shoulder, the way nurses do in a manner that says, "I'm sorry. I wish I could stay with you, but I can't. There are too many others."

I pushed aside the curtain. The room was dim with only the muted glow of counter lighting. Madge lay on the gurney, the backrest partly elevated, looking smaller than I remembered, as if she'd somehow shrunk since I'd last seen her. A thick gauze dressing was wrapped around her head, and a plastic bag of IV fluid hung from a pole, the tubing leading to her hand. A pinpoint light in the blue controller box winked every few seconds.

Hospital people must think pink gowns, like the one Madge wore, make patients look less ill. Not true. Her milky pallor was frightening. Tears blurred my vision. Why did he have to hurt a defenseless old woman? She was no match for him. All at once my anxiety gave way to fury. He didn't *have* to hit her. He could have taken the phone away, jerked it off the wall.

I moved to her side and put my hand on her shoulder. "Madge?" Her eyelids fluttered, but didn't open. I felt a surge of hope.

I heard the curtain rustle behind me and turned to see a dark-skinned man with a clipboard of papers under his arm. He was solidly built with muscular shoulders and wore green hospital scrubs. I figured he was another technician arriving to take Madge for another test. I was wrong.

"I'm Dr. Parker," he said and motioned for me to follow him. Outside the curtain, he leaned one shoulder against a pillar in the corridor and flipped through the pages of the chart.

"The good news is the scan didn't show any bleeding inside her head. That doesn't necessarily mean there isn't any. A slow bleed wouldn't show up at first. She'll need another scan in twenty-four hours to be sure. The blow left a U-shaped laceration which I've repaired." Despite his youthful appearance, weariness in his voice made him seem older.

"And the bad news?" I asked.

He lowered the chart and looked directly at me. His manner wasn't cold or distant, only matter-of-fact. "The bad news is that she has a concussion, possibly severe. It will cause her brain to swell some, even if there is no bleeding."

"Which means?"

"It's a wait-and-see game. She'll be in the care of Dr. Bahari. He'll want her kept quiet to minimize swelling." He tapped his pen lightly on the chart. "Her reflexes are normal right now and vital signs are stable, but her age is not in her favor." He straightened, a signal our conversation was over. "The transport team will be here soon to take her to the neuro unit." He turned to leave.

"Can I stay with her?"

"Check with the nurses upstairs," he said over his shoulder.

Buzz came through the outer door, evidently let in by the receptionist. I suspected he'd used his badge to get past her. I was so glad to see him I nearly hugged him.

"I think she's responding a little," I told him and pointed to the cubicle. He moved to Madge's side and took her hand, his jaw working. He leaned close to her ear. "We'll get whoever did this to you, Mrs. Hatcher. I promise."

Her lashes fluttered again, and I was sure she'd heard him.

A fellow dressed in blue scrubs with "Transport" printed on his shirt flung the curtain aside and stepped into the space. He twisted Madge's ID bracelet and studied a sheaf of papers in his other hand. "I'm taking Mrs. Hatcher to the third floor. If you go around to the front, you can catch the visitor's elevator." He tucked the chart under her pillow, released the brake on the gurney with his foot and maneuvered it out and down the corridor.

As I watched her disappear around the corner and out of sight, I realized I'd been holding my breath. I closed my eyes, remembering the day an ambulance took my mother away. I had the same sick feeling. Only that time, I was seven years old and my fear was justified. I could still see my father's face, the knowing eyes. I never saw her again. It was later I understood about the cancer.

Maybe Buzz thought I was about to faint. He put his arm around my shoulder. "Come on." He guided me toward the door. "We'll find that elevator and make sure she's settled. I imagine someone from Security will let us in."

He was right. A man in a blue uniform opened the door. The hospital gift shop was dark and locked. I glanced at the schoolhouse clock above the information desk. It was half-past ten. We were the only people to enter the elevator. I leaned against the back wall and stared at my feet.

"Are you okay?" Buzz asked. It wasn't really a question. By the softness in his voice, he knew I wasn't okay. He was just trying to be a friend.

"Today can be counted among the worst days of my life, that's all." I looked up at him, tears blurring my vision.

"I have some good news."

"I could use some good news."

"Jeff is going to be fine, no skull fracture or other injuries. I held him while the vet sewed his ear. He was really good. He's a great dog."

I couldn't help but smile. "I know."

"The vet said he didn't think the dog was ever unconscious, just knocked silly and his equilibrium disrupted. He'll stay overnight to be observed."

The elevator stopped, and as the doors opened Buzz handed me a paper with the pet hospital address on it. We approached the desk at the nurse's station.

Two women dressed in identical blue scrubs sat behind a counter with their heads together, conversing in low tones.

"Mrs. Hatcher's room?" I asked.

The dark-haired one looked up. Her glasses reflected the light from a desk lamp. She raised her hand and pointed to the right. "The corner room. I'll be with you in a minute," she said and resumed murmuring to her colleague.

I entered the room, Buzz trailing behind. A second bag of I.V. fluid had been added, tagged with a red label. The head of her bed was elevated. She looked so peaceful and dead-like, I caught my breath until I saw her chest rise and fall.

I went to her bedside and leaned over close to her ear. "Aunt Madge, it's Deena. I'm here with you." I watched her face. Her lashes fluttered. She moaned, but didn't open her eyes.

"You're in the hospital. You have a banged-up head." It was a gross understatement.

A hand touched my elbow. I straightened. It was the dark-haired nurse. She was short and chubby and her name tag read "Carolyn." She motioned us to the doorway. "She's responding, but we want to keep her quiet. We'll keep the room dim and visiting brief. Dr. Behari called in orders. He'll be here later." She explained everything they were doing for Madge, but five minutes later I couldn't have repeated it even if my life was at stake.

After lingering several minutes, I turned to Buzz. "Let's go back to Madge's house. I need to find her insurance cards for the admissions people."

"Morning ought to be soon enough. You shouldn't stay there tonight. I don't think it's safe. I have a spare room. You and your little dog can stay at my place. He's waiting in the car. He'll be glad to see you."

We left Buzz's phone number with the clerk at the desk and returned to the parking lot the same way we came in.

As soon as Mutt saw me, he began pawing the car window. "I think you better drive," I said.

Buzz nodded and went to the driver's side door.

As soon as I climbed into the SUV, Mutt alternated between licking my face and stuffing his head under my arm. I stroked his back and ears and after a few miles he settled in my lap.

I felt a lot like my dog, shaken and wanting to hide my head from all the ugliness. Was that what I was doing by going to Buzz's place— hiding my head under his arm? I decided it didn't matter. I simply wanted to feel safe, if only temporarily.

Chapter 29

After we stopped at Madge's home long enough for me to find her insurance cards and grab a change of clothes, I followed Buzz to his ranch with him in the police cruiser and me in the Explorer.

About ten miles east of town we turned off the highway. I trailed behind him along a bumpy dirt road that snaked between orchards and ended on a low hill next to a white clapboard house with tall pines in front. It was close to midnight when we arrived, and even though the moon was bright, I really had no idea where I was. I parked next to the cruiser, and with my clothes in one arm and Mutt in the other, followed Buzz inside.

He grinned as he showed me around, evidently hoping to make me feel comfortable. His home was a tidy three bedroom, one bath. The old west décor lent a warm atmosphere.

After a bit of awkwardness about the use of the bathroom, we settled ourselves for the night.

Despite the fact Buzz was a gracious host, I didn't sleep much. Besides the disturbing events of the evening and the strange surroundings, Buzz's ranch was in a remote and eerily quiet part of Delta County. Mutt must have felt the same because even though I gave him my coat to sleep on, he whined until I allowed him to curl up on the covers at my side. The sound of Buzz's gentle snore in the next room filtered through the thin wall. I stared at the bedside clock and at last drifted off, only to be awakened by a hoot owl in a tree outside.

At some point, I slept soundly, and when I woke sunshine was coming through the bedroom window. The house was quiet. I dressed and went out to the kitchen. Buzz was gone. I felt sure he'd be going over evidence collected at Madge's house.

A note left by a pot of hot coffee told me to help myself to anything in the refrigerator. I found a package of cinnamon rolls and opened it. They tasted fresh. I gave Mutt a sample and he agreed. With a cup of coffee in my hand, I strolled into the living room. A row of windows on two adjacent walls were perfectly situated to reveal a stunning view of the Sierra. A slope in the foreground led to a horse corral and barn. On the other side an open pasture stretched to a steeper hill. As I enjoyed the view, I understood why Buzz loved his home. It was a serene retreat from the hard edges of his police work.

There were three horses and a colt in the corral. Like a scene out of *Country Magazine*, the colt stood on spindly legs beside its mother. I had no idea what their breed might be. For a moment, I pondered what my life might have been like if I'd married Buzz after we left high school. I'd probably be living right there and have a couple of kids. I'd be pitching hay to the horses and mucking out the stables instead of searching through records in musty courthouse books. I shook my head as I pictured myself with a shovel. The theme song from Green Acres, the long defunct TV show, ran through my brain.

I finished the sweet roll and coffee, then rinsed my cup before retrieving my belongings from the bedroom. I was anxious to find out how Madge was doing, and I needed to ransom Jeff at the animal hospital. As soon as I opened the door, a Border collie, who'd been lying under a tree in the yard, jumped to his feet. Mutt started to bark and bare his teeth at the other dog. I snatched him off his feet. "Pick on someone your own size," I said as I climbed into the SUV.

It was a cool morning with no sign of more rain. The high fog that often covered the valley at that time of year had been washed away, and the sky was a faded blue. I followed the dirt road leading back to the highway. The road didn't seem as long by daylight, and twenty minutes later I pulled into the parking lot at the animal hospital. I left Mutt in the SUV and went inside.

Jeff nearly wagged his stubbed tail loose when he saw me. The vet opened the cage and deftly clipped a leash onto Jeff's collar as he lunged in my direction. I knelt and gave him a big hug. He put his front paws on my knees and lapped my face. Our joy was mutual.

The vet gave me instructions on Jeff's wound care, and I pulled my checkbook out to pay the bill. As I stood at the counter writing the check, Jeff leaned against my leg, his weight nearly buckling my knees. As soon as I loaded him into the rear of the car, Mutt began sniffing him, checking out his pal.

When I reached Delta Hospital, I had to circle the parking lot three times before finding an open spot. I parked and lowered the windows to give the dogs some air, then fished a couple chew toys from under the seat to keep them entertained.

I had to wait my turn in the admissions office where I left the information they wanted, and then took the elevator to the third floor.

When I approached Madge's bed and spoke to her, she opened her eyes, blinked as though confused at first, but managed to focus on my face. A dark stain had seeped through the thick gauze still wrapped around her head. I placed my purse on the bedside chair and reached for her hand. Her color still wasn't normal despite the extra oxygen she was getting.

"Deena," she whispered.

Relief erased my fear. She recognized me. I barely choked out, "I'm right here, Madge."

She closed her eyes. "Dizzy...no sense...I'm...afraid." She took a breath between each word.

"You don't have to be. No one is going to hurt you. You're safe here."

She gripped my hand. "Deena, I have to...tell you...something...before..." She tried to raise her head. "I owe you...the truth."

I laid my hand on her shoulder. "No. Just rest. You don't owe me anything, Madge. You're going to be all right."

She slumped back on the pillow as if the simple act of raising her head took every ounce of energy she could muster. She motioned with her index finger. "Come close," she whispered. "It's important."

I leaned forward.

"The truth...is..." She took several breaths before continuing, "You were...adopted." That said, she closed her eyes.

I stiffened. For a second I thought I'd misunderstood. "Adopted? Is that what you said?"

She gave a faint nod. "Later," she whispered. "I'm...so tired."

"Sure, Madge. Later." It wasn't what I wanted to say. I wanted to shout, "What do you mean, adopted?"

Right then, out of the corner of my eye, I caught a glimpse of someone in the doorway. I swung around and saw Irma. From the expression on her face, it was obvious she'd overheard.

I went to the door. "You heard her?" I asked, forcing myself to keep my voice low.

She nodded, stone-faced. "It must be the drugs talking."

"Don't give me that. Is it true? Did you know?"

She pursed her lips and nodded again. I took her by the arm and led her down the hall. "My parents weren't my parents? Who was then? And why was it a secret all these years?"

Irma raised her hands, palms out, as if to ward off a blow. Turning her head, she closed her eyes. "I don't think it's my place to tell."

Anger bubbled to the surface. "You better tell me everything you know." No matter what, I wanted to know the truth. Then, like an avalanche, it hit me. "The estate." I let go of her arm. "Lottie's estate. Oh, my God. Lottie was my mother? No!" I glared at Irma. I pictured Lottie, with her stringy, iron-gray hair, her dirty black coat, ratty shoes, and all those cats. "No! It can't be."

Irma started to move away from me, but I grabbed her arm again. "The Westons were my parents?"

"Not exactly."

"What do you mean, not exactly?"

"Only Lottie."

"You mean Lottie and my father?"

She shook her head with vigor. "No."

"Who was it?"

"I don't know." She jerked her arm from my grip, marched away and disappeared into the elevator. I watched her go, unaware my mouth was gaping.

I couldn't wrap my mind around all the implications. I'd seen my birth certificate. It clearly documented that my parents were Louise and Wallace Powers. If what Madge said was true, my father wasn't my father, and Madge wasn't really my aunt. It was all a lie. Other thoughts crowded in. If Lottie was my birth mother, it meant Irma and I were related—sort of. I remembered the two gossips at the library. Lottie had twins, they had whispered, and gave one away. Was that me? Was Freddie Weston my brother? The kaleidoscope had shifted again. I leaned against the wall for a couple of minutes to gain composure. I returned to Madge's bedside and saw that her eyes were closed. The skin of her face appeared loose and sagging. I put my hand on her arm and spoke her name. She didn't respond. Grabbing my bag from the chair, I left. I knew where to find an answer to one question—the cemetery.

Fifteen minutes later I stood in front of Freddie Weston's grave stone. The date verified what the library gossips had said. His birth date and mine were the same. If he'd lived, he'd have been forty in July, like me. I tried to picture what Freddie would look like as a mature man. Tears fogged my vision. I closed my eyes. Why was it such a secret? What was everyone so afraid of? Did my parents fear that if I knew, I'd go looking for my birth mother? Or was it part of a secret so shameful it needed protecting? What had Lottie done other than steal Baker's money?

I returned to the Explorer, sat and stared at nothing. I'd arrived in Four Creeks psychologically bruised but intact. Now I was shaken to the core. I was the same person but somehow not the same. The knowledge that Lottie was my mother altered my focus. There was no turning back. I had to know the whole story. Who was my biological father?

I looked up and glimpsed that damn white pickup as it crept past at the intersection. It intruded on my misery and triggered my fury. I turned the key and set my jaw. Determined to find out who he was, I pulled out and floored the accelerator. But when I reached the stop sign, it was nowhere in sight. Crap!

I drove to Madge's house with my thoughts in turmoil. Why had Madge felt compelled to tell me about the adoption, even if she feared she was dying? Nearly forty years had passed. What difference would it make? Then again, truth has a way of weighing on one's mind.

As soon as I arrived, I let the dogs out of the car. They wandered around the yard, returning to my side every few minutes, as if sensing my disquiet. Questions whirled around in my head like flies. Who else in town knew about the dreaded secret? Who told the librarian?

My ponderings were getting me nowhere. I diverted my attention to restoring order to the house. The dogs followed me inside and from room to room while I tugged the mattress back on the bed and wiped black fingerprint dust off surfaces. As I worked, Lottie's motives commenced to jell. She likely regretted giving her baby girl away and thought she could make things right. Why else did she put me in her will? That must have been the reason for the argument between Madge and Lottie in the library the day before her murder.

My parents' wedding picture was on the dresser in a scrolled wooden frame. I reached for it. Though it was a black-and-white, it was clear and distinct. Who did I look like? I leaned toward my reflection in the mirror. Did I look like Lottie? Her picture would be in Madge's high school yearbook. I laid the picture aside and went to the living room bookcase where I coaxed one of the yearbooks off the top shelf. I flipped open to the senior class and found Lottie's picture. Yes, I had to admit it, her mouth and the shape of her jaw was much like my own. I returned the book to its place, my thoughts bouncing around like ping-pong balls.

Madge's dried blood was still on the kitchen linoleum. I went to the broom closet for a mop. Jeff followed, but stopped and pawed at the stain.

By the time I finished the floor, I was aware I hadn't had anything to eat since the sweet roll at Buzz's house. I found a can of vegetable soup in the cupboard and rolls in the bread box. I opened the can, filled a bowl and heated it in the microwave. Taking it to the kitchen counter, I sat and tested the temperature. As I ate, another idea surfaced. Lottie was dead and couldn't explain, but I still had the key to the lock box. There had to be a really good reason for leaving the key for me. Perhaps she'd left a letter—an explanation. Creekside bank was the next on my list.

I felt agitated. Someone had killed my birth mother. Buzz said there was no proof Eddie Lee did it, in spite of the lottery ticket. There had to be proof somewhere at Lottie's house. I made a snap decision.

Buzz wouldn't like it, but I had to go back to Lottie's to look for evidence.

The sun was getting low in the western sky. I realized I'd have to hurry if I was going to get to Lottie's house before dark. I gulped the last swallow of soup and stuffed an extra roll in my purse to munch on the way. I changed clothes, slipping into a thick sweatshirt. It was still winter, I reminded myself. After I laced my boots and stuffed my pockets with items I might need, like lock picks and Swiss Army knife, I grabbed my camera and purse.

Mutt and Jeff would have to stay in the kennel while I was gone. I put out fresh water and food for them, but it wasn't much of a consolation. They whined when the gate closed. "I won't be long," I promised. "I'll be back before dark." In retrospect, I should have gone to the bank instead.

Chapter 30

Dusk was settling in when I pulled off the road opposite Lottie's house. It stood dark and uninviting. What was I expecting to find? I had no inkling, but the fact she was actually my mother had changed my perspective. I realized I no longer thought of her as a stranger I had little interest in. Her murder had become more personal. My hope was that the investigators missed something—besides the money under the rug.

I shoved my purse under the front seat, took a flashlight and my camera from my bag, and stepped out of the SUV. No need to bother with the front door, I decided. Messing with the lock would take too much time. And it might draw attention of someone passing, someone who'd dial 911. Nearly everyone in town knew Lottie was gone.

The dead grass, still wet from recent rain, squished under my feet as I rounded the side of the house. The screen door in back wasn't locked, but the inner door was. With the flashlight tucked under my arm, I used my picks to open it.

Inside, I noticed the cat odor had dissipated somewhat. Standing in the doorway between the back porch and the kitchen, I swung my light slowly across the kitchen floor and back again, then around the door frame. Turning around, I did the same to the back porch, starting in the farthest corner at floor level, and worked my way around. Nothing but cat hair. The cat that had been on the shelf the previous Monday was gone, probably caught by the SPCA, courtesy of Buzz Walker.

I considered turning on a light, but it wouldn't be a good idea. It would attract unwanted attention. Besides Treadwell had probably ordered the electricity turned off.

I stepped forward, knelt in the doorway between the kitchen and living room and swept my light across the living room floor. The beam revealed a herd of footprints in the dust. If the killer's shoe prints were there, they'd been obliterated by others made by the police.

Standing again, I flashed my light on the bookcase where the figurine had been. It held a fine layer of fingerprint dust.

Across the room was the wood burning stove. I stepped forward and flashed the light into the wood box. It held a few woodchips. I turned around and faced the kitchen doorway. The scene unfolded in my mind. Her wood box was empty. My guess was that Lottie had gone to the woodshed to replenish the supply. The front door must have been unlocked, and when she returned, she found the intruder. He must have caught her in the kitchen doorway. One of them knocked the figurine off the bookcase. Or possibly he hit her with it, sending shards flying.

I knelt in the doorway and swung my light across the kitchen linoleum. A bit of white under the refrigerator caught my attention. It looked like a tooth broken out of a comb. I moved closer. It was about an inch long with a sharp tip, tinted brown. Blood? It could be, if her attacker hit her with the figurine and cut her scalp in the process. Or perhaps he'd been cut when it broke. Either way, there'd be DNA. I took two snapshots, one from the doorway to establish the location and the other a close-up. It wasn't much, but I'd tell Buzz where to find it.

I hung my camera on the door knob as I moved toward the back yard again. Little daylight lingered. I stepped out and I swung my light back and forth across the grass. The nights were still cold, and Lottie would have needed wood for a fire.

Maybe she went for firewood every evening at the same time. Her killer might have watched and known her habits; he might have waited for her to leave the house. Various possibilities raced through my mind. He could have shattered her skull with something he'd brought with him. But it didn't make sense if the figurine was used first. Conjecture, was all it was.

I swung my light around to the path in the grass. There were numerous footprints—the police again. But the deepest prints were in the center along with the tire mark from the wheel barrow, indicating someone pushing a heavy load. A plaster cast of those shoe prints would have been made by the detectives. Where were the shoes Eddie stole from Jonesy? Would they match?

The murder weapon could have been tossed into the field. Like a hound dog sniffing out a trail, I followed the path and sent a beam of light into the wild grass. Before long I stood next to the canal.

I walked along the bank and scanned both sides with my light, soon ending up where the culvert ran under the road, and where I figured Lottie's body had been. If her killer left the scene from that end of the property after dumping her body, the wheelbarrow would have been left behind. It wasn't. It had been returned to the house. Why did he do that? Maybe because it would draw attention, or maybe he hoped her death would look like an accident?

I turned to retrace my steps and paused as I considered another option. He might have tossed the weapon into the water, figuring it would sink and go unnoticed. I flashed my light on the murky stream. It caused a shadow where something near the edge stuck out of the water. Could I be so lucky as to find the murder weapon? I carefully side-stepped down the bank. As I stooped to pull the item from the mud, my shoes sunk into the soft soil. I didn't let it stop me. I pulled a chunk of wood out of the muck and almost shouted with joy. Though covered with mud, it looked like it matched the firewood Lottie kept in her shed.

That's when a hand slapped across my mouth.

A surge of adrenaline sent my heart rate rocketing! I sucked air through my nose and tried to emit a scream, but it was muffled. The piece of wood fell from my hand as I twisted and clawed at the hand, so large I knew it belonged to a man. I stepped back hard with the heel of my right shoe, aiming for the bridge of his foot, a move I'd learned in a self-defense class. A lot of good it did me. The soft earth cushioned the impact. His other arm squeezed me tight against his chest. I sucked air in through my nose and bit the fat finger that was across my mouth. He jerked it away. I opened up to scream, but got out no more than a yelp because an oil-scented rag was stuffed in my mouth. A second later, a piece of tape held it in place. I had to fight the impulse to gag. At the same time, I tried to club him with my flashlight, but he grabbed my wrist and shook it loose. It rolled into the water.

He twisted my arm behind my back with a painful force, then caught the other and kicked my feet out from under me. I went down. I rolled. I didn't care if I ended up in the canal. But as I rolled, he grabbed my wrists from behind and a wide piece of tape strapped them together. He jerked me up by the back of my jeans beltline and gripped the back of my neck like a vise. Hauling me around to face the street, he gave me a shove. "Walk," he growled.

Was this Lottie's killer? Had he seen my light and been alerted? My thoughts raced through all the scenarios I'd heard or read about trying to fend off an attacker. If a kidnapper is allowed to take you from the initial scene, you're dead. Panic rose in my chest and adrenaline flooded every cell of my body. Somehow, that was *not* going to happen to me.

I flopped on my butt, spun and kicked, connecting with his ankle twice. But he was tough. He grunted and didn't try to avoid my blows. He put his foot on my chest, grabbed my ankles, slipped a piece of rope around them and pulled tight, knotting it. He grabbed my belt again and in the next instant, hoisted me over his shoulder like a sack of potatoes. His strength was impressive and frightening. I fish-tailed my rear-end in an attempt to loosen his grip on my legs or throw him off balance, but it didn't work. He kept moving toward the road.

The only thing I could see was the back of his legs and the heavy boots he wore. He stopped as soon as he stepped onto the road and from behind me, I heard a vehicle door open. He dumped me into the rear seat of a pickup truck—a white pickup—and pulled me to a sitting position. Shit! I was going to die!

In the light of the moon, just before he stuffed a paper grocery bag over my head, I caught a glimpse of the tattoo on his arm. I heard the sound of tape tearing, twisted and flung myself across the seat. I raised my feet and thrust them toward him. I wasn't fast enough. He pressed my knees against the seat and secured the sack to my bare neck. He had complete control.

The door beside me closed. I heard footsteps, and then the door on the driver's side opened. He slid into the seat, the door closed and the locks clicked. He fumbled for something. Another click and cigarette smoke drifted my way. The engine started.

In spite of the cool air, sweat trickled between my breasts, my hair hung limp, and my muscles ached from the effort to free myself. As I tried to swallow, the taste of motor oil seeped from the gag in my mouth. I kicked at the door in frustration. Fool! Stupid, stupid, stupid! How could I let myself get into such a fix? I knew better. Buzz's words rang true. Never go alone!

I had to calm myself and be alert. Think. Anticipate. I struggled to gain a comfortable position—difficult to do with my arms trussed behind my back—and decided to concentrate on the direction he was driving. I sensed a left turn, then a right turn. I recalled Dad telling me that if you keep your head, you can get out of almost every situation. I wasn't so sure about it this time.

The pickup had been parked headed east. I hadn't sensed turning around, only left and right, so I reasoned we were still going in the same direction. I listened for noises that might indicate our location, but heard nothing over the sound of the engine. He made several stops I figured were at stop signs, and turns, as if he were travelling the back streets.

Finally we were on a straight road. The pavement was smooth—a highway, but which one? I still felt like we were headed east. I counted and calculated ten minutes had passed when he turned onto a gravel drive or road.

After another minute, the truck came to a stop. My heart raced again. I heard him get out and his footsteps approached the door. A cold draft swept over me when it opened. Grabbing my feet, he pulled me toward the door, took my arm and dragged me out. "Stand," he commanded. I stood.

I heard him fumble in his jeans pocket. Next thing, he cut the restraint on my ankles. I tried to knee him, but missed. From in back of me, he caught my belt again and pushed me ahead. "Walk," he ordered. I sunk to my knees and made as much noise as possible around my gag.

"Shut up." He hauled me to my feet. "That won't do you any good. There's no one around to hear." He shoved me forward.

I counted twenty-five steps.

"Stop," he commanded.

A door squawked in front of me. He gave me another shove and I stepped into a building. Another shove. I stumbled. He grabbed both my shoulders and guided me until I bumped into something solid.

I smelled tobacco on his breath as he forced me around and pushed my back against what felt like a post. "Sit," he said. I kicked. He slapped my leg aside and punched my shoulder. "Knock it off!"

Pain shot across my shoulder and into my neck. I slid down and kicked at him again but missed. I felt his arm across my chest, holding me from behind the post. Then a cord surrounded my waist and was pulled tight. Next he had my ankles. I pulled and kicked, but he fastened one ankle to the floor with his knee and grabbed the other. He bound them together again. Next, his fingers were at my throat, digging the tape loose. The bag was pulled off my head. I blinked.

The room was dark except for moonlight streaming through a ribbon of large windows on the far wall. I glanced around. Folding chairs and tables lined the adjacent wall. The ceiling had bare rafters. Three posts supported the roof. I was tied in the center. It looked like a social hall for a trailer park.

I heard the sound of a creek or river in the distance. That meant I was right. We'd traveled east to somewhere near a branch of one of the rivers flowing out of the mountains. If it was one of the vacation parks near Sandy Cove, there might be people around. I might have a chance of drawing attention to myself.

He moved to the shadowy corner next to the door with his back to me and pulled a cell phone from his belt. After a few seconds, a conversation began. "I got her. It was easy."

A pause. "No, I haven't questioned her yet."

Another pause. "What you want me to do with her after that?"

After a couple seconds. "Okay, you got it. I know where to dump her." With that, he snapped the cell phone shut and moved in my direction.

Chapter 31

Panic! He planned to kill me. Questions? What questions? He approached, a giant hulk from my vantage point. Kneeling on one knee in front of me, he stuck his hand in his jacket pocket, pulled out a pistol and laid it on the floor in front of me. The threat was obvious. It was the right size for a .38, but in the dim light I couldn't tell for sure.

"Here's the deal Miss Lady Detective. You're going to tell me where the tape recording is—the one your old man made the night Dennis Colton was stupid enough to offer him a cut of our business. You *sabe*?"

Holy shit! He wasn't Lottie's killer! Recognition dawned as I remembered the tattoo. This was the guy I'd seen at the store the day I went to get the dogs from Francie's. Except his mustache was gone, and he'd changed the color of his hair to a lighter shade. Even in the dim light though, I recognized the s-shaped scar on his left cheek.

He ripped the tape off my mouth. It felt like three layers of skin went with it. I spit out the gag. "You son-of-a-bitch!"

His back-hand lit my left cheek on fire. "It's useless to scream. No one's here. The park's empty. Caretaker's gone." He snapped his fingers. "Now, where's the tape?"

"I don't know anything about any frigging tape."

The second slap was hard enough to make my teeth rattle. Reaching out, he wound a few strands of my hair around his fingers and pulled straight up. "You better change your mind or you'll be bald before I'm through." He gave a jerk. A chunk of hair came loose. I gritted my teeth. It felt like a hornet sting and brought tears.

"Why is it so damned important? Probably just notes. That's all."

He gave a snort. "You lying bitch!" He slapped me again. "You know all about it, or you wouldn't be hiding it."

"How would I know? My father had dozens of tapes. I had no reason to listen to them. What date are you talking about? If I knew I might be able to find it for you."

"You're lying." He cuffed the side of my head, making my ears ring. "You know, all right. You know Colton offered him a piece of the action, but he wouldn't bite. He was too damn straight." Another snort. "But I fixed his wagon. Too bad that little accident I rigged didn't kill you too."

I tried to mask my surprise. My crazy dreams weren't crazy after all. This bastard ran us off the road. The second set of tire tracks belonged to him.

Despite my stinging face and the ringing in my ears, fury rushed in. My senses sharpened. Somehow I'd see this guy got what he deserved—if it killed me.

"Ah ha!" He picked up the pistol and stood. He paced back and forth in front of me, passing the weapon from hand to hand. "You didn't know. I can see it on your face. Hah! You fell for that shit about black ice. There's lots you don't know. Like, the fire was a cover. Like, the boxes in that warehouse held bags of chemicals for meth. We had a good deal going till Colton screwed up. The stupid ass. He panicked when he saw the DEA in town. Thought they were following him. Told me to fire the place. Then the jerk decided your father had some evidence all sewed up and was about to blow the lid." He leaned over and grabbed my nose. "Where's the tape?" He gave a twist.

"Ouch!"

I clamped his little finger between my teeth, bit down hard and held it. It was his turn to yell.

Swift as lightning, he whacked the side of my face. I let go.

With a cavalcade of obscenities, he gave my hip a fierce kick and pocketed the pistol. He marched back and forth again, rubbing his finger, his eyes hooded in shadows as he stared down at me.

Then he leaned over, fingering the earring in my left ear. "I think Hester would like those little pretties." He straightened and took a jackknife from his jeans. "I think I'll take those and a bit of ear with 'em." He opened the knife and reached for my ear.

I had no doubt he'd do just that. "Okay, okay. The recording you're looking for is in the tape deck of my SUV." It was a lie, of course. Buzz had it. But if he went to look for it, I'd have a chance to get myself loose. If not, I was a dead woman.

No such luck. He stepped to the corner by the door again, produced the cell phone and flipped it open. After a moment, "It's me. Go over to the Weston place. Her SUV is there. The cassette is in the tape deck in her car. Get it and take it to Hester's. I'll pick it up later." After several seconds of silence. "I don't care what you think. Just do it!" Another pause. "Listen to me, Eddie. If anything goes wrong, I'll make sure someone knows what you did over there." He snapped the phone shut and turned to me. "Very wise of you to give it up. I'd cut off both your ears and you know it."

He stepped behind me. I felt him test the knot in the rope around my waist, and then he moved toward the door. "You sit tight. I'll be back." He chuckled as the door closed, no doubt thinking of the Terminator.

Seconds later, his truck door opened and closed. Flashes of light hit the windows. I expected him to come back inside, but he didn't.

I dug at the sticky tape on my wrists with my nails, and finally raised a corner. Frantically, I teased it until I got a finger beneath the edge, then worked and worked it until I released one hand. I pulled the tape off the other wrist. With my hands free, I squirmed to get into my pocket for the jackknife, and then sawed at the cord around my waist until it broke.

Undone, I sliced through the tape on my ankles, dropped the knife and in a flash was on my feet and out the door, running up the gravel drive. Frantic, I glanced right and left. No lights anywhere. No telling how far I'd have to go for help. I'd cleared about twenty feet when I heard a crunch of footsteps behind me.

Shit, he moved fast for his size. He grabbed me around the waist. I screamed with everything I had and fought like a deranged wild woman, kicking and scratching. But he was damn strong. He bounced me over his shoulder like a rag doll. I grabbed for hair and kicked. He held both ankles with one hand and the back pocket of my jeans with the other. I pulled up his jacket and shirt and clawed his back, digging in my nails as hard as possible. He stomped past the building where I'd been held, cursing me all the way.

As he carried me down a slope, the sound of the river became clear. He jostled to keep me off balance and unable to dig deeper into his skin. I twisted, caught his ear and jerked hard. My efforts were fruitless.

I sensed his intentions. He was going to dump me in the river. The water would be freezing cold from snow melting on the high ridges. I was a good swimmer, but the river was swift and treacherous with sharp boulders and tree limbs under the surface. I'd get slammed against a boulder, or caught on a branch and be pinned under water.

He stopped. I heard the river roar below. A chill breeze swept over me.

He hoisted my hips high over his head with both his arms. I hung onto his shirt, but I couldn't maintain my grasp. He flung me over the edge. I screamed.

Several feet below, I hit the steep bank with a thud and slid on my belly. I dug my fingers into the soil and grabbed for anything to slow me down. My sweatshirt was raked up to my chin and my bare stomach scrapped against sharp rocks and sticks protruding through the dirt. I dug the toes of my boots into the bank and reached out a hand, searching.

At the precise instant my feet touched the water, my left hand found a young sapling. I grasped it and hung on. It held. My descent stopped. My heart hammered like a machine gun.

I gasped and looked up, afraid that when he didn't hear my body hit the water, he'd come down after me. I saw him silhouetted against a waning moon.

Abruptly, his body jerked, his back arched, and he flew forward, his arms pin-wheeling. He sailed over the edge of the embankment to my right, hit the ground once and tumbled into the river. He shrieked. I heard a moment of splashing, several shouts and then no more. It must have been a deep spot. I shivered. That's what he'd planned for me.

Confused by what I'd seen, I looked up again. A dark shape leaned over the edge. "Miss Deena, are you there?"

I recognized the voice. "Jonesy, is that you?"

"Yeah, Miss Deena. You hang on now. Help's coming."

Faint sounds of sirens could be heard in the distance.

"Hang on. I'm gonna go wave 'em down."

Within minutes, two firemen flashed a spotlight on me and a rope was tossed over the edge of the embankment. I heard more sirens as one of the men lowered himself to my side. A rescue basket followed. Before long they'd hauled me to the top and covered me with a blanket.

"Where's Jonesy?" I asked.

"Right here, Miss Deena." The little guy stood by my side.

"How did you know?"

"I saw him put you in his truck."

I clutched his hand. "You saved me."

"I found a cell phone in a trashcan the other day. Wouldn't work 'cept for 911. That's all I did."

I squeezed his hand "You're a hero, Jonesy," Tears filled my eyes. "You're my hero."

Chapter 32

The wailing ambulance siren didn't help my headache. But I was alive and so grateful for the warmth of the blankets that covered me that I hardly noticed the burning sensation from the scratches on my belly.

As soon as we pulled into the ambulance bay, I was wheeled into a room blazing with lights and transferred to a hospital gurney. The hospital staff swarmed around, all gloved and wearing plastic masks, as if I carried some horrible contagion. They cut off my sweatshirt, pulled off my boots and jeans and poked me with needles.

A woman in a blue sweater flitted like a hummingbird from one side of me to the other, all the while firing questions about advanced directives and insurance cards. She heaved a sigh of disappointment when I told her I had neither.

A doctor also asked questions—did it hurt here, did it hurt there—as he pressed on various body parts. Concluding that I didn't have any broken bones, he quizzed me about my facial injuries. I felt my puffy cheeks and suspected that I looked like a hamster. The doctor asked about my medical history. He was particularly interested in my previous concussion and said he'd order a CT scan.

A nurse in maroon scrubs handed me a cold pack for my face and asked other questions about allergies and my last tetanus shot. She gathered my clothing, stuffed the garments in a white plastic bag and scribbled my name on it. Soon, the same young man who'd taken Madge for her scan the night before came to get me.

When I returned from the CT scan, the room had cleared. Only the nurse in maroon scrubs remained to reposition the oxygen prongs in my nose and recheck my vital signs. "A policeman is here to talk to you," she said.

Buzz appeared from the other side of the curtain divider. He scowled as he moved closer. "I've been talking to Harlan Jones. You nearly got yourself killed this time."

"God, it's good to see you," I blurted and grabbed his hand.

His frown melted.

"Oh, Buzz, that bastard was the guy who ran Dad and me off the road." Tears came as I poured out the whole story and everything I'd learn from my kidnapper. My babbling must have sounded crazy. "I heard him talk to *Eddie* on his phone. It sounded like he knew Eddie killed Lottie. And he said Hester would like my earrings." I fingered my earlobes, glad I still had them.

"We have Eddie in custody," Buzz said. "One of our officers was making his rounds and caught Eddie trying to jimmy the door of your SUV, so he took him in. But unless he confesses, we can't prove he did anything except attempt to break into your car. Without your kidnapper to corroborate what you say, there's only your word."

"But there might be proof. When I was inside Lottie's house, I saw a piece of broken figurine under the refrigerator. It has a dark stain that might be blood. And I pulled a chunk of wood out of the canal bank. It looked just like Lottie's firewood. That could be the murder weapon."

His brow furrowed. "I'll send someone to take a look."

"Did the bastard who attacked me drown in the river?"

"We haven't found him yet. We'll renew the search in the morning. His truck's been towed in for a close examination."

"It would have been *me* in the river if Jonesy hadn't come along."

"Yeah, Jonesy's a clever guy. He told me all about it. When he saw the guy stuff you into his truck, he sneaked over the tailgate and hid in the dark. His cell phone had no signal, so he had to hike down the road to where it'd work."

"I don't know how Jonesy did it, shoving him over the embankment like he did. He's no match for a guy that big and heavy. And with a cast on his arm."

"Adrenaline, I suppose, and the element of surprise.

"I have his DNA under my fingernails." I held out my hands for him to see. The undersides of my nails were brown. "I clawed his back like a tiger. There must be some skin under the dirt."

"Don't let anyone wash your hands." Buzz pulled his cell phone from his belt and poked in a number. When he got an answer he asked to have someone come over to the hospital ER with an evidence kit to collect my fingernails. He listened a second and replaced the phone.

About then, the doctor came back into the room, and I recognized him as the same one who'd taken care of Madge. "Dr. Parker."

He smiled. "You remember me from last night. That's a good sign." He made a note on a clipboard that lay on the counter. "Your scan looks okay, but we'll admit you for monitoring overnight. The fact that you recently sustained a concussion puts you at risk for complications. You'll need follow up care. I'll write some orders, and then they'll take you up to the third floor. Dr. Bahari will look after you." He shook Buzz's hand and left.

"I better leave," Buzz said. "I want to question Eddie myself, and there's a lot of paper work to take care of. I'll get a formal statement from you tomorrow."

"Where's Jonesy? I want to thank him again."

"He was in the waiting room, but he's probably gone by now. I told him he could come in to see you, but he didn't want to. He said he was afraid the hospital people were still mad at him for sneaking out the other day."

The nurse in maroon scrubs entered the room with a small tray in her hand. She placed it on a stainless steel table beside the gurney, then picked up a syringe from the tray. "Are you sure you haven't had a tetanus shot in the last ten years?"

"I confess, I don't remember."

Buzz gave my shoulder a squeeze. "I'll see you tomorrow."

"Coward," I said as he disappeared around the curtain.

While the nurse polished a spot on my upper arm with a swab, I read her name tag. Kelly. Nice name. She gave the injection, turned and stuffed the syringe into a red box on a nearby counter. After a check mark on my chart, she lifted the sheet and gave my belly an appraising look. "I'll find someone to clean those abrasions. We're still waiting to hear about a bed for you."

I rubbed my shoulder. "Okay."

She slipped between the curtains and was gone.

Noises drifted in from the hallway. A phone rang, the intercom announced visiting hours were over, and in the distance, someone laughed. I lay waiting and watched the big clock on the wall click off the minutes. Somehow my adoption didn't seem very important anymore. I was alive. I could tell because the scrapes on my belly burned, and a dull ache filled my head. I closed my eyes and thanked God I could feel anything at all.

Several minutes later the curtain divider rustled. A young woman with a blonde ponytail came in. She flashed a sparkling smile, and I instantly thought 'student nurse.' I pegged her for twenty-something. She didn't have the tired eyes of experience like Kelly.

"My name is Sally," she said, "and I'm going to clean all those abrasions on your abdomen."

She deftly folded back the sheet, exposing my wounds and winced. I looked and saw dirt imbedded deep red scratches extending from my waist to the bottom of my bra line.

She filled a basin at the sink and poured in a molasses colored liquid. "I'm sorry," she said as she placed it on a stainless steel table beside me. "This is probably going to hurt, but if I don't get the dirt out, you'll have an infection."

She was right. It stung like fury—enough to bring tears. When she finished, she dumped the basin into a deep sink, then applied a light dressing to my wounds and covered me with a clean hospital gown.

I was about to tell her my fingernails contained evidence, when a middle-aged woman carrying a toolbox entered. Her iron-gray hair was Dutch-cut. She wore street clothes, dark rimmed glasses and a smile. She twisted my ID bracelet and said, "My name is Millie, and I'm here to collect evidence from under your fingernails." She slipped on a pair of plastic gloves and went to work.

Sally and I watched with rapt attention while Millie scraped blood and dirt from under each nail into a glass tube. She clipped a couple fingernails from each hand and added them to the mix, then marked the tube with a black pen. So much for my expensive manicure.

After Millie left, Sally handed me a wet cloth to wash my face and then soaked my hands in a basin of clean water. My palms were scratched and sore and would be tender for days. In spite of her best efforts, I could still see a slight stain under my nails. It gave me the shivers and I wondered how long I'd carry the remnants of the kidnapper's DNA around with me.

Chapter 33

I didn't sleep after admission. Besides the fact that every muscle of my body ached from the fight of my life, I couldn't stop reliving the evening's nightmare, plus about every two hours someone came in to see if my brain was still working.

When I heard the breakfast carts clanking outside the room, I slipped out of bed, put on a pair of paper slippers the hospital provided, and went to the bathroom mirror. I was a sorry sight. My cheeks had a bluish tint. I looked like I'd been beaten up, which, of course, was the case. I put cautious pressure on my abdomen. Not too bad. The lump on my hip where the bastard had kicked me still hurt, and my neck and head still ached. But my injuries could have been so much worse, I felt lucky.

I padded along the hallway to find Madge's room—all the while trying to keep my backside covered. I peeked in the door and saw that her color had improved. The gauze dressing was new. The drapes were closed against the morning sun, but she was awake.

I walked in and stood close to the bed, hoping she wouldn't notice the hospital gown, or that my face was puffy and discolored. The truth would upset her, and I couldn't think of a reasonable lie on short notice.

"You're here awfully early," she said. Her voice was stronger. She still had the oxygen prongs in her nose, but she breathed without difficulty.

"Thought I better check on you and see if you're behaving yourself."

"That's what Barbara Haskell and Marlene Wilson said when they came to see me last night. I don't see how I could misbehave, even if I wanted to.

"How are you feeling?"

"A good deal better. The dizziness comes and goes, but the headache stays. What happened? My memory's hazy."

"Someone broke into the house and conked you on the head. Do you remember anything at all?"

"I remember something upset your big dog. He growled."

"Jeff was trying to protect you."

"It didn't work, did it. There was a man. He was angry about something."

"He hit both you and Jeff."

Madge pushed herself up in bed. "Did he hurt the little dog too?"

"No. We found him hiding under my bed."

I wanted to talk about her revelation from the day before, but wasn't sure how to approach the subject. "Have you been up to walk yet?"

She shook her head. "My brain isn't working quite right and everything takes such an effort."

"I imagine they'll want to be sure you're steady on your feet before discharge."

"I expect so."

For a minute she stared at the wall and pursed her lips, like she did sometimes when trying to decide something. Then she reached for my hand. "I'm sorry about yesterday, dear." She faced me with eyes glistening. "I thought sure I was dying, and I didn't want you to find out about the adoption from Lottie's papers."

Lottie's papers. I still hadn't found the deposit box.

"Irma was over by the door and heard what you said. I made her tell me what she knew. She said Lottie was my birth mother. That's when the inheritance made sense. I don't understand why it was such a big secret."

"There's more to tell." Madge heaved a big sigh and leaned back, heavy against the pillow. "A lot more, but not right now."

"I went out to the cemetery and saw the date on Freddie's gravestone."

Madge nodded her understanding.

A girl wearing a pink stripped apron over her uniform came into the room with a tray of food. After a cheery greeting, she placed it on the bedside table and positioned it in front of Madge before leaving.

Madge gripped the glass of orange juice with both hands and took a sip. Her hands shook as she put the glass down.

"When I get home," she said, wiping her lips with the napkin, "we'll make ourselves a nice cup of tea, and I'll tell you how it all came about."

"All right, I've waited over thirty years. I guess a few more days won't matter." I figured she didn't have the energy for a long story. I gave her a peck on the cheek. "I'll see you later." As I was leaving her room, I glanced back. She was concentrating on her breakfast tray. The fact I was wearing a hospital gown hadn't registered. It was obvious Madge hadn't recovered as much as I wished.

When I returned to my room, I found my breakfast tray waiting. The only food I'd had since lunch the day before was a glass of orange juice I'd been given before I attempted to sleep. It didn't take long for me to polish off breakfast. Just as I swallowed the last bite of toast, a man entered my room. He was a short East Indian with a toothy smile. After introducing himself as Dr. Bahari, he pulled a penlight out of his breast pocket and checked my pupil reaction, then held out his index fingers. "Take my fingers and squeeze."

It was the same routine I'd experienced before. He had me walk from the bed to the door and back again, while he asked questions about my previous concussion: symptoms, my headaches and how long I'd been unconscious after the accident.

"You're doing well considering the short time since your initial injury. I'll discharge you. Call my office for a follow-up appointment." He started to leave. His whole visit had lasted less than ten minutes, the quickest neuro exam I'd ever had.

"Wait," I said. "What about my aunt, Mrs. Hatcher?"

He turned back. "Oh, Mrs. Hatcher is your aunt? I didn't realize that. Well, toughness must run in your family. She's doing better than I expected for her age. She'll be here a couple more days until we're sure she's stable."

"But you think she'll have a full recovery?"

"We won't know for another four to six weeks. Sometimes the after effects last a long time, as you've probably been told." He left the room.

The bedside phone rang. It was Buzz. He asked how I felt and then about Madge. I explained Madge's improvement. "I'm going to be sprung today."

"I'll pick you up," he said.

"I'll need something to wear. My jeans are filthy, and my sweatshirt is in pieces."

"I probably have something here. My daughter always leaves clothes behind. It won't be stylish, but it will cover your um . . . bareness."

I imagined him grinning over his quip.

"Where is my car, by the way?"

"Still parked opposite Mrs. Weston's house."

"Good. If you'll drop me off, I can drive from there to Madge's. I'm concerned about my dogs. I need to get back to take care of them."

"Oh, don't worry. I stopped by last night and fed them after I left the station. They were suspicious of me until I filled their bowls with kibbles."

"I appreciate that, Buzz. And everything else you've done."

"We aim to serve. I have to stop at the office first. I'll be there in an hour or so."

"Bless you." I replaced the receiver.

I wanted a shower, but knew I wasn't supposed to get my bandage wet. A basin of water and a wash cloth would have to do.

Afterward, I felt mildly better, and returned to visit Madge, but it looked like she was asleep. I didn't bother her. I spent the next hour enjoying hospital décor; bland cream colored walls and dull green drapes. From the tall narrow window in my room, I could see half of an evergreen tree and the gray exterior of another wing of the building.

About ten o'clock Buzz came in the door with a pair of jeans and shirt draped over his arm.

"Fantastic." I gave him a big grin and reached for the clothes.

"When do you think you'll be ready to give a formal account of what happened?"

"Right after I hug my dogs, shower and put on some of my own clothes. Then I'll do anything you ask."

He raised an eyebrow, and I caught the flicker of a smile. "Okay, how about we get it out of the way this afternoon?"

"Sounds fine. Any news on my kidnapper?"

"No sign of him, but Eddie was willing to give us a little information. He said the guy's name was Buck Harper, and he was Hester McKay's half-brother. Of course, Eddie denied he had anything to do with your kidnapping. My men found a half-pound of meth in a baggy stashed in a trap in the door of Harper's truck. My guess is that he was using it as a product sample to expand his business. We contacted Ortega Bay police. We should know a lot more about him by tomorrow. And his body will probably wash up somewhere along the river bank."

"Good riddance." I held his daughter's jeans up to me, gauging the fit.

"I'll go look in on Madge." He closed the privacy curtain as he left the room.

After doing my best to button his daughter's jeans, I put on the shirt and rolled up the sleeves. I dug to the bottom of the white bag that held my clothes and found my boots. They looked as dirty as my jeans. I shook off as much dirt as possible into the waste basket and pulled them on. They were still damp.

I found a tiny comb in the bag of goodies the hospital provided and tried to run it through my hair, but it was hopeless. I went to the bathroom mirror. I looked like a bag lady.

A moment later Buzz returned. He had a quizzical expression on his face. "I think the trauma has affected your aunt's emotional state."

"I suppose it wouldn't be surprising, but what makes you say that?"

"She said the oddest thing to me. She said she was sure that when you leave Four Creeks, she'll never see you again. I tried to reassure her, but then she said, 'When she knows the truth, it'll change everything.' Why would she say something like that?"

My heart sank. Madge thought I'd abandon her. Nothing was farther from my mind. But what did she mean by "the truth?" I thought I already knew the truth.

I started for the door. "I have to talk to her."

Buzz caught my arm. "What's this all about?"

I paused and explained what Madge and Irma had told me, and about Freddie's grave stone. He listened without expression.

"Lottie's murder took on a whole new meaning for me. That's

why I went to her house. I simply *had* to look for more evidence."

Buzz let go of my arm. His face reddened and he expelled a gust of air through his nose. "I can understand that, but you should have waited. I'd have gone with you or made arrangements for Mike to be there. You shouldn't have gone alone. You keep going off half-cocked. One of these days your bullheaded foolishness is going to get you killed."

Like a child being scolded by a parent, I bristled. "Look, I'm going to go reassure Madge. Then you can drop me off at my car and I'll go home. With Harper dead and Eddie in custody, plus things I found at Lottie's, this case should be over soon. I'll be out of your hair."

I was halfway through the door when he said, "Deena, wait, damn it. I wouldn't be so mad if I didn't care about you so damn much."

Chapter 34

I stopped and turned to face him. The depth of his feeling was apparent in his eyes. I remembered that look from years ago. It was something I didn't want to see. Back then, we'd argued and I turned my back on him. I was afraid of getting stuck in a town full of narrow-minded cliques. I doubted the town had changed all that much. Then again, the day before, when he put his arms around me, I felt protected. It felt right. But I'd always savored my freedom, pushed back when my father was overprotective. You can't have it both ways though—secure and free. I felt at odds with myself.

"Buzz, so much has happened. I...I need to talk to Madge." I left him standing there in the doorway looking ill at ease.

I went to Madge's room and saw the bed was empty. For a split second my heart raced. Then logic took over. Perhaps they'd moved her to another room. I went to the nurse's station. "Where is Mrs. Hatcher?" I asked the clerk at the desk.

"Downstairs for a repeat scan. She'll be gone about an hour."

I returned to where Buzz waited and told him where Madge had been taken. "I'll come back this evening and talk to her." I picked up the hospital bag labeled with my name. "Let's go."

After I signed my discharge instructions, we went down the hall and stepped into an empty elevator. I leaned against the wall and stared at my dirty boots. A flood of jumbled feelings bounced around inside of me. I didn't know what to say. I glanced at him, and he gave me a rueful smile.

"I'm sorry I popped off," he said. "I know you've been through a lot."

I swallowed my pride. I'd strained our fragile friendship. "I *am* impulsive sometimes. I should have listened to you. I really do appreciate everything you've done." The elevator door opened.

Outside, the cool air felt good. Buzz and I climbed into his Ford pickup. The faint scent of hay and leather in the cab hinted that he used the truck to haul feed for his horses. I placed the white bag at my feet.

He reached behind the seat, pulled out my camera and handed it to me. "Mike found it hanging on the doorknob in the Weston house when he went to check out the evidence you talked about. He figured it was yours."

"Thanks. After all that's happened, I forgot about it."

After pulling onto the highway, we settled into a subdued silence for a couple of miles. Then Buzz cleared his throat. "Buck Harper was a real bad character. He had a record leading back to his teenage years starting with a breaking-and-entering charge when he was fifteen. He served time in juvie and afterward moved on to assault-and-battery in a bar fight, and then armed robbery at a gas station. He evidently had an anger management problem. He not only robbed the kid in the gas station, he pistol-whipped him too. More recently, he spent some time in Corcoran for cocaine trafficking. He's been out about six months."

I swallowed hard. "So now he graduated to murder and beating up on dogs and women like Madge. I'm glad he's dead."

Buzz didn't say anything. He kept his eyes on the road.

"You must have listened to Dad's audiotape. Was it like Harper said, Colton trying to bribe Dad?"

"Yeah. How he linked up with Dennis Colton is still a mystery. I shipped your tape off to Ortega Bay PD and got a call back this morning. The DEA figures the warehouse was one link in a drug trail starting in Mexico or South America with a transfer point in Delta

County. From here it went to other parts of the west."

Buzz pulled in across the road from the Explorer. I dug in the hospital bag and opened the valuables envelope where the ER people had placed my keys for safekeeping. There was an awkward pause for a second. With my keys in hand, I opened the pickup door and stepped out. I sighed and glanced back at Buzz. "Thanks."

As he smiled back at me, I was reminded of a younger Buzz, a guy I'd been very fond of.

His smile disappeared. "Say, call me when you're ready. Let's get your statement over with. Okay?"

"Gotcha." I closed the door and he pulled away. I waited for several cars to pass before I dashed across the road to the Explorer, climbed in and settled myself. I pulled across into Lottie's driveway, backed around and turned toward Indian Hill and Madge's house.

On the way, I automatically glanced in my rear view mirror, half expecting to see Harper's white pickup. I wondered how long the ghost of it would cause me to be watching.

At a stop light, I reached in the glove box for the pistol and clip and slipped them in my purse, then turned my thoughts to seeing my canine pals.

The dogs recognized the sound of the engine and began their greeting as soon as I pulled into the driveway. When I let them out of the enclosure, they ran circles around me. A chill wind swept across the hillside, giving notice another storm was on its way. I hustled inside.

Mutt and Jeff followed me from room to room as I looked around. I headed for the bathroom to treat my resurgent headache, then stripped down and climbed into the shower. The hot water running over my body was just short of nirvana. While I washed my hair, I blessed the man who invented modern plumbing.

After patting my belly dry and smearing the scratches with ointment, I pulled on a clean pair of blue-jeans and a loose shirt, tossed my dirty jeans in the washer and the remains of my sweatshirt in the trash. Next, I went to Madge's kitchen, started a pot of coffee and made myself a ham sandwich. With it comfortably deposited in my stomach, I phoned Judy.

"Man, I'm glad to hear from you," Judy said. "I called last night, but no one was home. It must have been 8:30. I wanted to let you know about your insurance check."

"It arrived? That's good news. If I give you my account number, would you deposit it into my checking account? Then I can pay the hospital bill."

"I thought it was already taken care of."

"Um. Not this hospital bill."

There was a pause at the other end of the line, and I could almost hear her mental wheels turning. "What's going on up there? Who's been in the hospital?"

"Sit down. It's a long story." I started with Friday night and the assault on Madge, and went on to explain my ordeal. "I'm okay, but I'm not certain about Madge. She's still in the hospital. I'm going back to see her tonight."

"I'm glad I'm sitting down. Holy shit, Deena. What a harrowing experience. But now that what's-his-name, Harper, is dead, and the other guy's in jail, that should end the trouble. Right? When Madge gets out of the hospital, you should be able to come home."

For two seconds I debated whether to tell her about the adoption, but decided there was no point in putting it off. "There's one more thing," I said, before launching into my revelation.

When I finished and took a breath, Judy said, "I'm flabbergasted."

"I still have unfinished business here. My hope is that when I locate Lottie's deposit box, I'll find out who my father was. Let me read my account number to you. You're a peach for doing this for me." I dictated the number and we said our goodbyes.

Next, I phoned Buzz. "I'm ready to make my formal statement."

"I'll be waiting," he replied.

I slipped on my jacket, and ten minutes later was sitting at a table in the small conference room of Four Creeks P.D. The room was a twelve by twelve, painted white with one high window, a wooden table and four chairs. No wall decor.

Buzz took a seat opposite me and laid out a display of six pictures on the table. Each photo was a five-by-seven head-shot of men with grim faces. After he pressed the button of his recorder, he made a formal introduction, then said, "Look at each picture and tell me if you can identify the man who abducted you."

I examined each one as instructed, but it took only a second to pick out Buck Harper. I put my finger on number four. "That's him, but he changed his hair color. It was lighter, and his mustache was gone." His hair was black in the photo, as it had been when I first saw him. "I recognize the s-shaped scar on his left cheek. It's unmistakable. This *is* the man."

"Let the record show that Miss Powers identified Francis Buck Harper as her abductor," Buzz said for the benefit of the recording. "Now, Miss Powers, begin at the beginning and tell me what happened to you on Friday, February 13th."

I did as he asked, and by the time I was done, felt a sense of relief. It was as though going over every detail of the incident had erased my sense of helplessness from it. Buzz made some concluding remarks before pressing the stop button and popping the cassette out.

"We obtained a search warrant for Hester McKay's garage," Buzz said. "The DEA found residue from meth chemicals. Hester said she understood that her brother was transporting boxes of furniture for the company down south. He made regular trips to her house and put the boxes in her garage for someone else to pick up."

"What about Eddie? What did he say?"

"He denies he knew anything about Harper's trafficking. Only that he knew him because he was Hester's brother. I expect he figures he can hire a good attorney with the money from his lottery winnings. He'll need one. Hester, on the other hand, has figured out she can bargain her way out of being charged as an accessory in the drug dealing by being very cooperative.

"Ortega Bay PD picked up Colton. As soon as they played the recording for him, he lawyered up. They'll charge him with conspiracy, but it may not stick without Harper to testify. He'll probably end up with a plea bargain."

Buzz hadn't said anything about Lottie's murder. I was still convinced Eddie had killed her for the winning lottery ticket. "What about the weapon used to kill Lottie? Any news?"

"We're still working on it. We turned over the fragment from the figurine to the county crime lab. But it'll take weeks to get an answer."

I felt drained of energy. Nothing seemed to be working out. I stood, pushed in the chair and picked up my purse to leave. Buzz suggested we have dinner together. I begged off, telling him I planned to visit Madge and turn in early. I was very much sleep deprived, having not slept the night before, and I still had the lingering headache.

When I returned to the house, I took the dogs for a walk up the road to where a field of orange fiddleneck had started to bloom. I let them wander while I watched rain clouds creep across the sky. Afterward, as I brushed Mutt's long coat, I decided to leave the dogs inside when I went to see Madge. One nice thing about dogs when they reach adulthood; you're less likely to find your pillows torn to shreds when they're left alone for an hour.

The parking lot at the hospital was packed with visitors' cars that evening. I drove around and around and finally parked a block away and hiked the distance. The lobby was a hum of families with children. The gift shop was crowded. After waiting at least ten minutes to buy a bouquet of daffodils for Madge and a paperback book for myself, I followed the flow of visitors through the corridor to the elevator. People crowded in, maneuvering so as not to touch each other. I heard an older woman, a grandmother-type, bubbling over the fact a new baby was being named after her.

I found Madge watching television. I leaned over and kissed her on the forehead.

She clicked off the program. "I thought you'd be back to see me before this."

"I was, but they'd taken you for a scan." I placed the vase on the bedside table.

"Oh, my goodness. How pretty. I love daffodils. They always let me know spring is coming soon."

"The bulbs in your yard are sprouting, and the flowering quince is in bloom."

"The quince is the first thing to bloom every year." Madge took my hand, sat up and swung her legs over the side of the bed. "Two nurses came and took me for a short walk this afternoon. I did okay. And I only needed headache medicine once today."

"Did anyone say when you'll be able to go home?"

"I asked. The nurse said when the dizziness goes away. I'm going to be sick of this room by then. They insist I'm not to get out of bed by myself."

She sounded more like her old self. I decided to postpone any mention of what Buzz had told me she'd said earlier in the day. If she was really concerned about my affection for her, the subject would come up again. I was about to ask her what she had for dinner, when she said, "Did the police catch the man who attacked me?"

"I don't think so, but they're on his trail." The full story could wait. I didn't want her lying awake worrying about me. Ten minutes later we ran out of meaningful chit-chat. I gave her a hug and said goodbye.

It was dark when I left the hospital. As I drove back to the house, a heavy mist collected on the windshield, and by the time I pulled into the driveway it was sprinkling. I wished I'd left a light on inside.

Chapter 35

The rain was clattering on the patio roof when I crawled into bed at nine o'clock. I had the book I'd bought in the hospital gift shop, but doubted I'd read much of it. The dogs were curled up on their respective blankets beside the bed. I read less than an hour before getting drowsy. As I reached to turn out the light I heard Jeff emit a low growl. I looked over the edge of the bed. His head and ears were poised in attention. I strained to listen. The only thing I heard was the rain and the tinkling of Madge's wind chime on the patio.

Seconds later, both Mutt and Jeff jumped to their feet. Jeff growled deep in his throat and Mutt started barking. The crash of breaking glass made me bolt out of the bed. I dashed to the doorway between the hall and living room and reached around to feel for the switch to the overhead light. As I flicked it, Jeff bumped my leg and pushed past me.

The front door was wide open. Pieces of etched decorative glass were scattered on the entryway floor. Standing in the middle of it was Buck Harper with a crowbar in his hand. His hair was dripping, his shirt and pants soaked. The hate in his eyes was chilling.

My heart jack hammered in my chest as adrenaline flooded my system. I stepped into the room with my back to the wall. My pistol was in my handbag on the breakfast bar twenty feet away. Jeff continued to growl and positioned himself between Harper and me, his body low and threatening.

Harper raised the crowbar. "You bitch! I don't know how you did it, but I damn near drowned." His eyes were red-rimmed, his lips curled in a snarl. "I'm gonna kill you! To hell with the tape."

Mutt, in the hall doorway, set up a storm of yapping. I inched my way along the wall, my eyes focused on the fugitive.

Harper's gaze shifted from Jeff to me and back again. "I'm gonna kill that damn dog first!"

He knew he'd have to get past Jeff to get to me. I took a few more steps toward my bag. Harper caught my intention. He saw my purse and guessed I had a weapon. "Stop right there." He stepped forward— a mistake.

Jeff lunged, hit him in the chest and knocked him on his back. In a flash, the dog's teeth were at his throat. Harper let out a shriek. The crowbar dropped to the floor.

"Hold, Jeff. Hold!" I commanded.

Jeff froze, hunched over Harper's neck with his teeth bared. He continued his threatening growl. Mutt dashed into the room and started gnawing on the fugitive's pant leg. Harper flailed, shaking the little dog like a dust rag. But Mutt hung on. Harper groped for the crowbar, found it and raised his arm.

He was going to hit Jeff. I plunged my hand into my bag, pulled out the pistol and pointed it at him. "Don't you dare," I shouted. "Drop it!"

He didn't, but relaxed his arm in submission. "Get these damn dogs off me!"

With one hand, I grabbed the kitchen phone. "Hold still. If I give the command, my dog will tear your throat wide open." I dialed 911, told the dispatcher my name, and that the fugitive, Buck Harper, was in my house.

Like a frozen tableau, we waited with every muscle taunt. Rain splattered on the concrete walk outside the open door and wind buffeted the trees. In minutes sirens could be heard ascending the hill. Police cars swooped into the driveway, and two officers bounded to the door with guns drawn. It was Officers Gillford and Manning, the same men who'd responded to the attack on Madge. They took over.

I called Mutt and Jeff to my side. Mutt happily responded, but Jeff was reluctant to give up his prize. He backed off slowly, ready to pounce again, if needed. Harper didn't move.

Officer Manning holstered his pistol, rolled Harper over, cuffed him and hauled him to his feet.

"That damn dog attacked me, right through the door," Harper said. "I wasn't doing nothing."

"Yeah, sure." Manning said.

"Look at my neck. He damn near killed me. Shoot him. He probably has rabies. He's a vicious animal."

Officer Gillford pushed up Harper's chin and inspected his neck. "It's only a couple scratches. We'll take you to the ER and get them treated."

"We ought to get you a rabies shot too," Manning said, chuckling, as he pushed Harper toward the squad car.

I heard Harper cursing as the cruiser door closed.

Minutes later photos were being taken of the smashed door, and the crowbar was packaged for evidence.

As I put the pistol back in my purse, I began to shake. Officer Gillford noticed and stepped toward me. Jeff growled a warning. The officer halted and raised his eyebrows. He looked at my dog and then to me.

I patted Jeff on the neck. "He's still a little excited," I explained. "It's okay, boy. Sit." Jeff sat on his haunches, but remained wary. Mutt stood on his hind feet, pawing my pajama leg.

"Are you okay?" Gillford asked.

"I will be in a minute. Harper didn't know it, but my pistol wasn't loaded. I wasn't expecting a visitor like him. The clip is in the bottom of my bag. I didn't have time."

Gillford shook his head. He pulled a notepad from his shirt pocket. "Tell me what happened—from the beginning."

I took a couple of deep breaths.

"I know this was a harrowing experience," he said. "But I need to get some particulars. I gather you were in bed when he broke in, is that right?"

Suddenly aware I was standing there in a flimsy pair of pajamas, I folded my arms across my chest. "It's a good thing I wasn't in the shower."

A detailed account took only a few minutes and when we'd finished I said, "I'd like to clean up the glass now, if that's okay. I don't want anyone, human or canine, to get cut."

"Sure, go ahead. We'll take care of Harper." He moved through the debris and closed what was left of the door behind him as he left.

I put on a robe, then swept and vacuumed the glass. Afterward I searched the drawers in Madge's utility room for duct tape. With the aid of several layers of newspaper, I managed to cover most of the opening left in the door. By the time I'd finished, the rain had dwindled to a mist.

I was too worked up to sleep. Even the dogs had trouble settling down. I sat in Uncle Henry's big easy chair with Mutt in my lap. Jeff rested his chin on my knee, his big brown eyes pleading for closer contact. For the first time since he was a pup, I allowed him to climb into the chair with me. I'm sure it was a funny scene, and it didn't take long for my legs to feel numb from his weight. "Bedtime," I announced. They scrambled off my lap.

Around one AM, I settled myself in bed. Mutt turned around on his blanket several times and curled into his customary sleeping pose. Jeff sat nearby, apparently still feeling uneasy. When I turned out the light, he finally sought his usual spot and was quiet.

260

Before long they were both snoring. I envied them. Every time I closed my eyes, I saw Harper's angry face and the hate in his eyes. The s-shaped scar on his cheek wiggled like a worm as he ground his teeth and muttered vile obscenities.

Somewhere between three and four a.m., I drifted off, only to dream that Harper was chasing me in his white truck, about to run me over. I woke with a start and decided it was no use. As I switched on the light and crawled out of bed, Jeff raised his head and looked at me with heavy eyelids. I dressed and made a pot of coffee. Neither dog joined me.

I was sitting by Madge's picture window, hunched over my second cup of coffee and watching the dawn light fill a clear sky, when the phone rang. It was Buzz.

"I understand you had an unwanted visitor last night."

"I sure did. He was determined to finish the job he'd started. I think if it hadn't been for Jeff, he might have killed me."

"From what I hear, your dog was a real tiger. And you didn't do too bad yourself. We can celebrate—now that Harper's locked up." A pause. "You okay?"

"I think so. I'm relieved Harper is in jail, but I confess I haven't been able to sleep."

"I have a couple of kids coming for riding lessons this afternoon. Why don't you drive out and watch? Get your mind off it."

"Thanks, but I plan to visit Madge and then indulge in a long nap."

"Probably a good idea. I'll call you tomorrow."

As I put the receiver back, the yen for a jelly doughnut, one of my favorite stress reducers, crept over me. I put on some clothes, grabbed a jacket and called the boys. We piled into the Explorer. On the way to the doughnut shop, I decided to buy a few extra treats and leave them at the police station as a special thank you.

Though it was still early, the lights were on in the doughnut shop. As I pushed through the swinging door, the sweet fragrance made my mouth water. Behind the counter was a heavyset Hispanic woman wearing a white apron and a smile. I pointed out my selection and forked over the correct payment. With a big box in one hand and a cup of coffee in the other, I maneuvered my way through a growing line of morning doughnut lovers.

I climbed into the Explorer, placed my coffee in the cup holder and the box on the passenger seat. While backing out of the parking space, I noticed the shop's dumpster and thought of Jonesy. I pulled into the space again, dashed back inside for a second cup of coffee and then took a chance I'd find Jonesy at Avila's Quick Mart.

A couple of minutes later I pulled to the curb behind the store. There he was, dumpster diving, the toes of his shoes barely touching the pavement. I rolled down the window.

"Hey, Jonesy."

He looked up and gave me a snaggle-toothed grin. "Hi, Miss Deena." He extracted himself from the bin with a fistful of Mojos and trotted in my direction.

"Get in. Let's have breakfast together."

I cringed as he put the potatoes in his coat pocket. Between the cast on his arm and his short legs, he had trouble getting into the SUV, but with a little struggle, managed it.

"Here, I got a cup of coffee for you," I said as I handed him a Styrofoam cup.

He took it and carefully sipped. "Mmm, that's truly good. Thank you."

His cast, what I could see of it protruding from his coat sleeve, looked mud stained. "I'm glad I found you. I wanted to thank you again for saving my hide the other night."

"Oh, I was mighty proud to do it, Miss Deena. That guy was a mean one. I feared you was a goner."

"If it hadn't been for you, he'd have seen to it I ended up in the river. As it was, I suffered only a few scratches." I pulled out and turned the corner. "We can eat at one of those picnic tables in the park."

I coasted to a stop at the curb and let the dogs out. They made a bee-line for the nearest tree. I took the box of doughnuts, and we settled ourselves at a table near the barbecue pit.

I glanced at Jonesy's feet. "I see you found another pair of shoes."

"Sure 'nuf. People throw away good shoes all the time."

I spread several napkins out on the damp table, opened the box and offered Jonesy first choice. His smile widened at the sight of eighteen doughnuts lined in neat rows. He chose one with white frosting and colorful sprinkles.

The cake doughnut was for my four-legged friends. I broke off a piece and handed it to Mutt. The rest of it was for Jeff. After a couple of gulps, they were poised for more. But I coaxed them back into the Explorer with one of their favorite dog biscuits from a box I keep under the front seat. I didn't want to be caught breaking the leash law. Rejoining Jonesy, I sunk my teeth into the jelly-filled doughnut and took a deep breath. There's nothing like it to get my blood circulating.

"I dunno what happened to the mean kid over at the mini-mart," Jonesy said. "He used to show up and give me trouble, but now the owner leaves them Mojos on top fer me."

"You mean Eddie Lee. He's in jail, at least for now. Buck Harper, the man who kidnapped me, was talking to him on the phone shortly before he tried to throw me into the river. From what he said, it sounded like Eddie had something to do with Mrs. Weston's death. I don't know how long they can keep him. I expect he'll make bail. There's not enough proof to hold him unless Harper tells what he knows."

"Oh, he did somethin' to her all right."

"What makes you say that?"

"I was there. I seen him."

"You were there?" I drew a sharp breath. "What did you see?"

"I was in her pigeon pen and heard 'er scream. She came running out of the house and him after her. He hit her with a piece of her own firewood. I seen his face in the headlights when a car passed. He did it all right."

"You witnessed the murder? Golly, Jonesy, why didn't you go to the police?"

"I was scared they'd blame me. I'm nobody. I felt bad 'cause I couldn't help her none. But I saw 'im, I surely did."

"Jonesy, we have to go see Lieutenant Walker. You've got to tell him."

"Oh no, Miss Deena. I can't. When that Eddie gets out of jail, he'll kill me. I jus' know it." Jonesy wiped his mouth with a napkin and swung his legs from under the table. "I thank ya for the doughnut, Miss Deena, I surely do, but I gotta go now." He started for the street at a half-trot.

"Jonesy, please wait."

By the time I grabbed the box, dashed to the Explorer and started it, Jonesy had disappeared between two houses on the other side of the street. I circled the block looking for him. The little guy was gone. For fifteen minutes, I crisscrossed around several other blocks without any luck. Finally, I gave up and decided to take the doughnuts to the police station.

I found Elena at her post when I breezed in. "I brought the guys some doughnuts, an extra thank you for the quick response last night."

I placed the box on the counter.

"I can smell them. Mmmm. Only for the men, huh?"

I grinned at her. "Oh no, you're part of the team too."

She rose from her seat and took the box. "I'll put them in the break room." She moved toward the hall.

"I've found a witness to the Weston murder."

Elena stopped and stared at me. "You serious?"

I nodded. "There's a catch. He's afraid to talk to the authorities about it."

"Lieutenant Walker won't be in today. I'll call him and tell him the good news."

"Wait. I want to tell him myself, in person. He'll be surprised to hear who it is."

Elena raised an eyebrow. "Are you sure?"

I turned to leave. "Tell the guys I said they're the best," I said over my shoulder.

Even the best policemen wouldn't find Jonesy. There was no point in sending them to search for him. When he chose to, he could vanish like a ghost.

It was close to eight o'clock when the dogs and I returned to the house. I spent the rest of the morning catching up on laundry and making the house look tidy before driving to Delta Hospital.

Parking was the usual hassle. I wormed my way through traffic on one of the busiest intersections in the city and found a spot in a parking tower.

A cart of breakfast trays clattered as I stepped off the elevator. I found Madge walking in the hallway. She greeted me with a hug. "I'm ready to go home," she whispered in my ear. "The food here is terrible."

In spite of her complaint, she was in an exuberant mood. She hooked her arm through mine as we strolled to her room where she settled herself on the side of the bed facing me. I parked myself on a chair.

"What's going on in the outside world? The television here is closed circuit. The only programs I've been able to watch are reruns of The Golden Girls and The Love Boat."

"I have some good news. Do you remember Harlan Jones?"

"Harlan Jones?" Madge pursed her lips and tilted her head. "Let me think a minute."

Her hesitation was odd. Maybe her injury had affected her more than she was letting on.

A smile. She was teasing me. "Sure I remember him. Why? Has something happened to him?" Madge plucked a tissue from a box on the bedside table and wiped her nose.

"I said *good* news. I talked to him this morning." I told her what Jones had disclosed.

"Well, I'm glad somebody knows what really happened to Lottie. Why didn't he come forward before this? If he'd told the police right when it happened, a lot of misery could have been avoided. You think he can be persuaded to talk to the authorities?"

"I'm not sure. I have to locate him first, then convince him the police can protect him. It may be a tough sell." I jotted my cell phone number on a scrap of paper from my purse and handed it to her. "As soon as you find out a timeline on your discharge, call me."

"I sure will."

"I think I'm going to run along. There's a sale on at Penney's this weekend, and I'm in need of another warm shirt."

"Okay, dear. I'll call you as soon as I know."

When I pushed through the main door to the parking lot, I met Irma coming in. "Glad I ran into you," I said. "Are you here to visit

Madge? She could sure use the company. She's bored and anxious to go home."

"Actually, I'm here to see someone else, but I guess I could stop by and say hello."

"Say, Irma, do you ever see Harlan Jones around town?"

"Harlan Jones. Why would I ever want to see him?"

"I need to find him, and I wondered if you might know any of the places he hides out."

"I certainly do not," she said with a huff. "By the way, when are you going to get the contents removed from that house?"

"I'll get it done. I've been tied up with other things the last few days, and I'm still looking for the deposit box." It occurred to me to mention I'd been kidnapped and nearly killed, but the hell of it was I was too tired to go into details. "See you later," I said and headed for the car.

By the time I reached the store my legs were beginning to feel like rubber noodles. I wanted to replace the sweatshirt that the ER staff had shredded. After sorting through a half-dozen shirts, I chose one with a spring theme embroidered on the front. A rack of jackets caught my eye. Besides my all-weather coat, my only other choice of outer wear was my suit jacket and it wasn't very warm. Even with the sale, the jacket was a bit overpriced, but I bought it anyway.

Chapter 36

I had to endure the cold coming in around the makeshift cover I'd fashioned for the front door until the next morning. I wanted it fixed before Madge came home. It took one phone call. The owner of Golden Valley Glass Company cheerfully responded to my request.

While I had the phone book in hand, I checked the listing for Creekside Bank. It was located in a community between Four Creeks and Delta. I dialed and a recording told me the location and hours. I decided to make another stab at locating Lottie's deposit box as soon as the glass was in place.

The dogs had to stay in the kennel while it was being installed. I figured they'd take a dim view of another stranger. They were eager to run when I opened the patio door, but I rattled the Milk Bone box. After a few suspicious looks and more than one treat, I managed to coax them through the gate. By ten o'clock the temporary glass was in place and I was ready to leave for the bank.

Creekside Bank and Trust was in a small building with a stone façade. I pushed through the swinging door to the interior and glanced around. A waiting area near the door provided comfortable chairs and a television. Soft music played in the background. Three people were at the teller windows.

An auburn-haired woman seated at the highly polished customer service desk was in a conversation with a man. They spoke rapidly in Spanish. I took a seat nearby. Time crawled as I waited for my turn. As soon as he left, I approached the desk. She greeted me with a professional smile. I introduced myself, presented the letter and documents from Russ Treadwell and showed her the key. She slipped on her glasses, and after concentrating on the letter for several minutes, turned to her computer. With a few key strokes she accessed a screen, paused and nodded.

Her smile brightened. "Yes. We have a deposit box listed under the name of Carlotta Weston. The rent is paid until December first." She rose from her chair. "Follow me."

In my excitement, I almost knocked over the chair. She led me to the half-door that separated the public from to the teller's domain. She motioned to one of the tellers, who pressed a hidden release to unlock it. We entered the vault. She took my key and produced a similar one that belonged to the bank. She inserted them both into the small door of one of the deposit boxes. With it unlocked, she pulled out the inner drawer, then ushered me to a low counter with a chair.

"Let me know when you're finished," she said as she placed the box in front of me and returned to her desk.

I hesitated as I thought of my dad. Was I being disloyal because I wanted to know whose DNA I carried? But what I would learn wasn't going to change anything, I decided as I fumbled with the latch.

When I lifted the lid, I saw several envelopes and loose documents. I unfolded the top one. It was the deed to Lottie's property. Below was the pink slip to the Buick convertible. Next I opened an envelope. It was a copy of her will. My spirits deflated as I laid each aside and dug deeper. I'd held out the hope that the contents would answer all my questions. What I was finding was routine stuff. Mel Weston's death certificate was next and underneath was his Army discharge document. I laid it on top of the others.

An envelope, too large for the box, lay curled against the bottom and sides. It was yellowed with age. Instinct told me it was important as I carefully removed it and slid my finger under the flap. I extracted a single sheet of paper and smoothed it out. What I saw confused me at first. Faded blue scrollwork encircled the edge of a certificate. The wording was in Spanish. I scanned the page for a clue as to its nature. Two names were written in the body of the document: Frederick Baker and Rita Diamond.

It hit me as three words jumped out: Certificado de Matrimonio. Matrimony! It had to mean Lottie and Fred Baker were married in Mexico. Near the bottom was a scrawled signature. The date next to it was faded but readable. The marriage occurred less than a year before I was born—before *we* were born. Did this mean Fred "Bingo" Baker was my biological father? *Our* father? Or did it make Lottie a bigamist? But wait. She used her stage name, Rita Diamond, not her legal name. I remembered Baker had said he never knew her real name? That's why he couldn't trace her.

I sat slumped in the chair for several minutes, mulling over the implications of what I'd found. The Kaleidoscope shifted again. For every answer, another question emerged. If they were married, why did she run away with the money? Why didn't she meet Baker? Did she know he'd been arrested? And what drove her to such weirdness? Was it guilt? I'd probably never know unless Madge could provide an explanation. I searched through the envelopes again. Where was the record of her marriage to Melvin Weston? Its absence made me wonder if they were ever married. And where were our birth certificates? Surely they should have been kept with the other important documents.

I debated whether to take the contents of the box with me or leave it all where I'd found it. In the end I decided to leave everything except the marriage record. Since Madge knew about the adoption, surely she would unravel the puzzle for me. I motioned to the woman at the desk. She came, returned the box to its place, and I left, determined to ask Madge for the details.

Back at the house, I brought the dogs inside and after heating a cup of soup in the microwave, kicked off my shoes and relaxed in Uncle Henry's recliner. I put in a call to Judy. I needed a release for some of my angst, and there was no one better to unload on than Judy.

She answered on the first ring. We spoke for close to an hour as I described Harper's reappearance and the fact Harlan Jones had witnessed Lottie's murder. I rattled on until I nearly ran out of breath. It sounded like the plot for a TV soap opera.

"Anyway, I think Fred Baker is my biological father," I finally said, "though there's no way to know for sure, except with a DNA test."

"Are you going to tell him?"

"I think he has a right to know."

"It's going to complicate your life."

"True, but there've been too many secrets up to now. It's better to have everything out in the open. At least that's what I'm thinking at present."

The other end of the line was quiet for a moment. "Okay, it's your funeral. I'd think twice about it. Talk to you later." We hung up.

Judy's misgivings were well founded. She'd located a long-lost half-brother several years earlier. He'd moved in on her, and she ended up getting stuck with his bills. I'd have to take my chances—if I decided to go ahead and disclose my suspected relationship to Fred Baker.

Chapter 37

Early that afternoon Madge called to say her discharge was official. "Come and get me," she pleaded. I left the dogs in the house with a couple of doggie toys, knowing they felt at home and would behave.

It was an ordeal getting Madge released: the discharge instructions, the follow-up doctor's appointment, waiting for the obligatory wheel chair and getting the car into the pickup zone. When Madge was settled in the Explorer she said, "I'm bushed from all the rigmarole."

Her comment made me smile. During the drive to Four Creeks, I mentally rehearsed what I'd say about the events of the last few days—all the things I'd been keeping from her. Where to begin? The answer came quickly as we approached the front door.

Madge stopped. "What happened here?"

"It got broken," I said. "I had the glass company put in plain glass. You can choose something more to your liking later on." I reached to open the door. "I'll tell you all about it, but it's a lengthy story."

Madge scowled until Mutt and Jeff greeted us with wagging tails. She leaned over, patted Jeff's head and lifted his chin with her hand. "You're a *real* guard dog." She turned to me. "He's mighty smart. He knew the guy was up to no good the instant he came through the front door."

"You don't know the half of it," I muttered.

Madge placed her purse on the breakfast bar, leaned over and scooped Mutt from where he sat at her feet. She gave a deep sigh and looked around the room. "Golly, it's good to be home. I feel like I've been gone a month." She gave Mutt a squeeze. "I've missed you."

"A lot has happened. I didn't want to tell you about it while you were in the hospital recovering. Maybe you ought to get comfortable."

"That bad, huh?"

"Everything worked out, but there were moments when I had doubts."

She put Mutt on the floor and slid onto the stool at the breakfast bar. "Okay, shoot."

I started by explaining the night of her attack when I saw the front door standing open.

I hadn't gotten very far in the story when Madge said, "I didn't remember at first, but now I recall your big dog jumped at that awful man. He struck the poor dog with his flashlight." She reached down and patted Jeff's head again. "Seems like I wanted the phone, but that's all I remember."

"That wasn't the end of it." I continued, relating the trip to the hospital and the investigation, then proceeded to tell her about my search of Lottie's house, how I'd been kidnapped and everything I'd learned before being rescued by Jonesy. "That same man, Buck Harper, killed Dad when he ran us off the road and he meant to kill me too."

"What a despicable creature. I'm glad he's dead. But it doesn't explain the broken glass in the front door."

"There's more. We thought he had drowned in the river, but like a bad penny, he turned up here the next night and broke in." I nodded toward the door. "Hence the broken glass. He intended to finish me off. But Jeff took him down and I called the police."

Madge put her hand over her heart. "Good gracious. But he's locked up now, right?"

"Yes. I didn't have the tape recording he wanted anyway. I gave it to Buzz last week. And he sent it to the authorities in Ortega County. We can't be sure it'll be accepted as evidence, but Buzz said it incriminated Dennis Colton. It'll be months before a trial."

The phone's ring interrupted. It was Buzz. After a greeting, I told him Madge was home.

"How is she?"

"Seems like her memory has recovered. She remembers the attack."

"That's good, though I expect she'd rather forget it. Do you think she could spare you for a few hours tomorrow evening?"

I looked at Madge. She was examining Jeff's injured ear. "Is that Avis Walker?" she asked. "I'll bet he'd like to take you out on a date. Go ahead. I'll be fine. I have the best watch dog in the world with me."

"I heard her," he said at the other end of the line. "The Vineyard would be a great place to celebrate the end of Harper's criminal endeavors—good wine, good food, dim lights—how about seven o'clock?"

Madge gave a dismissive gesture.

"I guess it's okay," I said. "I'll leave the phone number with her and meet you there."

"Tell your aunt I'm glad she's home."

"Thanks. I will." I replaced the receiver.

I watched Madge walk into the living room and settle into her easy chair. Mutt jumped into her lap and she smiled as she stroked his ears. I had a hunch there'd been a good deal of fraternizing going on when I wasn't around.

"Why don't you make us some tea, dear?"

My heart flip-flopped. If she kept her promise, I was about to hear her side of the story about my adoption and the reason it had been kept secret.

"Sure thing," I said. I filled two mugs with water and put them in the microwave to heat.

Madge had several brands of tea in a canister. "What flavor would you like?" I asked her from the kitchen.

"I like the orange spice, but mint would be fine."

I submersed a tea bag in each cup and located a wooden tray on the top shelf of the cabinet. As I pulled it down, I noticed a box of Vanilla Wafers and decided a plate of cookies sounded good. The scent of orange spice drifted from the cups as I carried the tray to the coffee table. Madge reached out and picked up a cup.

"Be careful. It's really hot," I cautioned unnecessarily.

She put the cup on a coaster next to the table lamp. I settled myself in a soft chair nearby, picked up my cup and tested the temperature. Jeff plopped on the rug next to my chair. There was a long and heavy silence.

Madge took a deep breath and slowly released it. "I promised I'd tell you how you came to be adopted into our family. I guess it's time you know the details." She lifted her cup and took a sip of tea before continuing.

"The spring before you were born, I was home visiting my parents. I went to visit Lottie. She and Mel had been married only a few months, but it was obvious she was pregnant. She confided that she was carrying twins. She said she wasn't wild about having kids anyway, and sure hadn't bargained on two at a time. She figured one was all she could handle.

"I was shocked when she said that and asked how Mel felt about the babies. She said Mel wasn't particularly excited about it either. That's when she confessed Mel didn't know it, but he wasn't the father."

I grabbed a cookie and nibbled around the edges. I tried to appear relaxed, but actually felt as tense as when I'd opened the deposit box.

275

"Your folks didn't have any kids," Madge continued, "and it didn't look like they ever would. I contacted your dad and told him about Lottie's predicament. I suggested Lottie might be willing to let them adopt one of the babies. Lottie and Mel agreed and all the arrangements were made well in advance. In those days the sex of a baby wasn't known before birth. As it turned out, Freddie was big and strong, but you were smaller and a bit frail. She chose you for the adoption."

"It must have been quite a scandal," I said. "What did people think?"

"It wasn't common knowledge. She'd been careful to stay out of sight. Also, she went to a doctor in Valley Center, and that's where the two of you were born. You were handed over to your folks before she left the hospital. Within a year you grew into a healthy, happy infant. It seemed like everything had worked out fine."

"And Mel never objected?"

"Lottie never mentioned his viewpoint. I suspect he knew she'd tricked him, but decided to make the best of it. As part of the adoption agreement, she promised never to make contact with you or reveal the adoption in any way. Every time you came to stay in the summer, I made an effort to keep you away from any events where she and Freddie might be. But when your dad and you moved back to the ranch to help your grandparents and you entered high school, I couldn't control that. I felt sure she'd go back on her word, but she never made a fuss."

"Until recently?" I asked, thinking about the argument in the library.

Madge nodded. "That day in the library, she asked for your address. I wouldn't give it to her. I guess she thought she could remake her life. I figured you had the right to your own life without her."

I swallowed the last bite of the cookie, leaned back in the chair and sipped my tea as I contemplated my next question. "What about my biological father—our father?"

Madge was silent. I could almost hear the cogs in her brain turn, trying to figure out how to avoid answering. Who was she protecting? Certainly not Lottie.

"There's no way I could know for sure," she said as she studied the tea in her mug. "I only know what she told me."

"Did you know about the time she spent working in Las Vegas?"

She glanced in my direction. "Yes. I was aware of it." She looked away.

"Madge, I found Lottie's safe deposit box."

Chapter 38

I detected a slight change in her skin tone. She didn't look at me. For a second I was afraid she wouldn't tell me anything more, even though I was sure there was more to the story.

"Oh," she said. A pause. "I suppose the contents explained everything."

"I have something to show you," I said as I got out of the chair. I went to the bedroom for the marriage certificate. When I returned, I handed it to her. She set her mug aside, and squinted at it. Her eyebrows raised and then she scowled as she studied the document. I watched her expression.

"How did Lottie get mixed up with Fred Baker?" I asked. "Did you know about their marriage?"

She handed the certificate back, tilted her head and scratched her neck, then reached for a cookie. There was a long silence—too long.

I took my seat. "Madge, as far as I'm concerned, you're my aunt, adopted or not. I'll always love you, no matter what. Please tell me everything. Nothing can be so awful that you can't tell me."

She laid one arm across her chest and ran the fingers of her other hand across her forehead, as though considering how to continue. Another sigh. "All these years, I've tried to put that period of time behind me. Leave it to Lottie to drag out the old skeletons. I was *afraid* you wouldn't be satisfied until you heard the whole sordid tale."

Her choice of words puzzled me. I couldn't imagine my aunt being involved in anything *sordid*.

She took a deep breath. "Lottie and I graduated from high school the same year, and we both enrolled in college at Sacramento State at the same time. We even roomed together. We both planned on teaching careers. Before the end of the first year, Lottie's father died from a heart attack. In those days Social Security didn't amount to much. Her mother couldn't afford to send Lottie money for school any longer. She was afraid she'd end up back in Four Creeks working in a packing house.

"One of our classmates, a girl from Redding, told us there were jobs available dealing cards up in Stateline. Her boyfriend was a bouncer at one of the clubs. You had to be twenty-one, but he knew someone who could provide a fake ID. She said a dealer could make enough working during the summer to pay for college expenses. That's what she planned to do, and Lottie went along with the idea."

Madge paused and slipped off her shoes. "I went home during the summer and didn't see Lottie. But in the fall she came to the dorm late one Sunday night and told me she'd decided to quit college. She had auditioned for one of the floor shows at a casino. She certainly was attractive enough to be a showgirl. She had long, dark brown hair and a great figure."

I nodded. "I saw the picture she sent to Irma."

"A few months later Mama wrote to tell me Papa was sick with Valley Fever. Very few farmers ever thought of health insurance. That meant my parents would have to hire someone to do the ranch work until he was well. The result was I'd have to get a part-time job, Mama said. I wrote to Lottie about my troubles. When she wrote back, she said I could get a job dealing cards. She thought I could work weekends and continue my studies.

"So that's what I did. I roomed with her on weekends and worked through the spring quarter. I nearly drove the wheels off the '48 Ford I used to go back and forth to Stateline. I was a good student, but it was impossible to keep up, because of all night working on weekends, the drive and trying to study. My grades suffered. When summer came, I didn't go home. I worked at the casino full time."

"What did Grandpa and Grandma say when you told them?"

"I didn't tell them. They would have been horrified. At first I told them I had a summer job and everything would be okay. After that I lied. I didn't like it though. In the fall I decided to take a year off from college to earn enough money to pay for the next year. By that time Lottie had moved to Reno. She found a job in a bigger club with a better salary. She seemed to have plenty of money all the time, so I decided to apply at the same casino. I had experience, so I was hired, and I moved in with her. The money in my savings accumulated.

"Then she met Fred Baker. Fred was working in a small casino on the outskirts of Las Vegas. He filled her head with talk about Las Vegas glamour and convinced her she should move there so they could spend more time together. He found a rental for her. She wanted me to go along. We auditioned for jobs in a major production and thought we'd made the big time. But the rent was higher, everything was more expensive, and we didn't get the job we wanted."

My tea was gone and I'd eaten most of the cookies. It was an amazing story. You never know what lurks in someone's past, but there was nothing sordid about it.

Madge paused to finish her tea. "When Lottie told Fred we were unemployed, he introduced us to Dan Durango, his boss. Fred was a cage man at Durango's Dugout. He handled the money when people bought and sold chips and helped in the counting room.

"Durango was a very charming rat. He told Lottie and me he'd make us headliners at his place. He said his shows were small, but that it was only temporary, because he intended to expand. He thought we would help bring in customers and give him the increased business he needed. But there was a catch. We'd have to deal cards during the evening and do the late night shows too. It meant long hours, but we were young and if the casino expanded, I figured the arrangement wouldn't go on very long.

"Things ran smoothly for a few weeks. Fred introduced me to a new fellow who'd just been hired. His name was Murray. He was blonde, had dazzling blue eyes and a soft southern accent. We hit it off and the four of us spent our spare time together."

I broke in. "Oh my god! You were in those pictures." I let out a hoot. My aunt, the proper sixth grade teacher, had been an "escort" if Fred Baker was to be believed. It was the wildest idea, something I never expected. I hardly heard what she said next.

Madge squinted at me, not understanding my reaction. "We never used our real names. We didn't want anyone to know we were just a couple of hicks from rural California."

The full impact was stunning. I blurted, "You were Cuddles McGee, the girl Larry Bertram said he drove home one night because you'd had too much to drink."

Madge stiffened in her chair. "I don't remember any Bertram. I didn't intend to include every tiny detail."

Was that the secret she'd been protecting, the secret Lottie had threatened her with in the library? If that bit of history slipped out in Four Creeks, there would have been a roaring scandal.

Madge's brow creased as she continued. "Almost immediately, we realized Durango had a little *enterprise* going on the side. If the girls, a half dozen of us, didn't want to participate, he could get downright mean. That's how Lottie ended up with the scar beneath her ear. When that happened Durango and Fred had a big blowup. Afterward Fred and Lottie didn't show up for a couple of days. I imagine that's when they went to Mexico. She didn't tell me. When they returned, somehow Fred made peace with the boss and things smoothed out.

"But Lottie was acting strange—secretive. She hardly talked to me. One night I confronted her and asked what I'd done that she was so mad. She said it wasn't me and went on to tell me they were going to Mexico to live when they had enough money. They had a plan. It sounded risky to me."

I leaned forward. "What was it?"

"Baker had heard about a scheme some of the pit girls were running in other casinos. After the late night floor show, the pit boss would point out a guy who was alone and had plenty of money—a high roller. The girl would latch on to the guy and stick with him all night. The idea was to keep him drinking and gambling. It brought more money to the house. But while cuddling over the roulette table, the girl would pilfer some of the guy's chips when the pit boss was distracted and hide them in a pocket in her fur stole. In effect, she was stealing from the casino. Baker sold Lottie on the idea. Of course, she didn't have a fur stole, but she found a good substitute in one of the boutiques.

"Normally, at the end of the night, the mark would tip the girl with one or two chips before going to the room, but by that time he'd be so blasted, he didn't know what she'd done. The difficult part for Lottie was cashing in the chips without getting caught. She recruited me to help her and she'd give me a cut. Over the next few weeks, I met her in the ladies' room every night. She gave me her chips, and I'd turn them in. It was tricky. That's where Baker came in. As a cage man, he was able to manipulate the count. They didn't have all the electronic gadgets available nowadays.

"I guess the pit boss caught on and told Durango. Or maybe it was one of his other guys. A day or two before Christmas, Lottie packed a bag after the last show and gave me a hug goodbye. She wouldn't say where she was going. I knew things would get ugly around the

Dugout. I was right. Durango had half his goons out looking for her and Fred Baker. He badgered me about it so much I left too."

Madge was quiet for a minute. She finally said, "I caught the bus, went home for Christmas and reentered college in January. I had enough money saved. When I graduated, I took a teaching position here and put all of it behind me. I met Henry, fell in love and we got married. The rest, as they say, is history."

"What did you tell Uncle Henry? Did he know about my adoption?"

"He had to know that much to get his cooperation when you came to Four Creeks. But that's all. Lottie was the only one who knew about the sort of job I took to work my way through college."

I couldn't reconcile the picture of my family. The man who was probably my biological father was a thief, killer and ex-convict. It seemed like my birth mother was a bigamist, as well as a thief. I felt positively unhinged. Two weeks earlier I'd simply been an orphan.

"Did Lottie divorce Baker?" I asked.

"I don't know. She never said anything to me about it."

We sat in silence for several minutes. I don't know what Madge was thinking, but I was struggling to absorb what she'd told me.

Finally I asked, "Why did my parents keep my adoption a secret? They didn't have to tell me where I came from."

"It wasn't an issue when you were an infant. And when your mother found out she had cancer... You were about five. She wanted to have what time you had together to be as pleasant as possible to leave you with good memories. The timing wasn't right. And afterward, your dad probably figured it would be too much trauma. But when he called and told me that he and you were moving back to the ranch, I was worried. We talked about telling you. I begged him not to. I knew you wouldn't be satisfied. You'd be compelled to find out everything about your biological parents. And the trail would lead back to the rotten mess in Las Vegas."

"But your past is tame compared to what goes on now."

Madge held her hand up. "You were my surrogate daughter. I was probably wrong, but I couldn't face the shame."

"Aw, Madge. It never would have mattered to me. It doesn't matter to me. I'd love you even if the sky fell in."

A dog nose bumped my elbow. I looked down to see Jeff's brown eyes telling me it was time to go outside. I glanced at the clock over the fireplace. Through the dining room window daylight was fading. I rose from my chair and leaned over to give Madge a hug. "I'm glad you told me all about it. Don't worry; I'll keep your skeleton safely locked away."

When I straightened, she didn't look at me, seemingly thinking about another time.

I pulled on my jacket. "The boys need to have their evening run-about." When I opened the sliding glass door to the patio, Mutt and Jeff bounded out ahead of me.

Outside, any sign of the previous storm was gone. The wind had cleared the sky. It was cool, but not too cold yet. As I trudged out to the road and up the hill, the dogs raced through the weeds, stopping here and there to sniff out a marker. I paused to face the western horizon and watched the light fade.

I tried to imagine what Madge had gone through, the agony of protecting her secret and not just from me. Would I have done the same? Four Creeks was not a tolerant place. As far as these people would have been concerned, even the hint of such a scandal would have made her about as popular as a plague of locusts. A teaching position would have been out of the question.

When the dogs had expended their energy and came to my side, I returned to the patio to feed them. Afterward, I went inside for a long leisurely soak in the tub to relax and grapple with what I'd learned.

As I slipped beneath the billowy suds, I thought about Lottie, her strange life, her lies, and how she'd tried to make up for her bad decisions—all in vain. After a bit, having thought it through, I decided I was lucky to have been adopted. Lottie wasn't the kind of mother I'd have wanted. Then there was Irma. Would some of her bitterness die away? What is it they say about bitterness? It's like drinking poison and waiting for the other person to die. She must have figured out our relationship? Did she care? Probably not.

Chapter 39

The next evening, I stood before the closet and wished I'd brought a better selection of clothes with me from Ortega Bay. I pulled on my black slacks and donned a white knit top, then slipped into black pumps. I shrugged into my new jacket. It felt soft and warm.

The phone number of the restaurant was easy to find in the local book, and I wrote it on the telephone note pad for Madge. Jeff paced the floor and Mutt eyed me suspiciously. They sensed I was going out and leaving them behind.

Madge was in the kitchen methodically polishing the countertop. As I reached for the front door knob, she said. "Avis Walker is a good man, Deena. He's good-hearted, reliable, steady and a real gentleman. I think you should give him more consideration. You could do worse."

She was right about Buzz. He was all that she said. In the last few weeks I'd come to realize Dad had been my compass. Was Madge hinting I needed a replacement? Or was she thinking Buzz would keep me in Four Creeks where she wanted me? I didn't comment on her statement. "I won't be late."

I stepped inside the Vineyard Restaurant and paused to look around. It was decorated in a Mediterranean motif with a partially exposed brick wall. A mural of vines climbing a fence covered another, and a large watercolor of the same theme hung opposite.

Buzz was waiting near the door. He took my elbow and escorted me to a table for two near large windows overlooking a brick patio. He was wearing a blue suit with an up-to-date tie, not his usual western style. As he held my chair, I caught the scent of a new aftershave. He seated himself opposite me. I hung my bag over the back of the chair and stealthily peeked at his shoes. No cowboy boots. Golly, he *was* celebrating.

A smiling waiter brought menus and glasses of ice water. Buzz ordered a bottle of Pinot Noir. The waiter nodded and faded away to let us make our selections.

"Do you remember the restaurant I took you to on the night of our high school graduation?" he asked.

"I sure do. It was The Spaghetti Palace."

"It was all I could afford then."

"Come to think of it, it's not there anymore."

"An insurance company came in, tore it down and built their offices in its place."

"Too bad. The spaghetti was good."

The waiter returned. After we ordered I asked, "Not that I care all that much, but how deep were the wounds in Harper's neck?"

"Not deep enough to do much harm. They didn't require stitches."

"What a shame. Knowing he's behind bars pleases me beyond words. I suppose I'll have to testify at his trial."

"Absolutely, but Ortega County gets first crack at him. He'll try to work a deal for testimony against Colton. It'll be a year, maybe two, before he comes to trial here."

"I found Lottie's safe deposit box yesterday."

"That's good. Did it contain what you'd hoped for?"

"I found one thing of great interest, a Mexican marriage certificate for Lottie and Fred Baker. Except she used her alias. Makes me wonder if she planned to bolt all along. But the date on it seems to confirm he's my biological father."

Buzz's eyebrows lifted for a second. "Interesting. I suppose we should have guessed it from the story he told you."

"This afternoon Madge added what she knew of Lottie's earlier life." I gave him the short version, leaving out the "details" of her account that he didn't need to know. "It makes me sad that my family didn't think they could trust me with the knowledge earlier."

"They probably thought they were looking out for your interests. Parents are like that."

"I have more news," I said as I unfolded my napkin. "I had breakfast with Harlan Jones the other morning."

"That must have been a novel experience. How were those cold Mojos?"

"You know about that, do you?"

"I have an underground network you'd never suspect."

"Do tell. No Mojos. I bought doughnuts, found him over by the mini-mart and we ate in the park. But the interesting part is that he told me he witnessed Lottie's murder."

Buzz sat straight in rapt attention as I explained Jonesy's story. "Elena said you thought you'd discovered a witness."

"That's why he's been so afraid of Eddie. As soon as I told him he should talk to you, he took off. Even if we were able to convince him Eddie is no longer a threat, I doubt you could ever get him on the witness stand. Besides, a good lawyer would take him apart, and I'd hate to see that happen."

Buzz's expression was thoughtful. "Maybe you can talk him into giving a deposition. I'll talk to the D.A. and see what we can work out. His situation wouldn't make him a convincing witness."

The waiter brought the wine and opened it. Buzz did the customary tasting and nodded. Our glasses were filled. We clinked them together and smiled at each other.

"To happy trails," I said.

He tilted his head a bit to one side and his smile faded. "What does that mean?'"

I took a sip, but he held his glass without moving.

"You're leaving," he said. "Now the danger has passed and your puzzle has been solved, you're going back to the city."

Our salads arrived. I picked up my fork. "You jump to conclusions. I don't know how long Madge is going to need me to stay with her."

Buzz put his wine glass down. "I was hoping you'd stay, maybe find some work locally, and we could have time together without distractions."

"I have unfinished business in Ortega Bay. I want to talk to the police investigator about the burglary and the accident. I'll probably never be able to prove Harper's involvement, but it's worth a try. Also I plan to visit Fred Baker again. He doesn't know he has a daughter."

"Maybe he doesn't need to. What would it change?"

"I'm not sure, but I think he has a right to know."

We ate our salads in silence. I sensed Buzz's festive mood had melted like ice in hot dishwater. I knew Madge wouldn't need me more than a few days. Should I restart my life in Four Creeks? I had to make up my mind. I couldn't waffle much longer. If I walked away from him again, there might be no way back.

The waiter took away our salad plates and returned with the main course. I'd chosen a small filet mignon and baked potato while Buzz had a T-bone and fries. He cut into his steak and added catsup to his plate. He ate without a word, eyes on his food, as if contemplating every bite.

After several minutes he raised his eyes, his mood brightened. "Before you leave, you should come out to the ranch and see that filly of mine. She's quit a beauty now."

"Sure. Maybe this weekend."

"She's gentle and alert. I think she's going to be a great horse. Wish I had another like her." He continued describing her expected height and conformation when she was grown.

I could only nod as though I understood. I didn't, since I knew so little about horses. Dogs, I understood. "What's your dog's name? He's a border collie, isn't he?"

"That's right. I call him Charlie. He likes to herd, but the horses don't take kindly to his ideas, and sometimes they level a warning kick in his direction. That sends him off to lie in the shade."

When we finished our dessert he said, "I'd take you clubbing, except Four Creeks doesn't have any like the ones in the city."

I laughed. "That's okay. I haven't been to a nightclub in so long, I wouldn't know how to act anyway."

After he settled the bill, we strolled out toward the parking lot. He slipped his arm around my waist as we approached our vehicles. He glanced upward. "Look at the sky. Remind you of anything?"

I searched the sky. The moon was in a declining phase and hundreds of stars were visible.

"It reminds me of our date the night after we graduated," he said. "You remember?"

"Yes, I do."

"Deena, I'm feeling sentimental tonight. I'm going to kiss you—for old time's sake, of course. I've wanted to do it ever since you stomped into my office."

In a movement I couldn't describe later, he pulled me into his arms and sandwiched me between himself and the Explorer. Our lips met, and for old time's sake, of course, I kissed him back.

He placed an elbow against the car next to my head and leaned to nuzzle my neck. It felt so natural. I looked up at the moon. "Are you trying to seduce me?"

"Uh huh." He kissed me again before snuffling my ear and laying a series of kisses down to my collar bone.

My physical reaction was predictable. "You planned this, didn't you? You were plotting while chewing your steak."

"Uh huh."

I recalled the night of our graduation; the moon, the stars and him. But it was no teenage girl who felt the warmth of his body on this occasion. "I know. You figure if you can get my clothes off, I won't leave Four Creeks."

"Uh huh. Is it working?" His hand slid down low on my back.

"We should talk about this."

"No talking."

After a long, lingering red hot kiss my reservations were melting like butter on hot popcorn.

"Deena," Buzz said in my ear. "Come live with me on the ranch. I know we'd be a good team. You'd love the country, if you give it a chance; the quiet, the hills, the horses. It's peaceful."

I put my hand against his chest and gave him a gentle push. "Wait. I just remembered something."

"What?"

I recalled the picture I'd had of myself mucking out the stables. "Buzz, I'm very fond of you, but I can't see myself on Green Acres. I never could. That's why I left Four Creeks the first time."

"But Deena, things are different now."

"I don't think so. This valley is as hot and dry in the summer as it ever was."

"I have air conditioning."

I took three sidesteps to the door of the Explorer, opened it and slid in, putting the door between us. I lowered the window and leaned out. He came close and I took his hand. In the light from the street lamp, I could see his puzzled expression.

"Buzz, I think you're the greatest guy in the world, and although my body is telling me to hop in the sack with you, my brain says not tonight. In the two weeks I've been in Four Creeks, I've nearly ended up dead—twice. I've found out my parents weren't really my parents, my biological father is an ex-con, and my birth mother was a weird cat-harboring woman who was probably a Las Vegas call girl in her previous life. Plus, I had a twin brother I didn't know about. My whole self-concept has been disrupted."

"No room for me in that picture?"

"Right now, I can't say. You were right. I am going back to Ortega Bay. I have unfinished business. There's a crippled old man in a wheel chair who doesn't know I'm his daughter. He didn't seem like such a bad guy, in spite of his past. And his sister is my aunt too. I'm sure I'll be back here because I love Aunt Madge—who isn't actually my aunt. And then there's Harper's trial. On one of those trips, you might find me knocking on your door for a roll in the hay—if you're still willing."

Buzz laughed. "Oh, I'm sure I'd be willing. I've been in love with you since I was seventeen. Time hasn't totally run out, but don't wait too long. I'm not getting any younger." He leaned forward, slipped his hand behind my head and kissed me again. I responded.

Then I turned the key in the ignition and backed away. At the sight of him standing alone in the parking lot next to his pickup, my heart ached with longing. But I knew I'd made the right choice. I needed time and space to reconcile my conflicts before letting go.

Epilogue

The first thing I did when I returned to Ortega Bay was to look for a different place to live. I was lucky enough to find a house with a yard near my old grammar school. It was a one bedroom, one bath cottage in need of some updating. The backyard was the clincher—more space for Jeff. After experiencing the open fields at Madge's, it would have been hard to turn him into an apartment dweller again.

I stayed with Madge another two weeks. By then she'd taken over all of her own housekeeping chores and didn't complain of any more headaches. Madge had become so attached to Mutt that I decided to leave him with her. Both Jeff and I would miss him, but he'd be a good companion for her. However, she swore she was going to change his name. I told her, "Good luck. He's answered to Mutt his whole life."

My nightmares vanished, and though I still didn't remember precisely what happened on that mountain road, I was able to piece it together from my bad dreams, what Buck Harper had said to me, and what Buzz told me was on Dad's tape recording. A murder conviction for Harper wasn't possible according to the D.A. Insufficient evidence. But between his attack on Madge, his attempt to kill me when he kidnapped me, plus the drug trafficking charges, he'd be spending a good deal of time in prison.

I expect the episode at Lottie's will stick with me for many years, and I've vowed I won't get caught in a similar situation ever again. I still find myself glancing behind my back when I'm out after dark.

I suspected it was Dennis Colton who had placed the tracking device under the Explorer the day I pulled off the road after starting to listen to Dad's tape recording. When I saw a picture of him in the newspaper account of Harper's arrest, I was certain. And I was convinced he was the person Harper phoned that night in the trailer park before he tried to pitch me into the river. I had a hunch there'd be a lot of finger pointing when it came time for deal-making and plea-bargaining before his trial.

Incidentally, the warehouse that Harper set on fire belonged to Colton's brother-in-law. It actually did contain furniture for his store. The insurance money couldn't be recovered. It was already spent on rebuilding and replacing the contents. As a result, I never was paid for the remainder of Dad's expenses.

No one knows why Lottie didn't meet Fred Baker with the money they stole. We can only guess. Other than Baker, there was no one alive to explain its origin. Charles Dirk had been killed in a prison disturbance up in Pelican Bay. Consequently, after it was determined the hidden money had nothing to do with Lottie's murder, it was turned over to her estate. Even then it took two years before the probate was completed and the court released the funds to me. I had to do some soul-searching before deciding what to do with it. Though I don't believe in curses, it had caused a lot of trouble for so many people, I felt uneasy about it.

The Salvation Army was happy to take all the furniture in Lottie's house. I boxed her photos. I offered a few to Irma, but she declined. The last time I talked to her, she told me there was a for sale sign in front of Lottie's house. She sounded pleased.

Jonesy's shoes were never found. Everyone figured Eddie Lee dropped them into someone else's trash and they were buried in the landfill.

The investigators blocked the water in the canal long enough to search the bottom. They located the chunk of Lottie's firewood. It had several gray hairs imbedded in it. An attempt was made to compare them with specimens taken during her autopsy, but they were too degraded. There was no doubt in my mind that it was what Eddie Lee used to crack her skull.

The blood on the piece of broken figurine turned out to be Lottie's. I was really disappointed about that because it didn't sound like there'd be enough evidence to indict Eddie. However, Hester was the key witness. The evening after I overheard Eddie talking to Hester in the market, he showed her the lottery ticket and bragged about what he'd done. She bargained her way out of a jail term by agreeing to testify against him. And since there's a law regarding profiting from a criminal act, he didn't get the lottery winnings.

It took a week's worth of doughnuts to convince Jonesy to agree to talk to the D.A. about what he'd witnessed the night of Lottie's murder. After that I took him to the veteran's hospital to get his cast removed. They still had his records from when the bull trampled him. Because of his Korean War injuries, the doctor certified him as partially disabled and eligible for a small pension. Whether or not it changed his lifestyle, I don't know, but at least he wouldn't have to dig in trash cans for food anymore.

I did visit Fred Baker again. He acted pleased to know I was his daughter. I'm not so sure Helen felt the same way. I told them about what Lottie did with the stolen money. I didn't feel right about keeping it so I gave it to him, hoping it would redeem Lottie somehow.

I knew I'd never have the same feeling about Fred as I did about my dad. No one could take his place. For a long time, when I thought about Dad, I still choked back tears. I'll always miss him.

As far as Buzz Walker was concerned, I considered the possibility we could connect on some level again. I wasn't sure exactly when. After the two weeks of discoveries in Four Creeks, I felt like I had a new identity. I needed to stretch a bit and see how it was going to blend with the old one.

Gloria Getman

Bird of A Feather

Petite fours, lemon drops, tea, and a deadly stabbing normally don't go together, especially at a colonial high tea.

Deena Powers is back in Four Creeks to attend the annual event put on by her aunt's chapter of the Women of Colonial Heritage. But when her aunt's closest friend is murdered, Deena finds herself drawn to investigate a tangled web of misappropriated chapter funds, adultery and long-held secrets and she soon discovers that sins of the past are never left behind, no matter how carefully the trail is covered up.

Helping Lieutenant Avis "Buzz" Walker acquire vital evidence leads to rekindled feelings, but when a killer steps in, it might just be too late.

~ ~ ~

Gloria Getman grew up in Southern California and graduated from California State University Bakersfield with a BSN in nursing. She's been published in Yesterday's Magazette and Reminisce Extra. A few of her short stories can be found in the anthology, *Leaves from the Valley Oak*. She is a member of both Central Coast and San Joaquin chapters of Sisters in Crime, plus the Tulare-Kings Writers. She lives in Exeter, California.

She may be reached via email: ggetman5592@verizon.net.

Check out her blog: http://www.gloriagetman.blogspot.com/

Made in the USA
Coppell, TX
22 July 2022

80328356R00168